MW01141042

The Steel Lady

Jane Perrella

For Patrick

Prologue

The first computer did not have transistors. It had cogs.

Charles Babbage invented the Analytical Engine in 1837. He designed a machine that could calculate and loop back on itself, just like a modern computer. In 1843, his friend Ada Lovelace wrote the first program – for a machine which did not exist.

History was not kind to either of them. Funding was withdrawn from Babbage's invention. Ada stopped her work with Babbage as her life was consumed by illness and gambling. The first mechanical computer was never built.

What if it had been?

For Charles and Ada, the change would have come too late. But not for her daughter. And not for his son.

This is not history. This is what might have been.

I

The Analytical Engine has no pretensions whatever to *originate* anything. It can do whatever we *know how to order it* to perform. [...] Its province is to assist us in making *available* what we are already acquainted with.

~ *Notes*, Ada King,
Countess of Lovelace~

"It will work this time."

The room had high ceilings, and might once have been a bright and airy drawing room. Instead, it contained no furniture and had an oily, metallic smell. Nearly all of its space was consumed by a gargantuan machine, so large that it could only have been assembled in the room itself. Towers of brass cogs, like columns in a great temple, curved away from the door of the room and towards the windows. A drum that was feeding punched cards into the machine was crammed awkwardly into one corner. The carpeting had been removed, and the bare wooden floor was no longer polished. The gouge marks and black scars on the oak boards no longer mattered.

Annabella King looked up at the Analytical Engine, tracing its height to the ceiling. The cogs towers soared several feet above her head, and spanned a good six feet from her in either direction. She glanced down at the row of bells that had been attached to the Engine by bars and levers, and frowned. She tapped the wrench that she held in one hand against one of the bars, and pushed back a strand of her dark hair, as it slipped free of its ribbon.

"It should work this time," she murmured, almost to herself.

"It should have worked every time, Miss," a grumpy voiced returned from behind the machinery.

Annabella grinned, her dark eyes glittering. "One last time, Sarah. For me."

Sarah's theatrical sigh was swallowed by the metallic sigh of the Engine. There was an initial shriek of brass on steel, followed by the clicking of the cogs in the machine's many towers. Punch cards shunted into place like so many train cars, and numbers flew up on the paneled display from right to left. They flicked back across the panel, and began again, rifling upwards through their numbers. Slowly, though the din, came a noise barely audible, and yet profoundly strange – the delicate, twinkling sound of bells.

"Sarah!" Annabella's voice, soft and high and twinkling itself, was breathless with excitement. "It worked! It actually worked!"

Sarah, Annabella's maid, popped her head out from behind the machine crank. She had on her dark maid's uniform, and a white cap pulled over her light brown hair. She gave Annabella a crooked smile. "Was that what it was meant to do all this time, miss? Those little bells?"

"Little bells!" Annabella's voice would not rise loud enough for her speak her joy; she stood instead utterly breathless, as the delicate bells continued to play as if touched by the hand of a ghost. "Sarah, it truly worked! Music *composed* by a machine! Do you realize what this means?"

Sarah raised her head from the crank. "You may have made some fine music, Miss, but you still need a mule to drive her."

Annabella laughed, as the bells slowed and fell silent. She bent her head over the now-still machine, twisting her wrench against the bar that held one of the bells.

"The industrial ones are steam powered, Sarah! The Engine can run the steam engines, and they feed back into-"

"Annabella."

Annabella spun away from the machine towards the doorway, and her hair tumbled from its ribbon.

A tiny woman stood there, her delicate hands folded across her waist. Her dress was a shining green, that made her look like a fairy. She had dark hair, like Annabella's, and eyes that reflected back like pools of black water.

"Mama!" exclaimed Annabella, seizing her mother's unresisting hands. "It worked! The algorithm for choosing the sequence of bells! Listen! Sarah, one more time for Mama!"

Annabella stood back, watching her mother's face now instead of the machine itself. She couldn't resist a grin in anticipation of her mother's reaction. As the machine began to trickle numbers back and forth, Ada King,

8

Countess of Lovelace, gave a small, fond smile, as one might when watching a child perform an easy trick. When the first bell began to play, her expression changed to one of awe.

"How did you..." she trailed off as the waves of chimes continued, and her expression became stone faced anger.

"Stop that nonsense, Sarah!" she said sharply, as the machine slowed enough for her to speak. "Annabella, get dressed, and put up your hair. Your father tells me that we will be having guests."

"But Mama, I-" Annabella began to gesture towards the Engine, when her mother interrupted.

"Don't call me that ridiculous name."

Annabella took an involuntary step back at the sharpness in her mother's voice. "Yes, mother," she said softly, as she watched Lady King's retreating back.

She glanced back at Sarah, who gave her a small, helpless shrug. "I don't know, Miss," she said, to the question that Annabella hadn't asked. "She's always hated the Engine."

"No," Annabella said darkly, looking through the door where her mother had gone. "Not always." She sighed. "Come help me dress, Sarah."

Henry Babbage slammed the palm of his hand into the edge of the massive machine before him, and swore under his breath. He had been trying to convince the Analytical Engine to work for the past several hours. He had thrown off his jacket long ago, and sweat was prickling along the collar of his shirt. Hours of work in the sweltering room had left him feeling like he was even farther behind than when he had started. When they cooperated, the Engines made his engineering infinitely easier; when they didn't, they made him feel like a small child trying to move a steamship.

Henry ran a hand through his hair until it stood on end, and turned his grey green eyes upward to survey the Engine. He was tall, but even so, the Analytical Engine loomed large above him. He wasn't really looking at it; he was trying to decide how he could get around what was staring him in the face.

"It's the cogs in the mill, Master," a voice yelled next to him in a heavy northern accent.

Henry turned to look at his lead hand, a mechanic named Bentham. He liked Bentham. He knew the Engines better than nearly anyone, almost as well as Henry did himself. He was smart and capable and quick about his work. He wasn't an engineer, but he should have been.

"And there's no way we can fix it without taking it apart altogether," Henry said with a heavy sigh.

Bentham shrugged. "Unless you've invented a way of cutting them while they're still in the Engine, no, Master."

Henry slammed his fist into the Engine again.

"Won't go any faster for you breaking your hand, Master."

Henry gave a weary grin. He adjusted his waistcoat and began to roll his sleeves back down. He picked up his coat. "Very well. Take it apart. I'm going for some air."

Bentham nodded and went back to work.

Henry stepped back from the Engine, and threw a glance around the works, the sprawling factory where the Engines were built. It was lit by pane windows high up in the roof, but by the time the thin light reached the floor, it may as well not have tried. Gas lamps made up for the deficiency, enough that the workers could see, but what really made the factory seem so dark was its contrast. The red-hot vats of metal that seethed around the vast room made the rest of the place look as black as pitch.

Moving amongst the fiery orange and black were figures dressed in what Henry presumed to have once been blue clothing, but which were now also black. They looked like smiths, as they worked on cogs and wheels, pieces of a greater, and ultimately more dangerous, whole.

Henry looked back again at the incomplete Engine. It didn't look beautiful – it was several tons in weight, all gleaming steel and whirling cogs – but it was so beautiful, in its precision and its strange intelligence.

Henry shrugged his shoulders into his jacket, and walked out of the large front doors, doors that always stood ajar, even in the coldest weather, for that precious gasp of air. He climbed the exterior stairs of the works, and then the ladder that climbed to the top of the brick building. He swung himself onto the roof, and turned his gaze out to the city.

The air that London provided couldn't be called fresh. A light breeze lifted smells of mud and tar and filth from the Thames, along with a host of other scents – hemp and wood from the ships, spices and rum and spilled wine, the scent of a hundred cargos from a hundred places around the globe. From the rail yard out the back of the works come the smell of grease. There lingered under it all the ever-present smell of coal that overlaid every surface in the city with an opaque layer of black dust. On the horizon came the clean, hopeful smell of rain.

Despite the ever-present smoke, Henry could see the other works and factories lining the river, and up river, the graceful dome of St. Paul's cathedral. Looking down on the yard of the works, he saw, striding between the wooden outbuildings, two well-dressed figures. He recognized the pace of both of them; one was expected, one was not, but they were both, undoubtedly, looking for him. He sighed, and stayed where he was.

He didn't have long to wait before Bentham's face appeared on the edge of the building, looking faintly annoyed.

"Master Brunel wants to see you, though I 'spose you already saw that," Bentham growled.

Henry sighed. "I did, thank you, Bentham."

"He's in the office. Your father's with him."

Henry pushed open the door of his employer's office, and waited in the doorway of the small room. Isambard Kingdom Brunel stood behind his desk, talking animatedly at Henry's father, Charles Babbage, who sat in a chair opposite him.

"So we're in agreement, then," Brunel said. "We will show them not a machine, but an idea." Brunel was not a big man, but he always seemed to vibrate with poorly controlled energy.

Charles sighed. "I'm getting too old for this, Isambard."

"You'd better not be," Brunel replied. "You invented it." He looked up as Henry entered. "You took your time. Indulging your preference for roofs over solid floors again?"

11

"What is it, Brunel?" Henry said shortly.

Brunel glared at him. "You do know that I'm your employer, Babbage? That I'm capable of removing you?"

Henry raised an eyebrow at him. "Theoretically, yes."

Brunel turned away, but not before Henry caught a half-hidden smirk on his face. Brunel was less his employer and more of a second father to him, and even if he hadn't been, he was hardly about to fire him. There was only one man who knew the Analytical Engines better than Henry Babbage did, and he was sitting in Brunel's office.

"Father," Henry said with a nod.

Charles Babbage inclined his head. He looked weary, and Henry only had a moment to wonder why before Brunel spoke.

"Take a seat, Henry, we have business to discuss," he said, seating himself behind his desk.

"I'll stand, thank you," Henry replied. "I have work to return to."

"You have work to do here," Brunel said sharply, "and I have already had to battle one stubborn Babbage this afternoon, so I would appreciate it if you would sit."

Henry glanced at his father, raising an eyebrow, but Charles Babbage volunteered no information. Henry took the seat opposite his father.

"Charles and I have been discussing showing the Analytical Engine at the Exhibition," Brunel said, without preamble.

"Hadn't we already discussed that?" Henry said with a frown.

The Great Exhibition of the Works of Industry was Brunel's current consuming passion. It was to feature displays of machinery, engineering, and curiosities from throughout the Empire, and was to be housed in an enormous glass structure in Hyde Park. The idea belonged to the Prince Consort, but Henry had the sense that Brunel had a heavy hand in it, whether officially or not.

"We did," Brunel nodded. "But this is, ah, a different idea."

"Mr. Brunel and I have been discussing having a woman present the Engine," Charles said gravely.

"I – beg your pardon?" Henry said, staring at his father, certain he had misheard.

12

"We intend to use the Engine in a dramatic presentation of its capabilities, and-"

"Not that," Henry said, interrupting Charles. "Why a woman?"

"It has to be presented as simple," Charles said bluntly. "A woman would be well suited to the task."

"I assume that was your idea," Henry said, shooting a glare at Brunel.

Brunel held up his hands helplessly. "And why do you assume that, Henry?"

"Because it's showmanship, and showmanship is what you excel at," Henry replied with acid in his voice.

"Yes," Brunel replied, undeterred by Henry's tone. "And showmanship is what we need right now. Our audience has a ... shall we say, limited appetite for technical details. We need someone who can encourage those who don't understand engineering – no, more than that, who don't *care* about engineering, to care enough to use the Engine."

Henry glanced at his father. "And it would have to be a woman who understands the Engine well enough to run one. You were thinking of Lady King? The Countess of Lovelace?"

"No," Charles Babbage said softly, as if he regretted the necessity of saying it. "Lady King has been instrumental to the creation of the Engine, but she is not right for this particular task. Her knowledge of the Engine was hard-won, and would still be too... technical. The understanding must be that of a *user* of the Engine. It must seem natural. I intend to ask Miss Annabella King."

"I – what?" Henry said, louder than he meant to.

"I told you he wouldn't like it," Brunel muttered.

"Lady King's daughter. You can't be serious." Henry said flatly, looking between Brunel and his father.

"Entirely serious," Charles Babbage said solemnly.

"She's a child!" Henry exclaimed, getting to his feet.

"She's not," Charles replied. "She's nineteen. The same age her mother was when she worked with me on the Engine."

Henry opened his mouth to speak, and then closed it in surprise. He had met Annabella many times, and he couldn't deny that he had been

13

impressed with her quick understanding and eager mind, but he still envisioned her as a young girl. Between his time in the army and his work with Brunel, it had been a long time since he had seen her.

"Brunel has yet to see Miss King's abilities with the Engine," Charles pursued, "but you know of them, Henry. I believe she learned many of them from you, did she not?"

"No, I-" Henry cleared his throat. "I showed her what I knew the machine could do. God knows what she's done since."

"What do you mean?" Brunel asked, leaning forward.

"Miss King, like her mother, believes that the machine has capabilities other than creating numerical tables," Charles Babbage put in. "She likes to innovate on it, as I understand."

"She sounds perfect," Brunel said.

"Most of her ideas don't work," Henry pointed out, turning to his father.

"Most of *our* ideas don't work," Charles put in sharply. "We have learned as much from our mistakes as from our successes."

Henry resisted the temptation to roll his eyes. "All that is beside the point," Henry said, shaking his head. "The idea itself is absurd. You're asking the public to accept a woman presenting a piece of machinery."

"Women are not the producers of machines, it is true, but there's no reason they shouldn't be their users," Brunel pointed out. "They ride trains, they take ships, they use shops – they are the beneficiary of most of the places that the Engine can go. A woman in that position inspires acceptance of it."

"A man would be much better suited," Henry muttered.

"Men have already been exposed to the Engine. We cannot ignore the impact of half the population; we need to make them know that the Engine is accessible even to women. We need to make them *see* it," Brunel pressed.

"Henry," his father said, gently, reasonably, in a tone that Henry couldn't stand, "I'm a scientist. Do you think for a moment that I haven't also had to be a politician, a preacher, a writer? I have never had the choice not to be – not if it meant the success of the Engine."

Henry looked at his father. He had often thought that his father only kept moving through the world because of the Engine. Since Mother had passed, and then Georgiana had died of scarlet fever, the Engine had been all that he could understand. The world could take his wife and daughter, but the Engine was logic itself – a logic that would respond and elaborate, but would never, ever leave.

"How did you get him to agree to this?" Henry demanded, glancing at Brunel.

"I pointed out the new and exciting possibilities for his Engine," Brunel said with feigned innocence. "There is work yet to be done, places the Engine can be used for the benefit of mankind. We need the public's acceptance and approval, as we always have."

"Fine," Henry said, running one hand through his hair. "Just so long as it's clear that she is to be overseen. By someone who knows what they're doing."

Brunel grinned. "Why do you think you're here?"

II

I love her from my boyhood – she to me
Was as a fairy city of the heart,
Rising like water-columns from the sea,
[…] And Otway, Radcliffe, Schiller, Shakspeare's art
Had stamp'd her image in me…

~ *Childe Harold*, Canto IV, Lord Byron~

"But it's not as though she doesn't let you use the Engine," Sarah said as she pushed a pearl studded pin into Annabella's hair.

"No," Annabella murmured, gazing into the mirror. There was that at least. Most mothers would have been horrified at the idea of their daughter doing any mathematics, much less writing algorithms for an Analytical Engine. Her mother simply didn't seem to care either way.

"Never mind, Sarah," Annabella said as Sarah finished her hair. "At least it works." Annabella allowed a grin to spread across her face, and left her room to go downstairs.

In the main drawing room there were three men with Annabella's father. Lord William King, Earl of Lovelace, was a tall, severe looking man, who Annabella knew to be gentle and easily swayed. He was dressed in a gray suit, and was speaking quietly to the other men who sat with him.

One of them Annabella knew well. Charles Babbage sat, as usual, with a hunch in his shoulders and a stoic glare on his face, and yet Annabella smiled on recognizing him, and stepped forward to take his hand.

"Mr. Babbage, how lovely to see you." Babbage rose as she approached him, and allowed her, seemingly against his will, to place a kiss on his cheek.

"Miss Annabella," he said, more softly than she might have expected. "Lady King."

Annabella looked over her shoulder, at her mother, who had entered behind her. Lady King stood stiffly, her lips flattened. Her hands were still folded over her stomach, as if she were trying to hold herself together.

16

"May I introduce," Babbage continued, averting his gaze from Lady King's, "my friend, Isambard Brunel?"

Annabella darted her eyes towards the compact man that sat beside Babbage. She couldn't keep surprise from her face, that this man, barely taller than herself, was the renowned engineer of whom her father had so often spoken.

He stood, and bowed his head to her and her mother. "Lady King, Miss King, a pleasure."

"And of course my son, Henry Babbage, who I believe you've met," Charles Babbage continued.

Annabella hid the surprise on her face this time, but not the colour that swam into her cheeks. Oh yes, she had met Henry Babbage before, on a visit to her parents' home in London, when she had not yet been old enough to be at the parties at Babbage's home. Henry had been a gangly young man then, only just able to be presented, but this was another creature entirely. This Henry was tall like his father, broad shouldered, with green eyes that were at once bright and serious. He was well dressed, but his hair stood on end as though he had just run his fingers through it.

He turned to look at her, and the gaze that met hers expressed the same wary surprise that she felt herself. Somehow, she felt that he wasn't happy to be there.

"So this is the young lady," Brunel said briskly as Annabella seated herself neatly on the sofa near her father.

"Yes," Lord King replied on her behalf. "What was it that you wanted to ask her?"

Annabella looked up sharply at her father. "Me?" she said, much louder than she intended to. Her father laid one of his hands over hers to quiet her.

Brunel continued speaking to Lord King, but gazed firmly, disconcertingly so, at Annabella. "We have a task for this young lady at the upcoming Exhibition."

"What do you mean? The Prince Consort's exhibition?" Lord King frowned.

"The very one," Brunel said, his excitement seeming to override any caution he might have felt in being faced with Lord King. "We need a lady to introduce Babbage's Analytical Engine for the Exhibition, and as we understand that Miss King is quite adept at-"

"You cannot be serious," Lord King said stiffly.

"King." The soft remonstrance, the voice of a friend, was Babbage's. Old and tired though he seemed, his voice was steady, and the look he fixed on Lord King inarguable. "She's perfect."

"She's a child," Lord King returned.

"Father, I-"

"Annabella." Ada King's composed yet hard voice stilled Annabella's objections.

Babbage leaned forward in his seat, gazing directly at Lord King. "Lord King, Miss Annabella has had time to work with the machine in ways that even I have not. She is elegant and accomplished and perfectly capable of presenting the Engine to an audience."

"My daughter will not be used like some … music hall girl to sell your machines," Lord King said sharply.

"We are not merely asking her to sell the machines," Babbage replied, completely undaunted by Lord King's refusal. "She would need to come the works beforehand, to be familiar with all aspects of the machines. In short, she would work with Mr. Brunel and Henry before the Exhibition began."

Annabella gripped her father's arm, to keep him from answering. He turned to face her, and she gazed up at him, her face full of excitement and delight. Not just one machine – not just the one that Babbage had given the family as a gift – but an entire *works* worth of the machines. It was a delight that she couldn't bear to be refused.

"The whole idea is ridiculous," Lord King said, but more softly now, as he looked at his daughter.

"The Exhibition is perfectly proper, King," Babbage prodded. "The Prince Consort and the Queen are to attend, and ladies are welcome at all the displays."

"But not *on* all the displays," King pointed out roughly.

18

"Miss King would not be asked to do anything improper," Brunel pursued. "The display would need to appeal to a wider audience. Something light, something playful-"

"Something like music," Annabella murmured. "If the machine could be displayed playing bells, then you could demonstrate-"

"What bells?" Henry said suddenly. Annabella looked over at him, and felt herself blush under his scrutiny.

"I have created an algorithm that will produce results that will then trigger mechanical arms attached to the Engine. These then play bells, and the machine chooses them within certain parameters. It's not a recognizable song as yet, but with time, I think I could manage to-"

"How is that any different from a music box?" Henry replied sharply, his eyes narrowed.

Annabella raised her eyes, and fixed them proudly on Henry's face. "It *chooses*. A music box is a set of numbered buttons; it is only capable of one song. The algorithm begins with input numbers from me, and then composes the rest of the song. I received some horrible stuff initially, but I narrowed the parameters so that the machine could only select within a certain range of tones, and could only have a limited number of choices when moving from one tone to another. The machine creates something new, just as it is designed to."

Henry offered no reply. He was, instead, staring at Annabella. His lips didn't move, and yet Annabella had the impression that he was smiling, as if something were causing his whole face to brighten and focus.

"Would you show us?" Brunel said, interrupting Annabella's thoughts. His hands were on his knees, as if he were ready to jump from his chair at the slightest notice.

Annabella broke her gaze away from Henry, and looked up at her father. He gave her the faintest of nods.

Annabella rose from her chair, and met her mother's gaze. Stiff and tight-lipped as ever, Ada's eyes were bright with anger.

"This way," Ada said smoothly, turning her back on her daughter, and leading the party through the house.

"My God," muttered Brunel as they entered the room overwhelmed by the enormous machine.

"Well then?" Babbage said, looking expectantly at Annabella.

Annabella gazed uncertainly from her father to Babbage and back again. She studiously avoided her mother's eyes.

"I cannot turn the machine by myself," Annabella said, trying to steady her voice. "I will need someone to help me."

"Yes, of course," muttered Brunel, as if he were taking notes.

"I will do it." Henry stepped forward, and Annabella forced herself to meet his eyes, and gestured him towards the crank of the Engine.

She turned to face Babbage and Brunel once more. "It has already been programmed, so Mr. Babbage has only to turn the crank-"

"A minute now," Brunel said, raising his hand just slightly. "What was that? How do you mean, programmed?"

"Sorry, when I say programmed I mean that the Engine is retrieving a previously executed sequence. It has a set of numbers, a set of punch cards, that it can retrieve from ones already punched," Annabella clarified, trying to ignore the many pairs of eyes fixed on her. "As you'll know, in addition to creating new songs and tones, it can also store the previously run sequences. I understand that it's used in the same way in railroads timetables." She turned smoothly to Henry. "Whenever you are ready, Mr. Babbage."

When the machine had finished, the group stood silent for long enough that Annabella began to twist her hands in front of her. Even her father gazed at her steadily for what seemed to Annabella an interminably long time, before heaving a resigned sigh.

"There, now, King!" Babbage said, with the closest to joy that Annabella had ever heard in his voice. "You cannot deny her now, and you know it."

"There are details that I will need to discuss with you, Babbage, " King said, though with the voice of one who knows he has lost.

"Papa!" Annabella breathed. "Do you mean it?"

By way of response, Lord King smiled at his daughter, and led Babbage and Brunel from the room. Ada King threw her daughter a glare and followed them.

20

Under the wave of excitement that overwhelmed them, Annabella had failed to notice that she now found herself alone in the room with Henry Babbage, after all the others had left.

"Mr. Babbage! We had best be following them," Annabella said. She was annoyed at how breathless she sounded. She hoped he took the cause to be her sudden and unanticipated joy, rather than his presence.

His eyebrows were knitted together, and he was gazing at the Engine. He seemed not to have heard her. "You achieve a different result every time?"

"Not every time, of course," Annabella replied quickly, taking refuge in what she knew. "I can retrieve previously played songs from the stack." Annabella bit her lip. "Mr. Babbage, hadn't we better-"

"Oh! of course, Miss King." He blinked, seeming to return to reality.

Annabella found herself staring at the arm he was offering her, as though incapable of comprehending its purpose. Tentatively, she laid her hand on his arm, and allowed him to escort her from the room.

III

All who joy would win must share it.
Happiness was born a Twin.

~Lord Byron~

Annabella had toured a works before, but none of the floating cotton factories of Manchester could prepare her for the shrieks of Brunel's Engine works. Everything here glittered – the sparks from the machines, the brass and steel products that they spat out, the molten metals that seethed in large cauldrons. The mass production of Babbage's elegant engine was far from elegant itself – it was hot, gleaming, and menacing.

Annabella waited in the entranceway, breathless with excitement, as though her corset was far too tight, and was crushing her fluttering breath. A real goal to program for, not just her games with the bells. A chance to work, to really *work*...

With Henry, a treacherous voice in her head reminded her. She flushed, and smoothed her hands over her blue linen dress. She informed herself firmly that it was silly to be embarrassed. Henry Babbage was after all a talented engineer, and there was plenty that he could teach her. There now, she told herself. That was that.

She raised her eyes, and saw a man striding towards her. He wore blue coveralls, and a grey cap over dark, curling brown hair. He was frowning, and moving his hands, and Annabella had the distinct impression that he was talking to himself.

As he lifted his eyes to her, his expression dropped to one of puzzled concern.

"Miss King?" he said. His voice had an accent to it that Annabella couldn't place.

She nodded nervously. "Yes. You were still expecting me, I hope?"

The man extended a hand to her. She tentatively offered her own gloved hand, and he shook it firmly.

22

"John Bentham. I'm the foreman here. We... yes, we're expecting you, only... I've just realized that we'll have some difficulty getting you thought the works. Your skirts, you see," he added, somewhat sheepishly.

Annabella felt her heart sink. Her skirts. Of course. How could she have imagined, looking into the clashing works, that she would possibly be able to walk through them in the massive hoop of her skirt? With its wooden frame, the skirt was at least five feet in diameter. Annabella could readily imagine the pale blue linen getting sucked into one of the unyielding machines, with terrifying results.

"Mr. ... ah... Mr. Bentham, is there a room, ... or an office that I might use?"

Bentham bit her lip. "You might use the outbuilding round the side Miss, but-"

"Just for a moment, Mr. Bentham. I won't be long."

Plainly uncomfortable with the idea, Bentham nevertheless led Annabella to a wooden building on the side of the works. He walked up the steps and hesitated at the door, but when Annabella firmly said, "Two minutes, if you please," he stepped aside, and closed the door behind her.

Annabella found herself alone in a large empty room, dark and shuttered. She drew a deep and calming breath. Now what? Clearly it was impossible for her to tour the works as she was, but what could she possibly do about it, in here, alone?

She grabbed hold of the light blue skirt of her dress and threw the bulk of the fabric over the desk chair to reveal the cotton underskirt. She pulled it up to reveal the heavy wooden and leather frame of her bell skirt. Squirming, she began to work the ties of the crinoline loose.

She was not used to such exertion, and she was starting to sweat, her corset rubbing awkwardly against her ribs. She could not in fact remember a time when she had done up her own clothes, and as she stood so close to the Engine works, this fact annoyed her. These men could run a railway empire, and she could barely remove her skirt.

The leather laces suddenly came free. They unraveled rapidly, and the wooden hoops of the crinoline crashed to the floor. Annabella gathered the bulk of the fabric in her arms, and stepped out of the circle of the hoop. She let the fabric of the skirt drop to the floor, and glanced down at herself.

The affect was not unpleasing. The dress hung closer to her body, but the sheer bulk of the fabric didn't allow anything improper to show. The bulk and length of the skirt pooled on the ground.

Annabella blinked, and realized that Mr. Bentham was still waiting for her. She stepped out of the room, onto the platform at the top of the steps.

Mr. Bentham turned and looked up at her. He didn't speak, but a slow smile spread over his face, and he seemed to speak before he meant to. "Oh, he's going to *like* you."

Henry Babbage reached for the ink well of his pen, and missed it by a couple of inches. The metal quill of his pen landed with a shriek on his desk, streaking a long line of blue ink into the leather surface. *Damn*. He glared at his pen as though it were its fault.

He looked up at the table across from his, and found Brunel smirking at him.

"Do I dare ask what you find amusing, Brunel?" he asked as he glanced down at his watch, and rose from his chair. He tucked his watch into his waistcoat pocket, and pulled on his jacket.

Brunel placed his own pen in its inkwell, and smiled at him. "Going to meet her?"

Henry glared at him. "You know I am."

Brunel raised his eyebrows. "Lovely, isn't she?"

Henry elected not to answer the question. "How much time am I to invest in her?" he asked instead.

Brunel looked up at him with surprise. "Would you ask that question if she were a man?"

"No," Henry said impatiently. "But she isn't."

Brunel waved his hand dismissively. "Start work on the Exhibition project. For the time being, that is your priority. If there is more that she can offer, we will discuss it. And you'd best be going. You're late."

Henry nodded briefly, and left Brunel's office. He walked across the yard, his thoughts on the strange Annabella King.

24

He would admit, if only to himself, that she had intrigued him the day she had demonstrated the Engine at her parents' house. Her enthusiasm was feverish; he felt swept along with her, caught up in her delight in what the Engine could accomplish. It made her look as though she had been lit on fire from the inside.

Henry stood at the entrance of the works, his back to the machines, and looked out over the yard. It wasn't raining, but even the brightest day couldn't lift the grimness off the yard of the works, its many wooden sheds and outbuildings covered in a fine layer of coal dust.

After standing there a few moments, Henry pulled out his watch. He twirled the chain over his fingers and flipped it, face up, into his palm. He frowned at it, and turned to look into the works.

His eyes widened as he caught a glimpse of pale blue linen moving through the machines. She was not late; she was in the works, dangerous as they were, by herself.

Henry gripped the cool metal of his watch as a means of choking back his anger, and stalked into the works. He threaded his way past the flying sparks of the machinists' stations, past the molten vats. He could feel his collar sticking to his neck, and his heart rate rising. The works always put him on edge, but now he felt the agitation of indignation and fear flowing through him.

He rounded the corner of a machine, and stopped. Annabella King was bent over one of the machinist stations with Bentham; her face was hidden behind a mask, and Henry could see only her mass of dark hair. There was something strange about her dress; it was slim and straight, and pooled on the ground at her feet. She was bent over the piece that Bentham was working on. Bentham lowered the machine into it, and sparks kicked out of it.

Henry leaped forward, and grabbed Annabella's wrist. He pulled her towards him, away from Bentham and the flying sparks. She reached up one hand and pulled off the mask to look up at him. She looked quite wild; her cheeks were flushed, and strands of her hair floated around her face.

"Master Henry!" Bentham called. He had left his machine, and moved over to join them.

"Why didn't you tell her to wait for me?" Henry demanded, rounding on the man.

"She didn't mean no harm," Bentham shouted back over the din. "She was asking me about the cogs, and you were late, and I-"

"It was my fault, Mr. Babbage," Annabella called, her voice swallowed by the noise. "I insisted on seeing Bentham's work immediately. I was eager to see what he could do."

Henry glanced back at Annabella, and met her gaze. Her eyes were wary but determined. He realized that he was still gripping her wrist, and released it. He twirled his watch over his fingers again.

"We'll discuss this in the office. Bentham, back to work."

The overseer's office where Henry Babbage led her was a small windowed box that allowed its occupant to observe all the works. There was a desk and two chairs, and a bookcase filled with rolled papers. The wood paneled walls shut out only enough noise that it was possible to hear another person speak at a normal volume.

Annabella's hands lay loose in her lap; her head was bowed, and she gave herself the task of examining the black smears from the soot and grease on the fingertips of her gloves.

Henry Babbage stood staring out one of the windows. Both his hands were behind his back; his left hand clasped his right wrist, as his right toyed with his pocket watch in obvious agitation.

He turned abruptly around, and seated himself in the chair opposite her.

"Why did you not wait for me, Miss King?"

Annabella looked up. His voice was hard, but it was low and controlled. His green eyes gazed calmly at her, but the flush across his cheeks betrayed agitation and anger.

"I apologize, sir," she said, more breathlessly than she meant to. "I did not mean to inconvenience you."

"That does not answer my question," Henry replied sharply. "Why did you enter the works without me?"

Annabella raised her head, and looked Henry full in the face. Her instinct was to offer neither explanation or resistance, but Henry's silent anger demanded an answer.

"I was speaking to Mr. Bentham about my ideas about the Engine," Annabella said, hoping that her voice sounded firm instead of faint. "He was kind enough to offer to show me how connecting pieces might be made for a second Engine. He was quite concerned about my safety."

"As well he might be," sighed Henry. "We do not have women and children in our works for a reason. This isn't a cotton mill - these are dangerous machines, and they need to be made to precision."

Annabella swallowed against his pointed criticism, but didn't reply.

"You do not walk the factory floor without permission," he said, laying his hands flat on the table. "You report to me first. Is that clear?"

Annabella folded her hands in her lap. "Perfectly. Sir."

A muscle in Henry's cheek twitched, and he leaned forward, pressing the heels of his hands onto his desk. "A second Engine," he continued slowly. "What did you mean?"

"Two Engines connected together."

Henry leaned forward, splaying the fingers of one hand on the desk. "Why?"

"We are seeking new places the Analytical Engine might be used," Annabella said, resting her gloved hands onto the table. "But it is, essentially, the Engine of a mathematician. If we connected two of them, one Engine could be programmed to continue to receive numerical commands, and one would receive commands that had been simplified for human use."

"The second Engine would receive the more complicated instructions," Henry said. He placed his right hand on the table, and absently twirled his watch in it.

"Yes. No. Wait," Annabella set her hand on the desk, and stared at her gloved hand as her thoughts ran ahead of her. "The second Engine would be able to do larger calculations, it's true, but actually, the first Engine would have the more complicated – the more *human* – instructions. Not every railway worker knows how to use an Engine on its own, but the two Engines together-"

"Could mimic the requests of a human, with a punch card associated with a request rather than a calculation," finished Henry. "It wouldn't be able to process the request, it would only be able to receive it."

"Yes," Annabella nodded. "It would be, in effect, a translator."

Annabella was suddenly conscious that Henry's gaze was focused directly on hers. His face was alight and alive, his green eyes bright and glittering. They seemed to see through her, past her. He blinked, and was now staring at her as if she herself were a truly remarkable machine.

"No, wait," he said softly. "We don't need two Engines for that. We just need a translator *program*. One that runs-"

"And creates new punch cards, the translated program, which can be fed back into the Engine," Annabella finished, flushing at her own excitement. "So there would be a set of Operational cards, a program, that could translate instructions from the Number Cards, and those could be-"

"Give me that roll of plans, there, in the corner," Henry interrupted. He gave her an eager grin.

IV

Still from the fount of joy's delicious springs,
Some bitter o'er the flowers its bubbling venom flings.

~Lord Byron~

It was nearly a quarter after five when Brunel pushed open the door of the overseer's office. Henry looked up at him. Annabella was seated, and Henry was standing, both bent over a series of drawing of the Analytical Engine. Henry had removed his jacket and his shirtsleeves were rolled back, and Annabella's gloves were being used to weigh down the plans. Henry glanced down at her; one thick lock of her dark hair had wound itself free and lay across the side of her face, tucked behind her ear. She looked as startled as he felt, as if they had both forgotten the turnings of the outside world.

Annabella rose quickly to her feet, looking like she was about to say something. Instead, Henry watched in horror as her face went quite white, and she reached with a fumbling hand for the back of her chair. She missed it completely, and before he had time to react, she staggered forward and crumpled to her knees, and was only saved from crashing to the floor by Brunel rushing forward to catch her.

"Dear God, man!" he exclaimed as he lowered her to the wooden floor. "What have you been doing to her?"

"Nothing!" Henry managed to gasp, staring dumbfounded at Annabella's limp body. She looked quite ill. "We've only been discussing the plans for the Analytical Engine, and I can't think what-"

"She's breathing," Brunel remarked briskly. "She must have fainted. Run across to the apartment and get my housekeeper, Rosie. Quickly man!"

As Brunel pulled off his jacket and tucked it under Annabella's head Henry rushed out of the overseer's office, and barreled down the stairs. As he rounded the last step, he found himself face to face with Bentham.

"You all right, Master?" he asked, looking at Henry.

"Yes, I,... no, Bentham, will you run across the yard and get Rosie?" Henry said breathlessly, turning towards the stairs again.

"I will. Everything all right with Miss King?"

Henry turned back. "I, ah, no. She has fainted."

Bentham gave a short laugh. "I'll be back."

Henry took the stairs back up to the office two at a time, and pushed the door open. With Brunel's help, Annabella was sitting up, but she looked very pale.

"When's the last time you ate, my dear?" Brunel said.

"I... I don't recall," Annabella said softly. She looked up at Henry. "I suppose I ate breakfast. Before I arrived."

Brunel threw a hard glance at Henry, who felt himself flush to his ears. "We were working, sir," he said weakly.

"Then you can stop," Brunel said briskly. He turned back to Annabella. "Mr. Babbage will see you home, won't he?"

Henry nodded. "Yes, I'm sorry, of course."

Brunel helped Annabella to stand, and Henry offered Annabella his arm. It seemed to him that she hesitated longer than she needed to, but she at last rested her hand on his arm, and looked up at him with a smile. Her face was pale, but her dark eyes were bright and alive.

"What on *earth* can you have been thinking?"

The last light of the day faded in the windows as it occurred to Annabella, not for the first time, that her mother had a remarkable range of voice for such a slight woman. She stood before Annabella now, thundering at her, and Annabella sat with her hands folded on her lap, looking at the curve of her fingers.

She wasn't really listening, of course. As her mother rattled away at her improper behavior, Annabella allowed her thoughts to retrieve the sights and sounds of that afternoon, perfectly punched out in her mind. She thought she had known so much, had understood so much, but seeing the machines bare, stripped of their final coverings, had simply served to show her how much she had yet to learn. She understood its numbers, its patterns, its results – but to see the Analytical Engine as it was being made was to see its ticking soul.

30

Brunel had been endlessly enthusiastic about her understanding of the Engine; indeed, had she gone into the works with no intention whatsoever of being a part of their plan, she would have walked out won over to their side. As it was, she felt so full, brought alive in a sense that no music, no books, nothing before had ever been able to give. And even as the wonder of that afternoon filled her, her need to see more, to understand what she could not yet see, overwhelmed her.

And though she didn't want to admit it, the thought of seeing Henry Babbage again was hardly unwelcome.

"Did you hear me?"

"Yes, mama," Annabella said softly.

"You simply cannot flaunt yourself in this manner! We have fashions for a reason, and rules of conduct for a reason. If you can't abide by them, you can't leave the house! For God's sake, William, look at her dress!"

The sound of her father's first name was jarring to Annabella's ears, and she glanced at her father, seeking an ally. Lord King glanced back at her, and Annabella had the sense that he couldn't have cared less what the state of her dress was, but that he had a vague sense that she had behaved in a manner not befitting his daughter. Annabella could see the strained expression as he searched for something to say.

It was little wonder to Annabella, in these moments, why her father was so often from home. Conversations between him and her mother descended into arguments or awkward silences more often than not. It had been particularly true since Byron, Annabella's older brother, had left for the Navy about a year before. It was rare that Byron even wrote, much less was home. Lord King sometimes sought Annabella's company, but mostly he sought escape, either in London at the Royal Society, or in wandering the countryside around his estate at Ockham Park.

Which left him, in a moment such as this, lost in his own home, unsure of what to say.

"I didn't do anything wrong," Annabella said, facing him directly, trying to make it sound like a statement of fact rather than a plea.

"Nothing wrong!" Ada exploded.

"Ada, please," Lord King said, his voice heavy with exhaustion. "I'm still unclear as to the circumstances of Annabella's decision, and I would like to hear them."

"It makes no difference why she-"

"I would like to hear them nonetheless, my dear." The hardness of Lord King's words cut through the room, and Ada sat stiffly on the edge of one of the chairs, her hands pressed against her stomach.

Annabella sighed. "It was impossible, papa, to tour the works as I was. There would have been some kind of accident if my dress had gotten caught."

"Exactly why you shouldn't be there!" Her mother snapped, rising to her feet. "It's utterly ridiculous to begin with! They are putting you up for disappointment. Charles is being foolish and sentimental."

As she had become older, it had occurred to Annabella that her mother's use of the word *sentimental* as some kind of curse was ironic, given her parentage. Ada's own father had been Lord Byron, the Romantic poet. Every story that Annabella had heard of him, good or bad, portrayed him as rash and emotional, the very things that her mother claimed to despise. Yet even in her insistence on logic over sentiment, Ada's rejection of emotion came with the passion that Annabella associated with her grandfather's poetry – poetry that she had read secretly, while enclosed in one of the window seats in the library.

"And besides, you can't even walk through a works decently!"

"But I will!" Annabella said fiercely, glancing quickly up at her mother, who stared at her. "The dress will need to be altered now. I can have my dress made smaller, more narrow, more old-fashioned -"

"Completely improper, you mean," her mother hissed.

"Ada," Lord King said, warningly. He sighed. "Your mother is right, Annabella. There are limits, regardless of how well you have come to know Babbage's machine."

Annabella gazed at her father in despair. This was not something that she could lose.

"You will not go near the works without a guide," her father continued, "and you will need to ask the tailor whether he can't make a slimmer dress that will allow you to be decent and practical."

Annabella raised her head, filled with irresistible hope.

"William!" Ada burst out. "You cannot possibly let this nonsense continue."

Lord King rose to his feet, and pulled down sharply on his waistcoat. "Charles Babbage is my friend *and yours, Ada*." Lord King's voice sharpened on the final words, bringing Ada's next objection to an abrupt halt. "He is bestowing a great honour on our daughter, and we *will* be sensible of it. I trust him to not compromise Annabella, and you will as well. He did as much when you worked with him."

"This is hardly the same as my work with Babbage," Ada hissed, pressing her lips together.

"You are right," Lord King said, with more force. "It is not. The world has changed a great deal since your work with Babbage, and there is no reason, in that world, why Annabella might not contribute her thoughts to this project. She will make the necessary alterations to her dress, and there will be no other incidents of this kind. Provided of course that she is properly supervised, which I'm sure Mr. Babbage and Mr. Brunel are capable of."

"Charles never goes near the works, you know that, William," Ada said in a tone of complete exasperation.

"I am sure his son is entirely capable of ensuring Annabella's safety. Charles has assured me that he will continue to do so."

Annabella bit her lip, to keep her elation from exploding out of her. The mention of Henry made her feel strangely lightheaded and at the same time as if a stone had dropped into her chest, but she remained silent, holding tight to the opportunity that her father held out to her.

"I think that will be enough for this evening, don't you, Annabella?"

Annabella glanced at her father, and took the hint. She rose carefully to her feet, and collected her skirts in one arm. She carefully walked towards her mother, as towards a horse that might bolt at any moment, and placed a kiss on her cheek. "Goodnight, mama."

Her mother offered no response, and instead turned away, and sat on one of the couches with her head lowered. Annabella hesitated, then kissed her father, and gingerly, careful not to upset the delicate balance that she had achieved, made her way out of the room. She had only just closed the door behind her when she heard her mother's voice.

"I hope you are happy," Ada said, her bitterness not concealed by the softness of her voice.

Annabella heard Lord King heave a weary sigh. "Ada-"

"*How could you?*" The words, when they came, were not in the storm of temper that Annabella had expected, but were soft, as if all their fury had burned out.

There was silence for a moment before Lord King spoke again.

"Ada, you should be happy for Annabella," he said softly.

"*How?*" she whispered. "How can I possibly be? You know, you of all others know, that you are giving Annabella all that might have made me happy."

"But Ada-"

"How could you?" She was louder this time, and Annabella heard her get to her feet, heard the sound of silk whispering behind the door. "When Babbage came to *me*, asked for *my* help, you-"

"Did what any other man would have done," returned King, unable to keep the aggravation out of his own voice. "I allowed you to published your *Notes*-"

"Not mine," Ada gasped bitterly in return. "Under his name. As if they weren't wholly mine!"

"So that's what this is about?" King shouted. "Your fit of temper over Annabella's dress, it's because she is working with Babbage and you are not? For heaven's sake, you got what you wanted. Your wonderful Engine works."

"Yes! Because of me," Ada continued, her voice strangled in her anger. "And I watched while my ideas lived, and I was forgotten."

Annabella heard her father breathing heavily, slowly. "Ada. Do not exaggerate. There was nothing more-"

"No," whispered Ada. "There was more I might have done, more I might have been, had I not been-"

34

She broke off suddenly. Annabella heard her father's heavy tread on the floor as he walked towards her.

"Had you not been what, Ada? Had you not been a woman? Had you not been my wife? Had I not made you Lady King? What is it *this* time?"

Annabella heard her mother sob once, and waited with a pounding heart.

"Ada," Lord King said in a weary voice. "I cannot change this world. Not for you. And likely, not for Annabella. But may I not permit her the same moment I permitted you – a moment of giving something to this world?"

There was a rustling as Ada moved away.

"You will only disappoint her," she said softly. "She will become like me, bitter and incomplete."

"She is young," murmured Lord King hoarsely. "She will have a husband, a family. She may forget all this in time."

Silence stretched out, until Ada spoke.

"I didn't."

Annabella swallowed, turned, and slipped quietly up the stairs. She had only been in her room a moment when there was a gentle and familiar knock.

"Come in, Sarah."

Sarah opened the door, and frowned at Annabella. "Your dress, Miss?"

Annabella smiled. "Yes. Um. I'm sorry, it may need to be cleaned."

"Are you… without your crinoline, Miss?" Sarah said, her voice becoming small and a little shrill.

"It was the machines, Sarah," Annabella said with a small laugh. "I'll need smaller dresses to go into the works."

"Shall I help you out of your clothes, Miss?" Sarah said, stepping forward to undo Annabella's buttons.

"Yes. No," Annabella said suddenly. She looked at herself in the mirror. "Teach me to do it myself, please."

Sarah stepped slowly towards her. "Are you… sure about this, Miss?" she said. Something in her voice told Annabella that she didn't just mean the dress.

Annabella looked up at her maid. There were not many people who asked such a question of her – none, actually, now that she thought of it. Sarah was looking at her with genuine concern, and it occurred to Annabella that Sarah might be the one person in her life who had any idea how she actually felt.

"Yes, Sarah," Annabella murmured. "I've never been more sure."

V

What a strange thing man is;
and what a stranger thing woman.

~Lord Byron~

Annabella sat with her head bent over her notebook as pale, sickly light filtered into the drawing room. In the weeks following that long first day spent with Mr. Henry Babbage, much of her work had been done here, surrounded by papers and tables, scribbling formulas and calculating paths that the translator program might take. Henry's letters were amongst the papers, with his assurances that he was speaking to his father, and that he would tell her as soon as he was able to whether or not their ideas could be accomplished.

Brunel had initially accused them of being completely mad. With under a year until the Great Exhibition, why change how the program operated? But as they had begun to explain the potential of the program, Brunel had been full of energy over the possibilities. He had enquired, in his brusque, efficient way, how such a program might be implemented into his own railways and works.

Annabella set down her notebook, and rose to her feet. She stretched her arms behind her, becoming aware of how stiff and tired she was. She tried to remember the last time that she had gone for ride, or a walk of any length, or even played her violin. She felt as if her whole life had become the Engine, its sketches and workings.

She walked across the room to where her violin sat propped in its stand, next to a stand of sheet music, that she had not touched in months. She lifted the violin to her chin, and picked up the bow.

This was familiar; as she fit her body together to assume the posture needed to play the violin, the tension eased out of her shoulders, and melted down her spine. Even standing straight was a relief compared to being sat at her desk. She plucked at the strings, and tuned them carefully. She shuffled the sheet music. Then she set her bow to the strings, and began to play.

The last thing that occupied her mind was playing the violin. That occupied her body; it swayed through her whole frame, and ached all the way down her hands. The strings hummed back up at her, and made her vibrate down to her feet. As her body played the swift rising and falling arpeggios, her mind flitted through what occupied it most.

Her mother.

Something was different. Ada pretended to act like her old self, and smiled and chatted, but all the time wore the strained expression of one whose mask was too tight, and was pinching her. She had gone out yesterday morning, and had returned, her face blotchy with tears and anger, to spend the rest of the day in her own room.

Her work.

It was not merely the mental acrobatics of the calculations, the programming, the constant tests and failures. More than anything, the strain of her work was the stares, the quiet implication that she didn't belong. But it was not all of them; since her arrival, John Bentham had been uncommonly kind towards her, while the other hands had maintained a guarded distance. Yet she knew that the only way that her suggestions held any true weight was if they were passed through Henry Babbage.

Henry.

The E string of the violin shrieked in protest as Annabella's thoughts raced through her mind and down the bow of the instrument. Henry troubled her even as he fascinated her. He was the only one who seemed to listen to her thoughts without diluting them with her femininity, and yet he so often assumed that she was brilliant *despite* being a woman. Yet even as she was irritated by his judging her as a woman, she knew that it was as a woman that she looked at him. She didn't judge him as simply an engineer, but as the man he was.

They ought to have been simply an analyst and an engineer working together – but they weren't. Most of Henry's employees didn't know the exact colour of his eyes, or observe the way his agile fingers toyed with his watch when he was thinking. She was not so blind as to believe that her being a woman had no effect on her work with Henry, however much the fact annoyed her.

If anything, it was work itself that drew her to him. When he was engaged in an idea, the otherwise stoic man was lit up from the inside. He became boyish and eager; he talked faster and burned brighter than he did at any other moment. The very moment when they might accomplish most together was the moment that she found him to be the most distracting.

"Miss?"

The voice, low and almost more of a throat clearing than an actual word, caused Annabella to jump and turn around. Bancroft was standing near the door, looking uneasy, and next to him, staring unashamedly at her, was Henry Babbage. He was dressed in a dark blue riding coat with brass buttons that reminded Annabella of a military uniform, and high black boots. His hair was ruffled and standing on end, as Annabella had come to learn it almost always was.

"Oh, Mr. Babbage, hello!" Annabella held her violin at her side, aware that she was entirely out of breath. "Tea, if you please, Bancroft."

"Of course, Miss, I'll tell Emily," Bancroft said with a short bow. He left, and closed the door.

For a moment, neither of them spoke. Annabella tried to catch her breath without plainly looking like that was what she was doing, while Henry simply gazed at her. He finally cleared his throat.

"I apologize for intruding. Bancroft was going to interrupt you earlier, but I... asked him not to," Henry said, the slightest evidence of a smile forming on his lips.

Annabella smiled herself, in spite of the tremor that she felt in her body. "I suppose you had been there quite some time, then?" she said, as she set down her violin and bow, and gestured for Henry to be seated.

"Enough to hear most of the first verse," Henry smiled. "*The Oak and the Ash*, wasn't it?

Annabella sat across from him and smiled in return. "You are familiar with it?"

"Not as familiar as you are, evidently," Henry replied. "You play beautifully. When do you ever find the time?"

"Not much of it anymore, I admit," Annabella returned, folding her hands across her lap. "I'm terribly out of practice."

"Not to my ear, I assure you," Henry insisted. "It was ... exquisite."

There it was, that fire, that desire to know more of what was beautiful and good. His eyes were bright and alive, flickered between green and a pale grey in the daylight that came through the windows.

"Thank you," was all Annabella managed to say. "It would make a useful demonstration piece for the Exhibition. But whatever we choose to demonstrate, we are going to need a team of people to learn it in order to program it."

"And you will have to teach them," Henry said, sitting back in his chair. "You haven't mentioned the school to Brunel yet?"

The idea of a school had come slowly out of their conversations together. They needed more people, not simply engineers, but those who could work at programming the Engine. Henry had suggested that they could be workers from the Engine factory, and that she could be the one to teach them.

"No, not yet. The workers that you have aren't likely to be thrilled that their teacher is a woman," Annabella pointed out.

"There are plenty of women who are teachers," Henry said dismissively.

"Of children. Of painting and spelling. Not of men and of technical matters," Annabella pointed out.

"You are, at present, the only analyst that we have. If they want to learn, they don't have a choice," Henry folded his hands on his knee, as if that resolved the matter.

"Have you asked your father about our suggestion?" she said.

"My father agrees that it should work, though I'm not sure that he entirely sees the point of a translator program," Henry said. "You and I will program the cards that are needed and try to have them work with the existing programs. The immediate goal is the Exhibition, so it needs to be something that can be a demonstration."

"I've been thinking about that," Annabella said. "What I showed you with the bells could be done on the Engine at the Exhibition."

Henry's eyes brightened. "Through the translator?"

"Yes," Annabella said slowly. "It will take months of programming, though."

"We have months," Henry mused.

"True, but there will need to be thousands of pre-programmed variables and instructions, and there would need to be parameters on the options that the Engine can choose, so that we don't end up listening to something that sounds horrible. Can you and I program both the music code and the translator?"

"On our own? I wouldn't have thought so," replied Henry. "But that's where we can use the school and the new analysts."

"Who do you intend to be the analysts?" Annabella asked.

"I have been speaking to some of the clerks in the railway department of Brunel's works," Henry replied. "Their tasks will soon decrease with the use of Engines, and we will have to find another use for them or tell them there is no work."

Annabella frowned. "Is that what becomes of clerks in all disciplines where the Analytical Engine is used?"

"To a degree," replied Henry. "The Analytical Engine is designed to do computational tasks, ones that would have taken a whole army of clerks much longer to complete, with much less accuracy. One of the main reasons why a large enterprise would pay the expense of the Engine is to eliminate that task."

"But what of the clerks?" Annabella pressed. "Where do they go? What kind of situations do they find?"

Henry shrugged. "Work as clerks elsewhere, I should think."

"But if every business were to have an Analytical Engine, surely those situations would not exist either?" Annabella found herself leaning forward.

"Yes," Henry replied, frowning somewhat at her concern. "That is one of the costs of creating such an Engine. Work will change or disappear in some cases, just as it did when the looms were introduced. Weavers lost work, but the production of cloth increased, and work changed from being homespun to being steam-powered work." He looked closely at Annabella's troubled face. "And it will here. The school will help to create new places for those same clerks. New roles for them that are more efficient than their old ones."

Annabella was silent for a moment, looking at her lap, twisting her thoughts over in her mind. "Suppose they cannot do the new work?"

Henry nodded slowly. "That is the cost of progress, I suppose. Not all of its changes are for the better."

It was unclear who was more relieved by the arrival of Emily with the tray of tea.

"Will you have some tea?" Annabella said after Emily had left, swallowing her uneasy feelings.

Henry visibly hesitated for a moment, and then he smiled. Annabella could almost see the tension ease out of him as he did. "Please, yes."

"Good. We can't have you fainting as well," Annabella said with a smile.

Henry gave a short laugh. "Brunel is convinced that I was slave-driving you that evening. I have assured him it was quite the opposite."

"Brunel accused *you* of being a slave-driver? I don't even think he sleeps, does he?" Annabella said cheerfully. She lifted the silver teapot, and poured out a cup for Henry. He took the delicate cup and saucer in his long fingers, and she poured one for herself.

Henry's laugh was more relaxed now, and lingered in a genuine smile on his face. "He does, but only because it increases efficiency." Henry nodded faintly to himself, and he lifted his solemn eyes. "He's a good employer. And a great man."

"Well, we all know that," Annabella smiled.

"No, it isn't just the railway, or the shipping, or his innovations. He is… it's strange, but he's a humble man. He never assumes that he knows better, that he can't learn from an unlikely source." Henry glanced up at her as he said it.

"Like a woman," Annabella said, more tightly than she wanted to.

Henry raise his eyebrows. "Would you have been surprised if Brunel had been less willing to listen to you?"

42

"I'm surprised he listens to me at all. I'm surprised that you do," she added, lifting her teacup to her mouth, breathing in the delicate smell of the Darjeeling.

Henry smiled. "I hadn't planned to. But you have proven to be... exceptional."

It was fully intended to be a compliment, but the comment rang like an insult in Annabella's ears. Annabella knew that she should have been flattered by his view of her as an exceptional woman, but she found it increasingly aggravating, even infuriating. She didn't feel exceptional. She knew many women with intelligence and wonder to equal her own, and she was quite sure they didn't feel exceptional either. She wasn't a hopeless optimist; she didn't hope that the average man would change his mind so quickly. Yet it seemed to her, given that Henry worked so often with her, that he at least might come to see her as the rule rather than the exception.

"There was something else," Henry said suddenly, setting down his teacup. He seemed suddenly, strangely, uncomfortable. "My father... is hosting an evening gathering in a week's time. He has asked me...ah... if I would personally extend an invitation to you and your family."

"I – oh yes, of course." Annabella's fought hard to keep her joy on her face, even when it was mixed with the disappointment that followed.

"Is there a problem?" Henry asked, with what seemed to be genuine concern.

"Well, no, not exactly," replied Annabella. "It would be wonderful if Father could come, but I think it's unlikely. I know that he intended to be at Ockham Park to see to some business on the estate."

"Your mother wouldn't like to come?" Henry asked.

"No, no, I'm sure she would," Annabella replied. *That was, in fact, the problem.*

VI

We were apart; yet, day by day,
I bade my heart more constant be.
I bade it keep the world away,
And grow a home for only thee;
Nor fear'd but thy love likewise grew,
Like mine, each day, more tried, more true.

~Matthew Arnold~

Annabella smoothed down the folds of her dress, and looked at
herself in the mirror. After several weeks of wearing her simpler work
dresses, the figure in the mirror looked like a stranger. The taffeta of the dress
was a vibrant green, and fell in three layers of flounces over her enormous
skirt. It had taken all of Sarah's considerable strength to pull her tightly into
the waist of the bodice, and she found herself fidgeting with the long dark silk
gloves.

"Only one more pin, Miss. Hold still, for Heaven's sake!" Sarah said,
as she viciously jabbed a jeweled emerald pin into the coils of Annabella's
hair.

Annabella winced, and let Sarah finish. She felt excited, and couldn't
quite decide why. This was not the company of people she was unfamiliar
with, and it was not the first party that she had ever attended. Perhaps it was
the combination of the two that delighted her, as though she were seeing her
friends dressed as strangers.

She shut down the treasonous part of her mind that said she was
delighted to see Henry. Because that was silly. She saw him almost every day.

She gathered a small drawstring bag, and smiled at Sarah. "Thank
you," she said, and walked hurriedly towards her mother's room.

"Mother?" she said gently, tapping her gloved hand on the door.
"Mother, are you-"

She pushed open the door, and stepped back in alarm. Her mother
was dressed, in a dark blue gown, but she was doubled over. She had one

44

hand on her waist and the other on the table, as though it were supporting all of her weight. The look on Ada's face was nothing less than alarming. Her mouth was pinched, and her eyes seemed to be looking far into the distance, struggling to retain their focus. She was breathing in fast, shallow breaths.

"Mama?" Annabella managed, bewildered by her mother's obvious pain. She reached for her mother's hand, but her mother waved her away.

"No, it's nothing," she said. Her voice was soft and hoarse. "A momentary faintness. It's from the rush of getting ready. I'm fine now." She lifted her head, attempting, it seemed to Annabella, to sound almost cheerful.

Despite Ada's protestations, Annabella reached for her hand, and guided her mother firmly to the chair in her room. She stepped back and looked around, unsure of what to do, certain that she had just been lied to.

"Mother, are you sure you-"

Ada gave a sudden cry of pain, and bent over in her chair. "Annabella, will you get Jennifer please. I need to be helped out of my clothes."

Annabella rushed in the hall, to find Sarah walking past. "Sarah! Will you get Jenny, please? Mother... she needs to change, to... rest." Not heeding Sarah's look of concern, she rushed back into the room.

"Mama, Jenny will come and help you, and I'll just change too-"

"No," Ada said, shaking her head. "You may go without me."

Annabella stared at her mother. She was unsure what shocked her most: her mother's rapid and painful breathing, or the fact that she was willing to let Annabella go to the party on her own.

"I- unaccompanied?"

Ada waved her hand at her, her face taut and exhausted. "I'm sure Charles Babbage can find suitable company for you."

"Mama, what-" Annabella tried again.

She stopped as her mother let out a heavy sigh. "It's all right, Annabella. You may go."

"What is the matter, Mother?"

It was out of her mouth before she had time to stop it. As she heard her own words, Annabella realized she was frightened, frightened *for* her mother rather than *of* her, frightened and completely uncertain on how to proceed with this new, passive, and worrying creature.

Ada looked at her for a long time. Her face was calm, and yet the strain around her eyes suggested a struggle – with what, Annabella could only guess.

"It's nothing, Bella. I would be grateful if you…" she paused, and drew a deep breath. "… would give my regards to Mr. Babbage, and explain my absence."

"I can't leave you like this. Do you need a doctor?" Annabella asked, kneeling in front of her.

Ada waved her away once more. "No. Go. They will be expecting you."

Annabella watched the barrier drop back down between them, and found herself once more shut out of whatever turmoil Ada King felt.

Annabella drew a breath, and stepped out of the carriage. She looked up at Charles Babbage's brightly lit house, and found herself feeling faintly sick. She shouldn't be here, not while her mother was at home with… She wished she knew what it was.

She felt vulnerable, and alone. Why on Earth had her mother permitted her to be here? She gripped her hands together in front of her, and walked towards the door, feeling strangely exposed.

The warmth and sounds of the house washed over her, and she became lost in a sea of faces, of brilliantly coloured dresses, of chatting voices, and of high, bright music. From the entrance she could see that Babbage's large hall had been cleared for dancing, and she could see Charles Babbage himself at the top of the stairs, greeting guests as they arrived.

Annabella hurried towards him, and he smiled as he saw her, and took her hand. "Miss King, how lovely to see you." He frowned. "I thought your mother would be joining us?"

"My mother regrets that she is unwell, and will be unable to join us," Annabella said with a stiff smile. "I must apologize for trespassing on your hospitality unaccompanied, I-"

"No, not at all, I'll see that you're well looked after," Charles said with a warm smile. He squeezed her hand, and let her walk forward into the high ceilinged room.

She felt once again cast adrift, as though this were a new world that she had never before navigated. It wasn't, of course; she had been to parties and dances before, even ones at this very house. The singing string instruments, the waltzing couples, the house lit with the yellow glow of gas jets – none of it was new. But it all had a new vibrancy to it, as though she saw it through new eyes.

She hadn't known she was looking for him, until suddenly she saw him. Henry Babbage stood to one side of the floor, speaking to another gentleman.

He looked bored, she realized, as she watched him listening to the men around him. Bored, and… handsome. His dress coat of black wool fitted close to his shoulders and waist, and the tails made him seem taller. The coat was cut away to show an ivory silk waistcoat underneath, and his collar closed high on his throat with a white cravat. His hair was uncharacteristically neat, and she could see him playing with his watch in one hand.

She discovered she had been staring at him only when he suddenly saw her, and a smile slid onto his mouth. He excused himself quickly, and walked towards her. She felt herself untwisting inside, feeling, even before they spoke, calmer and safer. Her heart warmed enough that she managed a smile of her own, and felt, by the time that he had reached her and taken her hand in greeting, that she had regained her composure.

She expected him to simply shake her hand, as his father had. Instead, he bent his head over it, and pressed his lips against the fabric of her glove. Annabella smiled, and reminded herself not to be breathless and stupid.

"Miss King," he said, as he straightened. His voice was reserved, but his face was warm, his eyes bright. He did not let go of her hand.

"Mr. Babbage," she said. She felt silly speaking to him like this.

He frowned. "Is your mother not with you?"

Annabella was suddenly conscious that she had not sufficiently erased the worry and panic from her face. Her heart fluttered in her chest, with the knowledge that it would pain her to lie to him.

"It's nothing," she said, forcing another smile. "It's only… Mother had a bit of a turn when…. She tells me she's fine now."

Henry frowned, and pressed his thumb tightly into her hand. "Is she ill?"

"No," Annabella said quickly. "No, she tells me she's fine. I think she might be a little tired, that's all."

"Are you certain?" Henry said, his gaze fixed on her.

No. "Yes, of course," Annabella replied. She could feel the scrutiny of his gaze, and hoped that she didn't look as scattered as she felt. She carefully drew her hand out of his grasp.

"Would you… are you permitted to waltz?" Henry asked softly, glancing towards the couples turning around the room.

Annabella was glad he was looking away, as she felt her cheeks become warm. She wasn't sure whether her stomach had disappeared, or whether the floor had fallen away.

"I… yes, I am," she replied.

"Would you allow me to ask for the next dance?" he said, lowering his gaze.

Annabella swallowed. His face was calm, but his throat betrayed a blush against the white of his collar. She was caught between finding him captivating, and wishing she could shake him free of this version of him that was not himself.

"Yes, of course," she replied with a smile. She could already hear the music slowing, changing to the next waltz.

Henry guided her by the hand to the other side of the room. As the music from the strings picked up, he rested his right hand against the small of her back, and took her hand gently with his left. She placed her other hand tentatively on his arm, and hoped that she wasn't blushing as much as she was sure she was.

Henry danced well – much better than she would have thought he could. The pressure of his hand on her back was gentle, but he guided her firmly around the room. He moved elegantly, almost effortlessly.

"You look lovely," he said softly after a moment, as though it embarrassed him.

48

It embarrassed her. It felt wrong, somehow, coming from him. "You don't have to treat me differently, Mr. Babbage. My mind doesn't disappear because I am wearing an evening dress."

She realized the venom with which she must have said it when Henry looked surprised, and, unless her gaze deceived her, a little hurt.

"Please forgive me. I did not intend to offend you," he said, his voice low, his eyes grey in the soft light.

She sighed. "My apologies, Mr. Babbage, I know you did not. I find myself being constantly reminded of the divide between men and women. For you,... even here, you are still yourself. While I am simply a colourful ornament again."

To her surprise, Henry looked genuinely distressed. "But that's only fashion, surely."

"Is it?" Annabella replied, turning her gaze around to the other couples. "What is fashion, if not a dictation of how we can or cannot behave? Is the fact that so few women have a profession anything but a fashion?"

"Of course it is," Henry said instantly. "A fashion would imply that it is fleeting, that it will pass. The position of men and women is more enduring."

Annabella looked at him sharply. "Then what am I? Do you continue to work alongside me, even while thinking that my position is to be kept at home?"

Henry did not stop dancing, but Annabella could feel his fingers tense against her back. "*Your* position? No. But you are different."

"Only in that I am lucky. In that I have been given education and opportunity," Annabella pressed.

"No," Henry said swiftly. Whether consciously or not, he pulled her closer to him. "You *are* different. You think differently than other women. You are clear, and logical. And brilliant." Henry's words came tumbling, staggering, and abruptly stopped, as if he had suddenly become conscious of having said too much.

"Even if these other women here thought like I do, how would anyone be able to see them? They would see only a beautiful dress. Just as you did." Annabella glanced away from Henry's gaze. She felt suddenly strangely warm, flustered by how close he was to her.

"That is not all that I see," Henry said, anger edging his voice. "I see your mind, as will everyone else."

Annabella raised her head. "At the Exhibition, you mean."

Henry cleared his throat. "Yes, that. And who knows what besides?"

They danced for a moment in silence, and Henry seemed to relax. Annabella felt her agitation ebb out of her as he turned her across the floor.

"How long has your mother been ill?"

Henry's question broke harshly through into Annabella's thoughts, and for a moment she considered not answering.

"I don't know," she said finally.

"Has she seen a doctor?" Henry said. His voice was softer now.

Annabella shook her head. "I know nothing about it. She would never tell me anything of that kind."

Annabella didn't meet Henry's gaze. It was easier to just let this moment continue, to drown in the music that surrounded them and forget all the people who made her feel shut out and alone. The music slowed, and Henry took her hand and led her across the floor.

He turned to her, and looked like he was about to say more, when a shrill voice called his name.

"Mr. Babbage!" The voice belonged to a woman some years older than her mother, in a pink dress with a great deal of lace. "So lovely to see you again," she said, extending her hand, which Henry took. "You remember my daughter, of course?"

Annabella turned, to see a woman about her age with blond ringlets in a pale blue dress, who was smiling at Henry.

"Of course," Henry said with a slight inclination of his head. "Mrs. Carson, and Miss Carson, may I present Miss Annabella King?"

Annabella extended her hand to the younger woman. "How do you do," she said carefully.

"I was telling Cecily," Mrs. Carson continued, "about your father's wonderful automaton. The Silver Lady, isn't it called? Perhaps you might be able to show us?"

50

Henry glanced between Annabella and Cecily with a look Annabella couldn't read. "Of course," he said. He inclined his head to her. "Would you care to join us, Miss King?"

His formality had returned; she could see it in the stiffness of his shoulders, in his slight bow to her. It didn't suit him; it stripped him of all that was brilliant about him and left only his manners intact, hard and cold and empty.

She smiled, and nodded. "Of course, Mr. Babbage."

Henry glanced between Miss Carson and Annabella, and finally offered Miss Carson his arm. Annabella watched them walk across the hall to his father's study and workshop, feeling drained even as she followed them.

She had seen Charles Babbage's workshop before. It was the mechanical equivalent of Frankenstein's laboratory. Half-formed creatures of brass and steel were scattered on tables. The Analytical Engine had once sat in the centre, clanking for audiences of dinner guests and investors. But there was no Engine there now, and the room felt strangely empty without it.

Henry let go of Miss Carson's arm and walked towards a beautiful silver automaton that stood on a pedestal near the desk. The Silver Lady, as Charles Babbage called her, was a clockwork figure of a dancer. Henry wound it, and the figure began to spin and dance with lurching grace, to the evident amusement of Miss Carson and her mother.

Annabella barely heard the chatter of their voices, or the subtle grinding of the mechanisms that could be heard from the Silver Lady. She watched Henry, as he stepped back from the automaton. She watched his face as Miss Carson wrapped her hand around his arm. He was looking at the dancing machine, rather than at Miss Carson. She said something, and laughed, and a faint smile brushed across his face.

Annabella looked at the Silver Lady, as its arm swayed over its head. She wished she didn't feel the blooming ache in her chest that she so clearly felt. Because that, she carefully reminded herself, was foolish. Of course other women were interested in Henry Babbage. He was wealthy and handsome and well-connected; it would be foolish for her to think that he was without prospective brides.

Yet she couldn't help but feel that seeing him here was like seeing a pale echo of the Henry Babbage she knew – the one with Engine grease on his hands, with codes and programs pouring from his mouth, in the moments when his mind was full of new ideas. To see him now, elegant and well-mannered and distant, was to wonder how little those moments meant to him, when they meant so much to her.

She glanced over at him. Miss Carson had left his side to step closer to the dancing automaton, and Henry was looking over at her. His eyes were clouded with a slight frown. She gave him what she hoped was a reassuring smile, and dropped a small curtsy before leaving the room.

All she wanted now was to go home.

VII

I might have known,
What far too soon, alas! I learn'd—
The heart can bind itself alone…

~Matthew Arnold~

With an aching shoulder, Henry heaved the final case up and over the edge of the roof of Brunel's works. He set it down as gently as he could, wincing as the wood scraped against the slate roof, and hauled himself up next to it.

The roof was scattered with boxes, shapes rolled in canvas, and what looked like long wooden poles. In the rapidly weakening light at the end of the day, Henry moved quickly, setting up a tripod on the roof, and snapping open cases around him.

London rolled out below him, lamplights beginning to be lit, but most of the city only offered a dim glow. The pale blue sky seeped into liquid black, as the first points of lights began to appear above him. He snapped open the large case.

Even in the shadows, Henry could make out the familiar form of the telescope. It was a gift from John Herschel to his father, one that Herschel had made himself. The edge of the lens was a little murky, not as clear as a newer one would have been, but Henry kept coming back to it, as though it were an old friend. He strapped the telescope into the mount of the tripod, and let his mind wander as he adjusted it.

It had been a strange few weeks working alongside Miss Annabella King. He had known her for the better part of both their lives, and yet she continuously surprised him. His training for the Analytical Engine had been from his father. It was rational, clear, and held him on a straight-line path. Hers was non-existent. For her, the Analytical Engine had no predetermined limit; when he had suggested that there were some things that a machine could not do, she had simply replied with "why not?"

She was not what he had expected when he had initially refused to work with her. Working with her wasn't just worthwhile – it was downright pleasant. When she thought no one was watching, she chewed on the end of her pencil, and hummed to herself. As the sound of the Engine subsided, he could hear her, as though she were singing to it.

He loved watching her work. But now, whenever he did, he couldn't keep from seeing her as she had been when they had danced – her eyes looking up at him, her cheeks bright with anger and indignation, the emerald pins glittering in her dark hair. The image was sufficiently distracting, and sufficiently at odds with who she was when she worked, that he almost wished he hadn't danced with her.

Almost, but not quite.

Henry put his eye to the eyepiece, and carefully adjusted it. A few blacks of coal dust had settled on the lens, but not as many as he had feared. He grinned as the disk of Jupiter came into focus, its four bright moons dancing around it.

"Hello there," he murmured.

It was the end of a dreary December day that Annabella stood with Henry outside of Brunel's office, waiting while Brunel spoke with a steel manufacturer from the North. They didn't speak, not from awkwardness, but from exhaustion – they had both spent the better part of the grey day writing out patterns and punches for the cards of the demonstration engine. So far, the punch cards that held errors vastly outnumbered the cards that held viable options for the program. Every time that Annabella felt sure that the code for the music was right, it jarred her to hear the machine produce the wrong sounds.

It wasn't just the Engine itself that caused tension in their work. One of the days they had been at the works, a foremen had taken one swift look at Annabella, and had asked to speak to Henry privately. Annabella had stood turning her notebook over in her hands as the two men spoke furiously and agitatedly to each other. If there had been any doubt in Annabella's mind as to what the problem was, it was erased by Henry yelling, "I work with her, and you damn well will as well!"

54

He had then stormed back to her, and offered her his arm. Annabella had wanted to decline, but in looking at Henry, and seeing the thundercloud that overcast his face, she had decided not to argue.

And then there had been the catch. A catch, Henry had explained to her, was a mistake; it had originally meant, quite literally, one of the cogs catching in the machine, but was now used by the hands to mean anything that went wrong. A wrong code, a wrong number, a mechanical problem, was a catch – something that needed to be corrected before they could continue.

Henry had discovered one in a cog tower of the store, where data was kept until it was needed. One of the new mechanisms was physically imperfect; instead of transferring the numbers seamlessly to the next tower, the carry arm would skip across the cogwheels next to it, causing the Engine to jam. After frustrating hours of attempting to correct their instructions, Henry had pulled the cog tower apart, to find that the cogwheels hadn't been made at precise angles. What had followed had been some of the most creative swearing that Annabella had ever heard. It was then that Henry had suggested that they stop for the day, and speak to Brunel.

Annabella held her hands firmly in her lap, and demanded of herself that she not play with her gloves. The request she had of Brunel was carefully reasoned, she reminded herself, and perfectly sensible. She glanced over at Henry, who was resting his head against the wall, and found herself staring absently at the line of his jaw.

The door to Brunel's office swung open, and a thin man in a grey overcoat stepped out. He extended his hand to Henry, who shook it, and then allowed his gaze to fall on Annabella.

"Is this your lovely wife, Mr. Babbage?" the man said in a very Lancashire accent.

"Ah, no," Henry replied, with a faint smile. "This is Miss King, our finest analyst. Miss King, this is Mr. Cropper, of Cropper Steel."

Annabella had risen, prepared to offer her hand to the gentleman. She looked at his face, at the poorly disguised look of disdain that he had given her, and held her hands firmly clasped in front of her.

"How do you do, sir," she said stiffly.

Mr. Cropper bowed his head only a fraction, and turned back to Henry. "Good day to you, Mr. Babbage."

Annabella stared straight ahead as Mr. Cropper stepped past her without acknowledging her, and drew a calming breath as he descended the stairs.

"I'm sure Mr. Brunel is waiting for us, we'd best-" Annabella broke off her sentence as her gaze met Henry's face. He was gazing down the steps after Mr. Cropper, his face showing undiluted fury.

"Miss King," he said, his voice sounding choked, "would you give me a moment to speak to Mr. Brunel?"

Without waiting for Annabella to answer, Henry stepped into Brunel's office, and slammed the door behind him.

Annabella stared at the closed door, fighting down her anger. As if slamming the door in her face were any different than Mr. Cropper's look of disgust! But Annabella had spent many years of her life getting her information from closed doors, and Mr. Brunel's office door did not close exceptionally well.

"… possible complaint can you have against Mr. Cropper?" she heard Brunel saying as she leaned close to the doorframe.

"He looked at her as if she were filth!" Henry exploded. Even if Annabella had not been close to the doorframe, she would have heard Henry's furious words.

"I can't control how a man looks at a woman," Brunel snapped. Was it Annabella's imagination, or was that remark directed at more than Cropper?

"But you can control the esteem that they hold her in," returned Henry.

"They *who*?" snarled Brunel. "I don't have to control the hands – Bentham does it for me. They have always treated her with complete respect. And the very fact that she is a part of this display is an attempt to let the world see what she can do. I cannot do more than that."

"She is the daughter of an *Earl,* who-"

"It makes no difference who she is," Brunel said forcefully.

Henry made a sound of exasperation, his voice rising. "You cannot permit her to throw every ounce of her energy into that Engine, and to continue to be treated like a common-"

"Henry Babbage!" snapped Brunel. Annabella heard what sounded like a chair scrapping backwards, and the sound of Brunel getting to his feet. "I am not her damn father, and it is not my responsibility to protect the young lady. And neither, might I add, is it yours."

There was a steely silence in the room for a moment, and then Brunel's voice said softly, "You may as well listen in here as out there, Miss King."

Annabella jumped, and felt a hot flush rise under her collar in spite of the cold. She swallowed hard, and opened the door.

Brunel was indeed on his feet, and Henry was leaning with one hand on Brunel's desk. His eyes were bright and his jaw was locked – he looked like he was grinding his teeth. He looked at Annabella, and his face softened, before a quiet flush of embarrassment rose in his cheeks.

"How much did you hear of-"

"Oh don't be an idiot, Babbage, she heard all of it," Brunel sighed, sinking into his chair. "Please sit down, Miss King. Your white knight here will presumably sit down when he finishes wearing a path in my floor."

Henry had indeed started to pace the office, playing with his watch behind his back. He shot Brunel a furious glare, and threw himself into one of the chairs.

Brunel looked from Annabella to Henry, and back again. When he finally spoke, his voice was gentle and calm, and directed mostly at Annabella. "If you feel that there is no room here for more delicate sensibilities, understand that it is not because I am ignorant of their existence."

"Mr. Brunel, I have nothing to complain of-" Annabella offered.

"I was not referring to you, my dear," Brunel interrupted with a wave of his hand. "Of course you complain of nothing. You have everything to lose, and everything to prove. It is you, Mr. Babbage, who need to understand that you do her no favors by running to her defense and strong-arming a place for her here. No one will ever accept her if she doesn't stand on her own merits."

"Merits that Cropper cannot possibly appreciate," Henry growled in return, his fist closing tight on his watch.

Brunel gave the smallest hint of a smile. "Obviously. Let it be for now. There will come a time soon enough when Cropper will envy you and her both. Now, the school."

Annabella smiled. Brunel could be strangely sensitive, but he was, at heart, always at his business.

"We, ah, we will need operators to program the Engine if it is to be ready for the Exposition," Henry said after a moment's hesitation. "The thought was that we should be prepared to train operators in its use, who could then be apprenticed to you."

"A mechanical school," Brunel nodded. He frowned at Annabella. "Do you think we'll manage to get many men to attend? Meaning no offence, my dear."

"I've been thinking about that," Annabella said. "I believe that if I can get some of the hands from the factory to enroll as operators, we would be able to encourage others in enough time to program the Engine. And they would need to be paid for their training."

Brunel raised his eyebrows. "Consider it an investment, Mr. Brunel," Annabella said quickly.

A smile played on Brunel's lips. "All right, then. Did you have anyone in mind?"

"Yes," Annabella said, before Henry could respond. "I want Bentham."

Both Henry and Brunel stared at her in surprise. She hadn't discussed this part with Henry – she hadn't wanted to hear no from him.

"Bentham? He's my best hand," exclaimed Brunel.

"Yes, and he's wasted at it," replied Annabella. "He has a brilliant understanding of the Engine, and he would be able to understand how modifications might be made in the cogs to speed the programming."

58

Henry grinned, clearly excited at the thought. "He would also encourage more hands to become operators. If he's willing, he would influence the others."

"And I'd lose all of them to you," Brunel said, throwing up his hands. "All right, we'll ask him. To begin when?"

"In the new year," Henry replied. Annabella opened her mouth to object, but Henry cut her off. "No, we will need the time to prepare the training room and the hands that are to be moving to it. And besides, you will need rest and time to prepare," he said gently to Annabella.

"How dare you presume to know-" Annabella began.

"Stop, children, please," muttered Brunel. "We've had enough indignation for one day. We'll start in the New Year. Now, Mr. Babbage, I presume you are still a sufficient white knight, to see Miss King home?"

Henry handed Annabella into the carriage, and got in opposite her. Annabella had come to feel quite at ease in a carriage alone with Henry, but today, she found herself staring at her hands in her lap.

"You are angry with me," Henry said softly.

Annabella raised her eyes, and met Henry's eyes, warm and gleaming in the dim carriage. "Do you often ask your employees whether they are angry with you? Do you not simply let them feel however they want?"

"I do not wish to tell you how you may feel," Henry said sharply. He swallowed, and looked at her with what seemed to be embarrassment. "I only wish to know... what it is that I have done."

Annabella broke away from his gaze, unable to hold his gaze any longer. "I am not ungrateful for your reaction. But what you said-"

"You were not intended to hear it," Henry said, anguish seeping into his voice.

"What you said was what... what you must have heard many times before. Did the foreman say something of that kind to you?" Annabella felt a sickening knot developing in her chest, a testament to the pain that she had been telling herself she did not feel.

"Annabella."

Henry's voice pleaded her name, her first name, and made her look at his face. Those brilliant, eager eyes were soft now with poorly hidden pain. "I cannot bear it," he said hoarsely. "To see them look at you with such derision when they aren't worth the smallest part of you."

"They will always be worth more than me. Just as you will be."

Henry sat silently for a moment, gazing at her across the carriage from him. "You are cleverer by far than any of those men."

"And yet still a woman," Annabella said softly. "Still weak, and meaningless. Still a creature to be shouted over and protected, but not listened to."

Henry opened his mouth to speak, and then lowered his eyes. "I had no right to speak so. I... please, forgive me, Miss King."

Annabella looked at the curve of Henry's mouth, at his lowered eyes.

"We are friends, Mr. Babbage. Please call me Annabella." She swallowed hard as soon as the words were out of her mouth, but still extended her hand to him.

Henry Babbage raised his eyes, and a smile broke over his features. He took her hand in his, her gloved fingertips resting in the palm of his hand.

"It's Henry, if you please."

VIII

As kingfishers catch fire, dragonflies draw flame…

~Gerard Manley Hopkins~

"How far have you got?" Henry asked from the other side of the Engine.

"I have nearly finished the last of this stack," Annabella replied from her side. She sat at a small wooden table in the workroom, making delicate marks on one of the punch cards.

"I think that should do it for today," Henry called back. "We're losing the light."

"Let's run them at least," Annabella protested.

"Who's the slave driver now, I should like to know?" came Henry's reply. "All right, punch them and then bring them around to me."

Annabella made her final marks, and walked to the puncher, a heavy contraption with a long handle. It took considerable strength to pull it down to punch a single card, but it wasn't nearly as tiring as it had been to begin with.

"Can I do it for you?" Henry offered gently, as he walked up behind her.

Annabella turned and looked at him. He had pulled off his jacket, and wore his shirtsleeves rolled back to his elbows. His hair was disheveled; he must have raked his fingers through his hair while he was working. He had a smear of grease across his cheekbone, and a wrench stuck into the pocket of his waistcoat.

She liked him like this, at his work, the smell of metal on his hands.

She blinked, and realized that she was still staring at him as he awaited an answer.

"No, thank you, I only have a small number to do."

Henry didn't move, but stood next to her as the heavy punch swung into the cards. She felt her face growing hot, and told herself that it was from the exertion of punching the cards, not from how strangely aware she was of his presence. She finished the stack, and handed them to him.

"Ready to run them?" was all he said. She nodded, and moved around to the front of the Engine.

Their demonstration Engine had been fitted with small and rather rudimentary bells. They were for testing only. They had managed the first few notes, but nothing that could even be remotely equated to music.

There was a shuffling sound on the other side of the Engine as Henry shunted the cards into place. He gave a call of "Hands off!" to indicate that the machine was about to start moving, and Annabella heard the hiss of the steam-powered driver starting.

The Engine thundered into life. Annabella stood in front of it, watching the bells, waiting as the mechanisms slowly began to turn. In their initial programming, they had instructed the Engine to begin playing immediately, but now the Engine ran calculations until it was moving at its full speed, before passing signals to the bells.

Annabella saw it before she heard it; close to her right hand, two bells moved simultaneously. Slowly it swelled, the first few lines of music, at a slow but even rhythm, chiming out melody and harmony in the same instant.

"Henry!" Annabella called. "It worked!"

The words were no sooner out of her mouth than she heard a too familiar screech – the sound of a cogwheel catching, scratching across the surface of its tower, and then clicking back into place. Annabella froze, as the machine, the bells, all the sounds resumed their pattern.

Annabella picked up her skirts and hurried around the back of the Engine. "Henry, what-"

She froze as she saw him. Henry had thrown his wool coat around his hands, and was reaching for the edge of the card stack in the pounding Engine. One of cards had caught fire, and would, in a matter of seconds, burn through its stack. Their first successful attempt would be entirely destroyed.

Annabella realized what Henry was about to do only a moment before he did. He was watching the Engine, timing it, waiting until the cogs shunted into position so that he could reach in without his hands being crushed.

"Henry, don't!" she cried.

He thrust his covered hands into the Engine, and yanked out the burning cards. The spinning cogs snapped into place where his hands had been. He threw the cards to the stone floor, along with the cloth, and stamped them out under his feet.

Annabella ran to the side of the Engine, and looked up at the mechanisms of its steam-powered driver. It was neither large nor particularly powerful, but it was impossible to stop it suddenly. Annabella snapped open the valves, standing clear as the steam hissed out of it. The Analytical Engine slowed only slightly.

She stumbled around the back of the Engine, to find Henry flicking aside the burnt pieces of card, trying to remove something usable from their remains. There was an angry red burn on his arm where he had had his sleeve rolled back.

"Henry!" she called over the slowing Engine, feeling breathless. "Your arm!"

He was suddenly on his feet, closing the distance between them, until he clasped her arm with one hand. "Are you hurt?" he said.

"No," Annabella said quickly. "But your arm…"

Henry didn't reply. His gaze lingered where his hand held her arm, his thumb pressing the hollow of her elbow. He glanced up at her, his eyes startled and bewildered.

Annabella looked away quickly, knowing all the emotions that her face would betray. She was suddenly painfully aware of how close he was to her, closer than when they had danced. She could see his quickened pulse throbbing in his throat, and the edge of an old scar, visible just above his collar.

Henry slid his hand down her wrist, down the back of her hand, and wrapped her fingers in his hand, holding it close to his chest. Annabella dimly knew that she should be shocked by his action, but she knew this through a veil of gradually receding panic and relief.

"Are you all right?" he said softly.

Annabella nearly jumped at the sound of his voice. "Yes, I… what happened?"

"There was a catch in one of the instructions," Henry said. His voice was low. She could feel the breath of his words on her face. "The cards jammed and caused the closest cog to catch. It sparked and lit the cards on fire."

"A catch in one of the … in one of my instructions?" Annabella said, looking up at him in horror. A mistake in one of her cards. Annabella glanced down at Henry's arm, and blood began to pound in her ears.

"Annabella, please don't think like that," Henry insisted. He gripped her hand tighter.

"My instructions were flawed… and your arm…." Her throat started to tighten, and the more she tried to calm it, the more she felt like she was gulping air. "Henry, I'm so sorry, I-"

"*No*, Annabella." Henry caught her by her shoulders, and forced her to look into his face. His eyes were soft, like rainfall. "It was a *mistake*. Perhaps yours, but it could have as easily been my own. Perhaps there was a mechanical flaw as well. There is no harm done."

"But your arm-" Annabella heard herself whimper.

"No permanent harm," Henry returned with a gentle smile.

He raised a hand towards her face. He stopped, and dropped his hand, his smile disappearing.

Annabella swallowed against the lump in her throat. What she had felt at the dance at Babbage's home, the feelings that she had been able to ignore, were screaming at her now. Her mind rioted with guilt over the puckered burn rising on Henry's arm, mixed with fluttering excitement at the feeling that his hands left on her skin. His face was close to hers, their foreheads almost touching, and she realized how little it would take for her to be wrapped in his arms. And she realized, with a thundering heart, that she wanted to be. It was a feeling that she had no promise of having returned, that left her in terror of the idea that she could ruin everything, all that she had worked for, and all that she had gained.

"*Please*, Annabella," he murmured. "Don't make yourself uneasy. I… I have no comfort that I can offer you that would not… disgrace me."

Annabella stood still for a moment, letting Henry's words linger. She pushed down her panic, as well as the ray of hope that flickered through her. "We had… had better-"

64

"Yes," Henry said, abruptly letting go of her arms and stepping away from her. "Tea for you, and a brandy for me, and then I shall return you home."

She lifted her eyes to look at him, and for a moment they stood still, locked in each other's gaze. He turned suddenly and walked to the door of the room. Left with no choice, Annabella followed him.

Henry sent one of the hands to request brandy and tea from the inn across the road, and left Annabella in Brunel's office while he collected strips of fabric to bandage his arm. Annabella had no idea where he had gone, but simply sat and shivered, staring the fire, until he returned.

She watched with a sick feeling as Henry poured brandy across his burned arm. He drew in a hissed breath as the alcohol met his skin, but his face betrayed no pain.

Henry looked up at her, and smiled. "Half for the arm, and half for me," he said, pouring the remaining brandy into a glass.

Annabella smiled weakly, and reached for one of the plain china teacups on the desk. Her hands were no longer shaking, but she felt weak and tired, and above all, useless. Before her was Henry, injured, and yet wrapping his own arm in a muslin bandage, while she found herself still shaking off her own shock. She put her teacup down on the desk.

"Can I help you?" she asked.

Henry looked up as he tucked the last piece of muslin into place. "It will do for now."

"How did you learn to do that?" Annabella asked, picking up her teacup again and cradling it in her hands.

Henry collected his glass of brandy, and sat heavily in Brunel's chair. "By having to do it too often," he said softly. "In the army." He leaned forward in his chair. "How are you feeling?"

Annabella shook her head. "Foolish. And worried. What are we going to do?"

Henry took a sip of his brandy. "About the Engine, you mean?" He set the glass down on the desk, and rubbed his thumb against the rim. He frowned. "It's something about the speed at which the cogs are running. If there's the slightest imperfection, the Engine jams. That could be what's catching in the codes. Especially at the speeds we're asking it to run to play the music."

"Can it even be done?" Annabella asked, tension beginning to ebb out of her.

Henry shrugged. "It isn't whether it can be done, it's whether we can do it in time." He looked up at her, and gave an exhausted grin. "Enough for now. It was a long day even before I lit myself on fire. We'll come back to it."

Annabella nodded, and for a moment said nothing, just looked into her cup of tea. She looked up, to find that Henry had tilted back his head and closed his eyes, his brandy glass cradled loosely in one hand. She found herself tracing the lines of his throat with her gaze, and coughed.

"You are aware that my family has required me to be at Ockham Park for the next fortnight?" Annabella said, feeling strangely fearful of his reply.

Henry opened his eyes and titled his head forward to look at her. "Yes, you said, until after the New Year." It seemed to Annabella that his voice was almost shy. "In fact, I may be joining you for some of it."

"How do you mean?" Annabella said, feeling warmth flooding through her from more than simply the tea.

"Your father has been kind enough to invite myself and my father to spend Christmas with your family. I was planning to accept on my own behalf, if you have no objections?" He lifted his eyes to her, with a need for approval that seemed so strange in him.

"Why should I object?" Annabella replied, without even bothering to stifle the eagerness in her voice. "I am delighted. And your father will come as well?"

Henry nodded. "I hope so. I have every reason to believe he will. We will be joining you a few days after your arrival, I believe, so perhaps we might yet find time to discuss the problem of the arm."

Annabella grinned. "Of course. Will I be given Christmas Day off, Mr. Scrooge?"

Henry smirked. "I suppose you will. 'It's a poor excuse for picking a man's pocket every December the 25th,' but as you are not actually paid, I don't see that that will be a problem."

66

IX

The beginning of atonement is the sense of its necessity.

~Lord Byron~

For what she was sure was the fiftieth time, Annabella smoothed the fabric of her wool skirt. For the forty-ninth time, she reminded herself that this was ridiculous; she was awaiting the arrival of Charles and Henry Babbage, two men who she had known since childhood. There was absolutely no reason to feel ill at ease, or self-conscious of her appearance. She hastily opened her book.

She knew that a portion of her restlessness stemmed from inactivity. She hadn't realized, before working on the Analytical Engine every day, how desperately *boring* her life had been. It was even worse here, at her parent's home at Ockham Park; without an Analytical Engine, she could not even work on the theories that came into her head. The notebook that sat by her side was the constant outlet of questions, scribbled diagrams, and punch card patterns that she maddeningly wanted to test.

Instead, the past few days had been taken up by frivolous things, like the time that it took her to dress formally for dinner each evening, only to eat in tight silence with her mother and father. Ada King took herself to bed in steely silence, and let her and her father to finish their meal together. Such moments were bearable, as Lord King showed a genuine interest in her work and the questions and puzzles that she had been pondering during the day. But then he too retired for the evening to his study, and Annabella was left with what seemed interminable hours before sleep.

Yet however distressing and fraught with discomfort those dinners might have been, it was the days that seemed so long to her. She had finally attempted to give herself a schedule of riding and playing the violin, so that at least her body could feel distractions, even if her mind couldn't. Reading was impossible. Mostly, the book sat open in her lap, as it had now done for the past ten minutes.

This was pointless. Annabella glanced out the window to check if it were raining, and then went to find Sarah to help her into her riding clothes.

Annabella had long found riding clothes more comfortable to wear than her regular dresses, and after not wearing her work dresses for so long, she was doubly relieved to have something that resembled them. Even so, the jacket fit tight to the bones of her corset, and breathing was its own form of exercise.

She turned towards the back of the house, ready to go down the back steps to the stables, when she heard the crunch of carriage wheels on gravel, followed by the opening of the front door, and sound of voices, one of which was her father's. She turned and ran several steps down the corridor, but stopped, and slowed her breathing, before walking calmly down the stairs into the hall.

Charles Babbage, who stood shaking hands with her father, was dressed in a brown suit under his great coat. Henry stood to one side, his hat tucked under his arm, wearing, to her surprise, his riding clothes. The tall black boots and long dark coat made him look particularly tall; his face was flushed from the cold. Surely he hadn't ridden all the way from London?

"Henry!" was out of her mouth before she could stifle it with the more appropriate "Mr. Babbage." She pointedly ignored her father's look of surprise, and walked down the stairs to take Henry's hand.

"Miss King," Henry said, pressing her hand. Annabella saw a flush rise up Henry's neck; evidently Lord King's look had not been lost on him.

"And Mr. Babbage," Annabella said quickly, holding her hand out to Charles Babbage. "So lovely to see you. I apologize that I'm not ready to receive you. I was just going out for a ride, but I will meet you in the drawing room once I've-"

"No, please," came Henry's eager reply. "I'm sure you have much to discuss with Lord King, father," he said, turning to Charles, "and I would be happy to accompany Miss King on a ride, if she would permit me."

"But surely you've ridden from London today?" Lord King returned, glancing between the two of them in what seemed to Annabella to be a suspicious way.

68

"No," Charles Babbage replied. "We travelled by train to Woking, and were met with the carriage and the horses there. Let the two young people go burn off some energy, William – I believe you and I can entertain ourselves over a glass of something."

Lord King glanced pointedly at Annabella, who studiously avoided giving anything away. "Certainly Charles. We'll see you both at dinner then."

Henry watched their fathers walk away for a moment, before grinning at Annabella, and offering her his arm. "Shall we go find our horses, then?"

It was not raining, but December could hardly be anything other than bitter cold and damp. Even through her wool gloves, Annabella found her fingers cramped and aching with cold. But the thought of going in, and trading Henry's quiet, thoughtful company for the steely silence of her family made the cold seem almost tolerable.

"Have you been enjoying your holiday from your task-master?" Henry asked as they moved out of sight of the house and began to follow the stream.

Annabella gave a short laugh. "Would my task-master consider me ungrateful if I said no?"

"Really?" Henry asked with a grin, drawing his horse closer to hers. "I would have thought you would have welcomed a break."

"I would have thought so too," admitted Annabella, "but I find myself unable to think about anything other than the Engine. Whatever did I do *before* I worked on an Engine?"

"That is the question, isn't it," he replied, with a short laugh. "What did we do *before*? It seems quite impossible now that a world ever existed without Analytical Engines."

Annabella glanced at him. "What did you do before? That is to say, you haven't always been an engineer. What did you-"

Annabella looked at Henry and abruptly wished that she hadn't asked. The sunlight had drained from Henry's face, and his mouth had tightened.

"I was in the army, as I believe I told you. In India."

Annabella waited for a moment before asking. "Why did you leave?" she said softly.

Henry's hands clenched into fists around his reins. "It was the battle of Mudki. I was a captain then. We had been collecting our troops on their border, so the Sikh army attacked."

Henry rode in silence for a moment, Annabella silent beside him. "At first, it went well, or as well as a battle goes. There were minimal losses, even with their artillery. And then night fell."

Henry's horse paced to one side, and Henry himself swallowed hard before he spoke again. "The Mudki is mostly flat, but with hills of sand, and in the night, you might not notice if the man you're shooting at is British-"

Annabella gasped, and immediately wished she hadn't, but Henry didn't seem to hear. "- or Sikh."

He looked at her suddenly, and swallowed. "I'm sorry. I shouldn't be telling you such horrid details."

"I did ask for them," Annabella breathed. "Was it the attack? That made you leave?"

Henry looked over at her, his eyes hollow. "I was promoted for that night," he murmured, a sardonic smile flitting across his mouth. "I became a Major. Apparently, I demonstrated valiant courage." He sighed. "It was dark, everyone was confused. I had been ... shot through the shoulder, and had become separated from the rest of my regiment. I was trying to make my way back to the British lines when I saw a shape, a person, lying with a rifle in the sand, and he was firing in the direction of the British." Henry looked down at his hands, gripping his reins. "I couldn't hold a rifle with my arm, so I ran across the sand, and stabbed him with my bayonet."

Annabella waited, feeling that there was more, not wanting to break the silence that had fallen between them.

"I knew it was wrong as soon as I heard him cry out. I could feel it in the dark... the coat, the belt... that it was a British uniform." Henry licked his lips. "But then a blast of artillery fire went off. Far enough away that it didn't harm us, but close enough..." He drew a slow breath. "Close enough that I could see his face. I... I knew him. He was from my own regiment. His name was Thackray. And... because of the light of artillery fire... I was able to watch him die."

"Was he..." Annabella hesitated. "The first that..."

70

"That I had killed?" Henry said wearily. "No. Not even the first one up close. Just... the first of my own."

"Did you tell the army, your officers, what happened?" Annabella said, after a moment.

Henry gave a humourless laugh. "Yes. They didn't care. One more dead soldier in a night of chaos," he said, seeping bitterness in his voice.

"What reason did you give for leaving?" Annabella said, hesitating to even ask.

"My shoulder," Henry said, his voice flat. "After it first happened, once I was over the fever... I could barely move it. I was useless to them, so no one thought it odd when I chose to leave." Henry glanced at her, looking numb. "You've seen me... play with my pocket watch?"

Annabella nodded. Of course she had.

"For most of the trip back to England... that was all I could do with my right arm. But it helped," he said simply. "When I do it now, it's mostly when... it gives me pain."

Annabella stared at him. His right arm was rarely still. How often was he in silent agony?

The silence dropped completely now, and neither of them could think how to break it. Wind whipped up and threw water off of the stream. Annabella felt the cold biting down on her, urging her to turn home, but felt incapable of doing so.

"How do you forgive the rest of us?" she said softly.

Henry glanced up at her, and frowned. "I don't understand."

"All the women you see," Annabella murmured, "who you must know have not seen what you have..."

Henry looked at her in confusion. "What is to forgive? They have done nothing."

"But exactly," Annabella returned. She leaned over and reached out her hand. She did not think it odd when he caught it in his own gloved hand. "We do nothing, and have no responsibility, and yet we profit from your suffering."

"It is not your place to go into battle," Henry said, shaking his head.

"Then why was it yours?" Annabella said.

71

"Because it was my duty," Henry snapped, with a harshness that surprised her. He pulled his hand away.

"Do I not share that same duty? Are British women unaffected by the duty of British men?" Annabella said.

Henry frowned. "We would never ask women to brave horrors of war with us. Even you must know that."

"But we might at least share your burden when you come home," Annabella found herself saying.

Henry looked straight ahead, and then back at her. "How can you – after what I have told you? How do you simply forgive me?"

"Because I was not there," Annabella replied, wanting to reach out to him again. "If I was not there, if I did not share your nightmare, how can I presume to judge you?"

"I killed … a boy," Henry said, choking on his words. "My own countryman, a boy,… miles from home."

"Because we sent you." Annabella replied. "Because British women, ruled by a British queen, sent you to a place where that was possible. As long as that is true, isn't your guilt also mine?"

Henry stared at her. "What on Earth have you been reading, Miss-"

Henry didn't finish his sentence before Annabella felt her horse take a sickening lurch away from him. Henry grabbed for her hand, and she felt his fingers close around her wrist, before they were suddenly wrenched away. She pressed herself down into her stirrup as her horse pitched forward. She barely had time to register her own panic before she slipped her feet free of the stirrup, and pushed herself away as the animal stumbled and rolled onto its side. She could hear Henry yelling, but she couldn't make out the words as she slid off the horse and staggered to her feet. Her boot slid on the riverbank mud, and she fell into the frigid water.

She gasped as her side hit the water, and struggled up as her clothes weighed heavily around her. Suddenly there were hands firmly gripping her upper arms, and Henry hauled her up the riverbank. She collapsed against his chest, shivering wet, and realized that his body was shaking with laughter.

She glared into his grinning face. "What on *Earth* are you laughing at, you horrible man?" She tried to pull herself away from him, but found his arms still tight around her waist.

"Only you," he laughed, drawing her up the bank with him. "With anyone else, we would have had an uneventful ride, and we would have talked about the weather."

Annabella let out a shivering laugh. "But with me, we talk about the war, and I fall into the river?"

Henry shook his head, still laughing. "Your horse threw a shoe in the mud. You did well to get off as fast as you did. If somewhat inelegantly."

Annabella gave him at wry grin. "Ever the gallant knight, aren't you?"

The laughter subsided in Henry's face, but the warmth did not. "If you would let me be."

Annabella suddenly became quite conscious that she had wrapped one arm around Henry's neck and the other on his shoulder. She could feel the strength of his shoulders beneath her gloves, and could feel his breath on her face. His eyes searched her face, and his mouth was achingly close to hers. She shivered, and Henry's face clouded in concern.

"We need to get you home quickly," he said, frowning. He helped her to her feet, and collected the reins of the two horses. "You can ride behind me, and lead your horse."

Shivering now, Annabella nodded. She was beginning to feel weak and tired and heavy, as if all the excitement and energy were leaving her, and evidently Henry saw it too. He took both reins in one hand, and touched her cheek with the other. "You look awfully pale," he murmured. "Come, let me help you up."

It seemed comforting to Annabella, rather than strange, when Henry rested a hand on either side of her waist and helped her up onto the back of the horse. He handed her the reins of her own horse, who was gingerly lifting one of its feet, and carefully pulled himself up in front of her.

He looked back at her, tense and shivering behind him. "You will need to hold onto me," he said softly, sounding embarrassed at needing to say it.

Annabella leaned forward, and wrapped her arms around his waist. She leaned close to him as the horse began to walk, and before long felt her head droop against his back. She could feel the coarse felt of his coat under her cheek, and breathed in the smell of the wet wool. She felt so tired, so drained, so unsure of her limit, of where she ended and he began. The cold seeped through her, and made her long for his warmth, and the feeling of being held by him.

She felt half asleep when Henry drew the horse to a stop, and looked up to see the outline of the stables. She heard Henry talking to the groom, and a gentle "Annabella, let go," as Henry took the reins from her cramped fingers. He gently took hold of her arm, and she slid off the horse into his awaiting arms.

"I'm quite well," she murmured, "I can walk." Henry's arm remained about her waist, and after a few staggering, uncertain steps, he placed her arm over his neck, and lifted her up. She curled into his chest, where she could hear his thundering heart, and closed her eyes.

Henry approached the house of Ockham Park with increasing dread, his arms and neck aching. He imagined what he would look like entering the hall: the two of them splattered in mud, him cradling Annabella, pale and exhausted and wet through, in his arms. There were certainly better ways of making an impression on someone's home, but currently, he couldn't think of any options.

As he entered the hall, his eyes met the wild and startled eyes of Lord King, and Henry groaned inwardly. His arms were shaking, and he had to gently lower Annabella to the floor as Lord King rushed to his side.

"What in God's name happened?" Lord King hissed at him, as he touched his daughter's cheek.

Henry opened his mouth to reply, as Annabella tried to sit up. "Papa," she murmured. "It was my fault, not Henry's. My horse-"

"I don't for a moment doubt it was your fault," snapped Lord King. "Mr. Babbage, please wait with my daughter while I go find Sarah. We need to get her warm."

As Lord King left, Henry pulled off his coat, and put it under Annabella's head. She smiled wearily at him.

"I'm quite well, Henry. I'm just so cold," she whispered.

Henry felt his panic rising at the sound of her weak voice, but tried to keep his own voice calm and reassuring. "You're safe now. We'll get you warm."

"I was always safe," she said drowsily. She reached out and touched his face with a gloved hand. Henry took her hand, and pulled off her glove, to feel her ice-cold fingers. He held it in his until the servants came to take Annabella to her room.

X

The Analytical Engine ... weaves algebraic patterns,
just as the Jacquard-loom weaves flowers and leaves.

~ "Notes," Ada King, Countess Lovelace

Annabella was not at dinner that evening, and Henry sat down to a
full table of Lord King's guests, anxiety resting like a weight on his chest. He
made as little conversation as it was polite to make, while his father
entertained the guests with descriptions of his many inventions.

After dinner, the ladies withdrew, and left the men to a glass of Lord
King's scotch. Henry twirled his drink absently in his hand, waiting for the
other men to join the women, before he could escape for the evening.

He glanced up as the conversation died, and the men began to leave,
and met the questioning stare of Lord King. Lord King gestured to another
guest to go on without him, and returned and took a seat opposite Henry.
Henry set his glass down on the tablecloth, and swallowed hard.

"An eventful day, Mr. Babbage," Lord King said softly.

"Indeed," Henry replied. "How is – how is she?"

"Well enough," replied Lord King. "She would have come down for
dinner, but I insisted that she keep to her room until at least tomorrow. Then
we will see." Lord King glanced up and seemed to take pity on him. "She has
told me what happened. I'm glad you were there."

Henry nodded briefly. "She told you-"

"That her horse threw a shoe, as well as some half-sense about you in
India."

Henry went pale, but when he tried to speak, Lord King waved away
his speech. "Nothing I didn't know. Your father has told me that it was not
just your injury that brought you back to England. I can't say I blame you.
Anyway, you were wasted in the army."

Henry registered with only vague surprise the fact that Lord King and
his father had discussed his return; he couldn't actually remember having
spoken to his father about it himself. Henry considered draining the remainder

of his scotch and excusing himself for the evening, when Lord King spoke again.

"She is desperately fond of you, as I'm sure you are aware."

Henry froze with his glass half lifted, and raised his eyes to Lord King. He looked away quickly, down into the glass, and felt his heart quicken.

He had been trying to pretend that it wasn't there, that the way Annabella looked at him wasn't a mirror reflection of what he felt for her. He wouldn't presume to know her feelings, but he wasn't in any doubt as to his own. If he had been, the lurch of fear that he had felt that day in seeing her fall from her horse would have told him how desperately he cared for her.

As it was, the look that Lord King gave him could elicit only one possible reply.

"As I am of her. As I'm sure *you* are aware."

Lord King smiled. "You are neither of you terribly good at hiding what you feel."

Henry was conscious of his face going scarlet, and drew a slow breath. "I apologize, Lord King, if I have given offence. I would understand if…"

He swallowed, unsure of how to continue. He knew he should say that he would understand if Lord King did not want Annabella tied to a man like him. He was suddenly painfully aware of how little he could offer the daughter of an Earl – no title, no great house, no land. He was not the aristocrat that Annabella so clearly deserved – he had only himself to give.

The words would not come. He might understand it, but he knew his own heart well enough to know that he couldn't accept it.

"You were going to say that you would understand if I didn't approve of your feelings for Annabella?" Lord King said mildly.

Henry glanced up, and gave a brief nod.

"I know you to be an honest and an honourable man, Mr. Babbage. And my daughter is fortunate in not having to marry for wealth. The choice is, and always has been, hers." Lord King rose to his feet. "I'm sure we will have more to say to each other on that subject. Good night, Mr. Babbage."

Lord King rose, and followed his guests into the drawing room, and left Henry staring at the liquid in his glass, flickering as it caught the light of the gas lamps.

Henry ate his breakfast the next morning as quickly as it was good manners to do so, and began to wander through the main floor of Ockham Park House. The house had warm drawing rooms mixed in with grand galleries and halls, and even some Italian details that suggested a warmer and cheerier climate. All Henry was looking for at the moment was one of its occupants.

He found her in an east-facing drawing room, with thin winter light coming through the long windows. She did not see him as he entered; she was on a chaise lounge, facing the window, with her feet drawn up beside her. She looked so different from the way he usually saw her. Her clean-lined work dresses were presumably not permitted here; instead, her dress had an enormous skirt, with flounces of ocean green silk and lace that made her look like she had fallen into a sea of softly lapping waves. Her hair, rather than being pulled up and away from her face, framed it instead, falling in large loose waves down her neck.

Yet it was still her, Henry thought, as a smile pulled at his mouth. She didn't have a piece of needlepoint or a novel in her hands as might have been expected; instead, she held her notebook in one hand and her pencil in the other, and she was surrounded by diagrams and equations. She might be dressed like any other elegant young lady, but she would always be infinitely more.

"Miss King," he said softly, almost unwilling to break the quiet of the room.

Annabella lifted her head, and a warm smile lit her face. "Henry! You'll excuse me if I don't stand to greet you - I'm under strict instructions to rest this morning."

Henry pulled up a smaller chair opposite her, and sat down. "I'm surprised you've been permitted to leave your room at all. Your father-"

"Fusses far too much over me," Annabella said with a wave of her hand, as she let the notebook rest in her lap. "I'm perfectly fine, and well

78

rested, even after making a complete fool of myself yesterday. I *can* in fact ride a horse."

Henry raised his eyebrows. "I never questioned that. Knowing when to get *off* a horse is a crucial skill in being able to ride one."

Annabella shook her head with a smile. "Poor Pythagoras. He's not going to be walking for a few days yet."

Without giving Henry time to digest the fact that her horse was called Pythagoras, Annabella threw open her notebook.

"I've been thinking of something. The running speed."

Henry blinked. "Yes?"

"It isn't going to work, is it? I mean, with the music. It isn't about the programming. It's about the mechanical ability to keep the pace we're setting."

Henry frowned. "I was beginning to think that, yes. The Analytical Engine can change notes, of course, but can it do so at a reasonable speed?"

"I was hoping to speak to your father about it," Annabella replied with a nod, "but at the moment, the answer appears to be no. And if the Engine can't make a song sound like music, then there isn't much point in trying to make it do so. At least, not before the Exhibition."

Henry nodded. "So we need another kind of output before the Exhibition."

Annabella bit her lip. "And we need to reprogram the system?"

Henry's eyes brightened. "No. That's what makes the program truly useful. We need to reprogram the output, and redesign how the output connects to the variables, but the variables themselves are just numbers. They can apply to anything. We might have to reprogram the translator slightly, but not entirely."

Annabella grinned. "That still leaves the problem of speed," she said, opening her notebook. "I was thinking, what about something where the speed is still evident, but where it won't trip up the Engine?"

"Such as?" Henry replied.

"Fabric," Annabella replied. "I've been thinking about this for some time. The Analytical Engine has all the properties of a loom – the punch cards are based on one. Why not let it create fabric, and let the spectators use our translator program to input patterns?"

Henry leaned back in his chair. "Programming a pattern into fabric... there would need to be an instruction per weave."

"Per thread, yes. As there would have been in the Jacquard loom. We can program in recognizable patterns, or even ones that are abstract. The user might not know the output of the fabric before they ran the program." Annabella said. She flipped over the notebook, and handed it to him.

On the page in front of him was a rose, drawn in pink and green pencil. Overtop of it was a grid, drawn in soft pencil, dividing the rose into tiny squares, each assigned a value. To one side of the page, was a list of the codes for each square.

"I see," Henry breathed. "But then, how is that different from a Jacquard loom to begin with?"

"Because it can be changed in a moment, instead of taking days to rethread it. The Engine can take in numerical code, or simplified, human instructions through the translator, and make the changes for the weaver," Annabella said excitedly.

He glanced up at her and nodded. "We need to speak to Father about whether we can attach the output of the Engine to an existing loom, but I can't see why we wouldn't be able to. I believe he's in his study. Would you – no, sorry, you're confined here, aren't you? Let me go find him. For his Engine, he'll be pleased to be interrupted."

Henry got to his feet, and as he did so, Annabella reached out a hand to stop him. "Wait. I-"

Henry looked down at her, and offered her his hand. She placed her notebook on the seat beside her, and rose slowly, the folds of her dress falling out into an enormous hooped skirt. She lifted her face to look at him.

"I just, wanted to thank you," she said haltingly. "Not just for pulling me out of such a foolish situation, but also... for your honesty."

Henry looked away from her. He didn't want to have to talk about this, to be reminded of what she knew about him, and how she might see him now. He most of all didn't want to be faced with the forgiveness of her eyes, which made it somehow worse.

"Please, don't... You have nothing to turn away from," Annabella said softly but firmly. "You did your duty, in the midst of a nightmare. No man could have asked more of you. No woman could have either."

Before he could tell himself not to, Henry took her hand, and pressed the tips of her fingers to his lips. "Thank you," he said. He gazed at the white tips of her nails, still unable to meet her gaze. "Perhaps what we work on together is a chance to make that right."

Annabella smiled at him, puzzled. "What do you mean?"

He looked up at her. His heart was in his throat, strangling all the things he wanted to say. "A chance to improve humanity, rather than destroy it," he said instead.

He dropped his gaze before she could reply, and softly murmured, "I shall go find my father," before turning and walking to the door.

XI

The great art of life is sensation, to feel that we exist,
even in pain.

~Lord Byron~

Henry's eyes searched the drawing room, filled with elegantly
dressed men and women, before resting on the figure that they sought.
Annabella was dressed in dark green taffeta, the neck of the dress revealing
her throat, the edges of her collarbone, and the contours of her shoulders. Her
right hand fidgeted with a fan decorated with peacock feathers.

She was standing next to a younger man with sand-coloured hair and
a carelessly tied cravat. He had an annoying manner of flipping his hair, and
as he approached them, Henry realized with a sinking feeling that he knew
him.

"Miss King, good-evening," Henry said, taking Annabella's hand,
and pressing her fingers to his lips.

"Mr. Babbage," Annabella replied.

Not Henry here, of course, he thought with a sinking heart. *Mr.
Babbage*.

"May I introduce Mr. Wilfrid Blunt. Mr. Blunt is recently returned
from -"

"Italy. A tour of inspiration," Blunt said with a condescending smile.

"Yes, Mr. Blunt is a poet," Annabella continued. "Mr. Blunt, this is
Mr. Henry Babbage. We-"

"Ah yes," Blunt interjected, and Henry saw Annabella's mouth
tighten at being interrupted for a second time. He extended his hand to Henry,
who shook it. "The famous engineer. We've met. Miss King tells me that she
has been contributing the occasional tidbit to your project."

Henry glanced at Annabella, and saw her swallow what was
obviously her anger. He couldn't imagine for a moment Annabella referring
to her work on the Engine as "the occasional tidbit."

82

"Actually," Henry said, trying to make his smile genial rather than strained, "Anna – Miss King has been invaluable in the programming of the Engine. She and I have been working on it together."

Blunt flipped his hair again. "So good for her to have a hobby, don't you think?"

"I would never presume to think that for Miss King," Henry said, smiling stiffly. He could feel himself clenching his fists at his sides.

Blunt smirked. "Of course. Excuse me." He bowed to Annabella, and moved across the room to speak to Lord King.

Henry let out the breath he did not know he had been holding, and turned to Annabella. She was staring across the room at Blunt. For a sickening moment Henry wondered whether it was with affection for the man, but then he saw the tears beginning to shimmer in her eyes. She was swallowing hard, trying to force down anger and frustration, but Henry could clearly see that it wouldn't be enough.

"Miss King," he said, loud enough for the guests closest to them to hear. "My father has shown me how we might manage the changes to the Engine that you suggested. He left some schematics in the library. Would you like to see them before dinner?"

Annabella turned her eyes to him. "Yes, of course, Mr. Babbage." She gave him a tight, but grateful smile, and led the way out of the room.

The library was mercifully close to the drawing room. Annabella stepped into the room, lit only by its fire and two small gas lamps, and Henry followed her in.

"Shut the door, if you please, Mr. Babbage," Annabella said, not turning to face him. Henry did as he was told.

"*Damn!*" Annabella exploded. She threw her hand outward, sending her fan spinning across the room. She moved quickly across the room, her skirt rustling furiously, and leaned her hands heavily on the desk. Instead of slowing, her breathing was only becoming more ragged. He watched helplessly as she walked towards the chair by the fire, and lowered herself miserably to the floor, resting her face and arms on the arm of the chair.

Annabella's initial outburst had so startled him that Henry had remained by the closed door, unsure of how to approach her. To see her curled in on herself wrenched at his heart, and he didn't bother to stop himself from running to her and kneeling by her side.

"Annabella," he said gently, laying a hand on her elbow.

Annabella lifted her head. Her eyes were red with tears, and her face was blotchy. She swallowed once, and pulled a handkerchief from her sleeve to dry her eyes and face.

"I'm sorry, Mr. Babbage," she whispered hoarsely. "Thank you for helping me to make an exit. I'm sure you must be wanting to return to-"

"Annabella!" Henry gasped, gripping her shoulders before he could stop himself. He became suddenly, vividly, aware of her bare skin under his hands. "Stop, please! You must know that I have no desire to return."

Annabella lowered her gaze, more tears threatening to fall. "I hate for you to see me so foolish and weak, and-"

Henry turned her to face him, forcing her to meet his eyes. His own heart was hammering against his ribs with anguish for her, anger at Blunt and a hurricane of emotions that he couldn't begin to identify.

"You are not weak," he said forcefully, "you are angry. You are right to be angry at the way he spoke to you."

"Spoke *about* me," Annabella choked out, "as if I weren't there. And he called my work, ... he said-"

"I know, Annabella," Henry murmured. "I was there. I could barely keep from telling him that he couldn't for a moment understand how brilliant your mind is."

Annabella sniffed, and Henry reached out to touch her jaw, and to raise her eyes to look at him. The firelight shifted over her features, throwing glittering light into her eyes and dark shadows to one side of her face.

"Do you understand?" Annabella murmured, laying a hand over his, where he held her jaw.

"Yes," Henry whispered.

He lowered his mouth to meet hers, and tensed his body to draw her against his chest. The full force of his longing hit him all at once, and he held her tight against him, her lips soft and fluttering under his. A soft gasp escaped her mouth, and she seized the collar of his jacket and pulled herself closer to him. His world melted. Every thought, every idea in his mind,

84

seemed inextricably entwined with her. Everything he desired was in that moment wrapped in his arms, and it seemed impossible that he could ever let go of her. He pressed his hand against her back, feeling the ribs of her dress under his hand. She leaned against him, her hands fiercely gripping the lapels of his jacket. He slid his hand around the back of her neck, and laced his fingers into the curls of her hair.

With a reluctance that was painful, Henry lifted his mouth from hers, leaving a lingering kiss on her lips. He brushed a stray tear off her cheek, and began to pull himself away from her. "Miss King, forgive me, I-"

"No," breathed Annabella, "please don't be formal. Not now." She held him around the neck, and leaned her head on his shoulder.

Henry grasped her against him, knowing he had to let her go, but afraid to, for fear that this moment would vanish entirely. He could feel his hands trembling, and wondered if she could too.

"Annabella, we have to… we have to go back," Henry murmured, hating himself for saying it.

Annabella gave a gentle smile. "Of course."

Henry stood, and offered Annabella his hand. He pulled her gently to her feet, but could not resist pulling her into his arms again. He lifted her face in his hand, gazing into her eyes, eyes that gazed back at him with an emotion he could hardly dare to hope was real.

"Annabella, can I, can we… can I speak to you tomorrow?" He felt stupid as the words fell out of his mouth.

Annabella smiled, and bit her lip. "Yes. Of course."

He wanted to draw her to him to kiss her again, but let her go instead. "We had better return."

"Yes. Do I… do I look as if I've been crying?"

Annabella sat between Charles Babbage, and, much to her distaste, Lord Blunt, at the long dining room table. The meal was coming to a close, with candies and fruits being passed around the table. She was vaguely aware that Lord Blunt was talking to her, but she was listening instead to the man sitting on the other side of him – Andrew Crosse – who was talking to her father at the head of the table.

85

Annabella had always liked Andrew Crosse; he had throughout her whole childhood been the "thunder and lightning man," constantly talking to her father about his ideas for testing and harnessing electricity. He was now in his late sixties, solidly built, with wild white hair. She hadn't heard him discuss the details of his projects and inventions for some time now, but then, that might have had something to do with the young woman sitting at his side.

Cornelia Crosse, a pale woman in her twenties, was Andrew Crosse's wife. She was pretty, with silvery blond hair and grey eyes, and was completely and utterly wrong for Andrew. In the brief time that she had known Cornelia, Annabella had not known anything sensible or relevant to have come out of her pouting mouth. In a sense, Annabella felt sorry for Cornelia; Andrew's thoughts ran far ahead of hers, and would have done even had Cornelia not been young enough to be Crosse's daughter. She was simple, but quite harmless.

Annabella looked down the table to where her mother sat. Her mother was not currently looking in Cornelia's direction, but Annabella was familiar with the look that Ada frequently directed at Cornelia. Annabella had no great respect for Cornelia, but for some reason that Annabella couldn't determine, her mother *hated* Cornelia. Ever since Cornelia had married Andrew three years ago, Ada had treated her with undisguised contempt, and Annabella had never been quite able to determine why.

Across from Cornelia Crosse was John Crosse, Andrew's son. He was a few years older than Cornelia. He was handsome, and knew it, with dark hair and piercing blue eyes. Annabella wasn't sure what he spent his time doing, but had heard her father make passing comments at his gaming habits. Annabella found there was something about him that assumed familiarity, especially with her mother.

Henry sat next to John Crosse. He was quieter, and Annabella could tell that he was listening mostly to Andrew Crosse and her father. Thinking of their conversation the previous day, Annabella noticed that his jacket was simply cut, but buttoned high to his throat, like a military tunic. Old habits, it seemed, died hard. He didn't have John Crosse's sharp good looks, but he looked instead like he was standing in a fresh breath of wind, with his ruffled hair and cool green eyes. She found she couldn't look at him now without thinking of his arms around her, couldn't watch his mouth move without thinking of his kiss. She felt a strange hunger to be there again, in that moment, and blushed to think of it.

"Well Charles," said Andrew Crosse, loud enough for the whole company to be listening, "I understand that your son and Miss King have been performing all manner of abominations on your wonderful machine."

Henry darted a quick look at Annabella, and she made a point of smiling back at him, reassuring him.

Charles Babbage laughed. "I don't know about abominations, Andrew, but certainly more than I would have imagined on it."

"How can it do more than you imagined?" Cornelia asked in a thin voice.

"That is the Analytical Engine's whole purpose," Ada said sharply, before looking back down at her meal.

"I don't understand," Cornelia said in a gentle whine.

"The Analytical Engine's design is that it can be suited to multiple purposes," Annabella said quickly, before her mother could reply. Henry had put down his fork, and was giving her his undivided attention. "What Henry- I mean, Mr. Babbage and I are attempting to show is the range of those possibilities. Not just mathematical tables in trains and navigation, but any number of applications."

"How does it change between applications?" John Crosse asked, lifting a glass of wine.

"Through changing its programs," Henry replied softly.

"Programs?" Cornelia said, her brow furrowed.

"The Engine needs to be told what to do," Charles Babbage said, turning to Cornelia. "The programs that Miss Annabella and Henry are creating are simply a set of instructions, a map if you will, that tells it which options to take. With a new program, a new map, the Engine can go a different path."

"It sounds so complicated," Cornelia said with a nervous giggle.

"To design, yes," Annabella said. "To use, it mostly takes practice. And Mr. Babbage and I are working on a program to make it easier to-"

"Is it true that the military has made use of your Engine, Mr. Babbage?"

Annabella turned to face Lord Blunt. He was leaning back in his chair, his sandy hair falling over his eyes. He was looking, strangely, not at Charles Babbage, but at Henry, who was staring fixedly at his plate.

"They have," replied Charles Babbage, assuming that the question had been for him. "They were one of its main contributors of funding, as is so often the case."

"They were using it to calculate artillery strikes during the ... oh, what was it called?" Blunt said, rolling back his head.

"The Second Anglo-Sikh War," Henry said in a low voice. Annabella could see the muscles of his neck tightening.

Blunt leveled his gaze at Henry again. "Yes, that's right. You were there, I believe,... Major Babbage?"

"Mr. Babbage, retired," snapped Henry. "And no, I wasn't. I was in India during the First Sikh War."

"So good they decided to have another?" Blunt said with an ugly smile.

"I think your contempt for the colonial wars could be discussed elsewhere, don't you, Lord Blunt?" Lord King said pointedly.

"Oh I don't know," Lord Blunt said, grinning maliciously at Henry. "We were discussing progress, and a machine that can heighten the precision of death is surely progress, is it not?"

"Yes, it is," Henry said sharply. Annabella could see brewing anger in his eyes. "Precision in battle would lead to less death, less injured. The battle would be over more quickly."

"Leaving more time for capture and slaughter?" Blunt replied, setting down his glass of wine.

"That is enough!" Lord King flared. "As I need no doubt remind you, Lord Blunt, Mr. Henry Babbage is a decorated member of Her Majesty's Army, and we are all sensible of his service to our country."

Annabella looked at Lord Blunt in horror, as he sent Henry a smug and victorious look. She looked from him, to Henry, watching the muscles tense in his jaw. Henry put his napkin down on the table, pushed back his chair, and muttered a short "Excuse me" to her father. He left the room, as a heavy silence descended over the table.

Without thinking of what she was doing, Annabella pushed back her chair and rose to her feet. She was about to move to follow him, when she heard her father give a low murmur of "Annabella."

She looked down the table and met his gaze, calm, but cautioning. He was telling her to stay where she was, and let Henry leave.

She wanted so desperately to go to him. Not only to be with him, but to keep herself from purposely spilling a glass of wine down the front of Lord Blunt's suit, just to see if it would erase his smug look.

She was spared from making a decision. Ada King rose with a soft "Excuse me," and followed Henry out of the room. Annabella took her seat, and stared after her mother.

She tried to avoid the look that Blunt was giving her. A look not only arrogant, but calculating.

Henry found his way through the dim halls of Ockham Park, and staggered into the drawing room. The room had large French doors that opened onto the frosty, sloping lawn; he threw one of them open and let the cold hit him in the face. He pulled open the high collar of his jacket, and gulped icy air into his lungs.

He knew Lord Blunt. He held membership at the same club as Henry in London, and Henry had seen him there more than once. He fancied himself a poet, and would quote lines to anyone who would listen, though not always his own. He was also known to be fiercely anti-imperialist. He advocated total withdrawal of the British from India, and frankly, Henry could hardly disagree with him.

"Scotch, Mr. Babbage?"

Henry whipped around, and found Ada King standing in the entrance of the drawing room. She had stepped over to a cart with a decanter and glasses.

Henry swallowed. "Lady King, I beg your pardon, I did not wish to give offence, I simply needed some air, I-"

"I have known you a long time, Henry Babbage," Ada broke in softly, as she poured two glasses of scotch. Henry stopped talking. "You are a talented man in many things, but one thing you are not, Mr. Babbage, is a liar." She turned towards him, and handed him a glass.

He took it, and stared into it. "I apologize for my behavior, Lady King."

"Why?" Ada said. She walked over to one of the overstuffed chairs and sat carefully on it. Henry walked over to the hearth to face her.

"I'm sorry, I don't-"

"Lord Blunt is a pompous idiot, who for political reasons has to be our welcome guest here," Ada said, taking a small sip of her drink. "You cannot think that anyone in that room thinks less of you because of what he had to say."

Henry lowered his eyes into his glass, watching the firelight flicker through the amber liquid. "No, of course, I'm sure you don't, I just…"

"That includes my daughter, Mr. Babbage."

Henry looked up at Ada King, and felt heat flush up under his collar. He wondered whether Lord King had told her something, or whether he was simply that obvious.

"Did you think that no one knew, Mr. Babbage? That the regard you have for each other wasn't perfectly clear?" Ada gave a humourless smile. "It wouldn't surprise me at all if that's why Lord Blunt said what he did. Because he knew that getting a rise out of both of you would be easy."

Henry looked up, and frowned. "Both of us?"

"I'm not here because I think you can't look after your own honour, Mr. Babbage. I'm here because if I had not come, Annabella would have been the one rushing after you. And that… well, even for you and her, that might be too obvious."

Henry flushed, feeling embarrassed and childish. "Lady King, I-"

"Mr. Babbage, please," Ada said soothingly. "I'm not telling you this to scold you. I'm telling you not to let anything that Lord Blunt has to say come between you and Annabella. You have…" Ada stopped, and swirled her scotch, looking into the glass. "You have shown her a world that is full of promise, and I know myself just how tantalizing that world can be." Ada stopped, and Henry waited for her to say something more, but she didn't.

Ada stood, and placed her glass on the table. "I hope you will join us again for tea?"

Henry nodded. "Of course."

Ada left the room. Henry stared at his glass, drank off the rest of the scotch, and waited a moment before following her.

XII

Sometimes we are less unhappy in being deceived
by those we love,
than in being undeceived by them.

~Lord Byron~

"Annabella."

Annabella looked up from the desk she was bent over in the library, and her face lit up with a smile to see Henry standing in the doorway. His dark suit and ruffled hair made him look as he always did when they worked together, but here he seemed softer, and somehow, less certain.

"Henry, I-" She took one hurried step to him, but hesitated. She wondered for a moment if the night before had even happened, and saw the same flicker of wonder in Henry's eyes.

"Annabella, Miss King, won't you sit down?" Henry gestured to the chair by the fire.

Annabella felt her face redden, and lowered herself tentatively into the chair, and waited for him to speak.

Henry pulled his watch from his pocket, and began to turn it over the knuckles of his right hand. She thought of what he had told her, and hoped that he was merely agitated. He gazed at his watch as he walked towards the fireplace.

"Miss King, first let me say, let me apologize about last night, I-"

"Henry," Annabella interrupted softly, smiling at him, "we can do without that, can't we?"

Henry looked at her, and smiled. He dropped to his knee in front of her, the chain of his watch wrapped over the back of his hand, and took both her hands in his. "Then let me at least apologize for not speaking to you of my feelings before. Last night might have been less of a surprise if I had."

"It was a surprise," Annabella murmured, her heart beating fast, "but not an unwanted one."

Henry raised his eyes to gaze straight at her. "You allow me to feel what I dared not feel all these months. I have long admired your mind, but I-" He stopped and pressed her hands in his. "I have also learned to love your heart, Annabella, and all that is good and warm in you." His words came tumbling out in a rush, and he drew a gasping breath before saying, "Annabella, will you be my wife?"

Annabella felt as though the air had gone from the room, that it wouldn't let her speak to break the stillness left by those wonderful words. But as a frown began to form on Henry's brow, she clasped her fingers around his left hand, and pressed a kiss onto the tips of his fingers, exclaiming, "Henry, of course I will!"

Henry was on his feet, and she was too, pulled to her feet and into his arms, standing on her toes to reach her arms around his neck as he kissed her.

"Annabella," he whispered, holding her against him when he stopped kissing her.

"Henry," Annabella murmured, lifting her head to look into his face as she caressed the line of his jaw. She pressed a kiss to his lips. "We will tell everyone here, won't we?"

"Of course. Your father and I... have spoken briefly," Henry admitted.

Annabella raised an eyebrow, but then grinned. "Whatever do you think Brunel will say?"

Henry laughed softly, and clasped her against him again. "He'll probably be furious that I've made him lose his best analyst."

Pressed against Henry's chest, Annabella felt the world tilt around her, and pulled herself away to look up at Henry's face. "What do you mean?"

Henry looked down at her, puzzled. "Well, we can't... you can hardly continue to work with me when we're married."

The tilting of her world became a definite lurch, and Annabella pulled herself out of Henry's arms. "I don't understand."

Henry twisted the chain of his watch around one of his fingers, looking confused. "Annabella, when we're married,... my wife cannot come to the works with me. You know that."

"But Henry," Annabella said, retreating a step back from him, "why would that be? I work with you now."

Henry stared at her, disbelief and distress unmasking themselves on his face. "Annabella… do not pretend that you do not know the rules of our society. That you have been allowed to disregard them for as long as you have is –"

"Is that what you think my work is?" Annabella said softly, taking a step back from him.

Henry reached for her, his eyes confused and hurt. "Annabella, you know that I think the world of your work, but you cannot continue to work publicly on the Engine when we are married."

Annabella stepped back once more, and Henry dropped his hand. She felt as though her corset were tightening, crushing the air out of her lungs. "Why?" she said hoarsely.

"Annabella, please, you know why," Henry said gently. "You were there when Cropper insulted you, and when Blunt did the same. It will only be worse if you are married, and how can I stand to have you sneered at and mocked, when-"

"So your plan is to mock me yourself instead," Annabella replied, feeling the words being forced out through clenched jaws.

"No! Annabella, please," Henry pleaded. He stepped forward, and caught her wrist before she managed to move away. "I can't bear to watch them treat you like that, when you are so much more than they are."

"But you're just like them!" Annabella burst out. She rushed on, ignoring the pain that crossed Henry's face. "You tell me that my mind is exceptional, that it is special, that I have ideas worth knowing about and sharing, and instead of letting me share them, you'd rather cage me-"

"No, Annabella!" he said urgently, his eyes pleading as he pulled her towards him. "I love you, I want you to be happy, but you can't have both-"

"You're *worse* than the rest of them," Annabella gasped, wrenching her wrist away and wrapping her arms around her aching chest. "You can say that you want me to be happy, but you are asking me to give up the work that *gives* me happiness. To give up the very way that I… came to love you."

94

Annabella might have imagined that when she told Henry she loved him, she would feel joy. Instead, she saw in his face the same misery that she felt, the same sense of rapidly losing what she had only just gained. His words didn't lessen the ache that she felt – they made it worse.

"You do not have to give up thinking, Annabella," Henry said, reaching for her again, then dropping his hand. "You can still work on the Engine, but you know perfectly well that you can't be working publicly if you are my wife."

"It would not be the same, and you know it," Annabella said. "Or maybe you don't – maybe you can't possibly understand what it feels to have everything that matters pulled out of your grasp. To be left out of a field where you have so much to offer and so much to learn! You cannot even explain-"

"I do not have to explain it to you," Henry snapped as he turned away from her. "It is the world we live in, and I cannot change it!"

"Yes you can!" Annabella cried out. "You change it every day. *We* change it together, every day. If a machine can be made to think, then how can you possibly tell me that what I'm asking is impossible?"

"Annabella," Henry said wearily, turning back to face her. "I can design engines, but I can't change the way our world thinks. Neither can you."

Annabella stood in silence, as she watched her thoughts, her love, the world that had allowed her to hope for so much, come crashing down around her. "Then I cannot marry you."

The words ached even as she said them, but not nearly as much as seeing their effect on Henry. His breath left him in a gasp, and his hand tightened around his watch until his knuckles went white. The pleading left his face, replaced only by despair.

"You cannot marry me," he breathed. "Because I cannot allow you to continue your work?"

"Because you will not," Annabella replied, as the tears spilled over her eyes and began to fall. "Because I am not strong enough to make that sacrifice for you, and because you are not strong enough to defend me."

"Annabella, you love me-" Henry reached out a hand for her.

"You are asking me to stop being who I am," Annabella said stiffly, holding back her sobs. "And I cannot do that. Not even for you. Especially not for you, because I would no longer be the woman that you love."

Henry stood very still, except for his watch, which he twirled slowly across his fingers. An action he did when he was in pain. "Forgive me then, Miss King, to have taken so much of your time. I-" He swallowed hard. "I will leave you in peace."

Annabella closed her eyes as he turned away, letting the tears burn out of her eyes. She heard him stride across the library, as she sank down and rested her head and arms on the chair. She heard his footsteps stop, and hesitate, then resume. She did not look up when she heard the door close behind him, but let herself dissolve into tears.

XIII

Still bent to make some port he knows not where,
still standing for some false impossible shore.

~Matthew Arnold~

When Henry had been shot in India, the round had caught him in the chest, and had lodged itself near his right shoulder. He had been lucky – it hadn't pierced his lung, and a surgeon had been able to remove the lead shot. His shoulder still ached some days, as did the long scar under his collarbone, but he still had his arm, and his life.

It had been, and was still, the worst agony he had ever felt. It had knocked him off his feet, and his shoulder had felt like it was on fire. His lasting memory of it was the feeling of warm blood pouring into his uniform, his life leeching out of him, leaving him exhausted and begging for it to end.

The memory came back to him now, unbidden, as he staggered into the halls of Ockham Park. He could feel his hope leaving him. He had managed to hold Annabella in his arms, and lose her again, all in a single day. He needed to get away from here, but he couldn't think of how.

He looked up, and found himself in the hall of Ockham Park. He wasn't sure how he had arrived here. He could hear voices upstairs, his father's and Lord King's, and suddenly his father was coming into the hall towards him.

"Henry," Charles Babbage said, his voice soft. "I think we had best make plans to leave soon."

Henry blinked. The words were music to his ears, but they were also utterly incomprehensible.

"It's Lady King. She's unwell. Lord King gives his apologies, but I think we should leave as soon as it is convenient."

Henry resisted the urge to heave a sigh of relief. "Yes, of course. I'll… can you see that my clothes are sent on? I'll ride to London now."

Charles Babbage looked at him and frowned. "I'm sure there's no need to leave so-"

"No, it's all right," Henry said quickly. "I have business I can attend to in London. There's no sense for me to linger." The truth of his words caused a lump to rise in his throat, at all the words that he had left unsaid.

Charles Babbage frowned, but nodded slowly. "Yes, of course. You'll stop part way, of course."

Henry nodded non-committedly, only thinking that he wanted, needed, to ride as fast as he could away from here.

"I'll see that your things are sent on to you."

"Yes, of course," Henry said absently to his father, and took himself upstairs to change into his riding clothes.

Henry's face felt frozen and raw, and his legs ached. What passed for light was dwindling from the grey sky, and still he stayed on his horse, feeling pummeled and bruised in ways that he knew had nothing to do with the long and exhausting ride. His eyes ached, as though he had been staring at bright light for too long. His chest felt tight, his extremities heavy and numb.

The exhaustion helped, but it still couldn't dull the whirling of his mind. He had been through his and Annabella's conversation more times than he could count. It had only replaced his despair with anger. He could think of a hundred ways it might have gone differently, but in no case could he see a way out of the ending. Of her wanting so badly to continue in their work, and of him being unable to agree to it.

Yes, unable. Not unwilling, he insisted to himself. Her words seemed to suggest to him that there was some way that he and he alone could change the nature of society, that he could make it permissible and acceptable for her to continue working, to be part of a trade. Reconciling that with the role of his wife was something that he couldn't do, in spite of struggling to.

And yet, reconciling Annabella herself with the image of the quiet, domestic wife… was not quite right either. He couldn't admit, even in his dreams, to having ever imagined her in any world other than the mechanical and the industrial. Just seeing her in Ockham Park, seeing her dressed for company and engaged in polite and appropriate pursuits, seemed constrained and fake. And strangely, the fact that he could only envision her alongside the Engine didn't make her less beautiful; it only made her more so. It was as if

98

her work had forged her into what she was – brilliant, fire-bright, and defiant of what she ought to be.

Dammit. She was right. In asking her to be his wife, and only his wife, he was asking her to be other than the woman he loved. And it seemed to him that there was no other option, that he couldn't pretend that it was possible for her to be both.

Unless he lied. And he couldn't, not to her. He couldn't pretend that he would allow her that freedom, when he knew he wouldn't. He couldn't create that trap for her, however much he wanted to hold onto her.

The grey afternoon light was streaming through the tall pane windows when Annabella raised her head from where she had cradled it against the chair. Her hair was pressed against her wet face. She had no sense of how long she had sat there; a glance at the mantle clock told her it had been several hours.

She sat up, and looked around her. Several hours, and no one had come into the library? That didn't seem right. Where were the guests? They were meant to be here for several more days.

Annabella rose to her feet, and smoothed the crumpled skirt of her dress as she stepped out of the library. The house was strangely quiet. She heard footsteps in the entranceway, and walked out into the main hall.

Charles Babbage was there, shaking hands with her father. He held a small bag in one hand, one that Annabella knew had been with him when he arrived. She heard her father say, "I'm sorry, I must leave you," before walking hurriedly up the stairs. It was then that Charles Babbage saw her, as she walked slowly out of the passageway.

"My dear, I'm glad that I have a chance to say goodbye to you," he said, holding out his hand.

Annabella took it in both of hers. "You're leaving us, Mr. Babbage?"

"Well, under the circumstances, your father has asked us to leave. Poor man," murmured Babbage.

Under the circumstances? That couldn't mean her, surely? Her father would never have so rudely sent his guests away for her feelings.

"I understand perfectly, though," Babbage said, a weight overcoming his tall frame. "When my own wife was ill, I could hardly bear the sight of anyone but her."

Wife? *Mother*? A sickening dread began to stir in Annabella.

"You must feel the same, poor child," Babbage said, straightening his coat. "Don't let me keep you from your mother. Henry would have been here to say goodbye, but he had business to attend to in London."

The mention of Henry's name elicited in Annabella both a painful tightening in her chest, and at the same time, a wave of relief. *He doesn't know*. It was possible then that her father didn't know either. Which made it possible, for a few moments longer, to avoid speaking of a subject that had abruptly become so painful to her.

"Yes, of course," murmured Annabella. "Thank you, Mr. Babbage. Hopefully we will see you again under more pleasant circumstances."

Babbage smiled, and squeezed her hand. "God bless you, child."

He walked out the door, and Annabella turned and ran.

Annabella slowed as she reached the door of her mother's room. She heard the sound of voices, gradually shaping themselves into words as she approached the door.

"...God's name, William, why *now*? When I'm ill?" Her mother's voice.

Annabella heard the sound of rapidly moving feet, of someone pacing the room. "Because you might actually listen." Her father.

"This is ridiculous, Charles had no right to tell you-"

"He had *every* right to tell me!" Annabella jumped back from the door at her father's outburst. "He had a *duty* to tell me that my *wife* is involved in a feather-brained gambling scheme! How could you be so foolish as to suggest using the *Engine*? What did you hope that that would achieve?"

"It would have won me back what I had lost," Ada returned, her voice becoming shrill. "If we could have calculated odds on the Engine, we would have had-"

"You would have *lost*, Ada! And you would have believing that that *bloody* Engine would give you the answer!"

100

"It would have, if Charles had helped me write the program for it," Ada said, her voice pouting.

"I cannot believe you are still defending this," Lord King muttered in frustration. "You have lost thousands of pounds, Ada. Thousands of pounds, and you flaunted all propriety by - "

"They were all perfectly respectable gentlemen," Ada interrupted.

A hiss of air escaped from Lord King. "Exactly. Gentlemen. And as for being respectable, no group that includes John Crosse can be called respectable."

"That is not true!" Ada shrieked. "He was here, you invited him to-"

"I invited his father, for whom I have great respect," Lord King interrupted firmly. "John is a reckless degenerate and is squandering everything that he has, which is evidently what he is teaching you to do!"

"I don't see how you can accuse me for *flaunting* propriety as you call it, when you allow Annabella to-"

"You will leave Annabella out of this!" Lord King snapped.

"You give her everything that she asks for, and every chance I would have wanted, and yet you can tell me that-"

"Annabella has the good sense to use the Engine to create things rather than to squander them, and she does so in the company of a much respected friend. Her activities are irrelevant and unrelated to yours."

Annabella swallowed, her hands pressed against the door. *Henry.* Even in the storm of what she was hearing, the thought of him made her want to sob.

"I have paid my debts, William," Ada said, her voice sounding weak.

"By selling your jewelry," Lord King spat in disgust. "You sold the gifts that I gave you without a second thought to-"

Lord King's voice broke off suddenly, and Annabella heard his rushed footsteps as he moved across the floor. "Ada," Annabella heard him saying. "Ada!"

"Let me sleep, for God's sake," came her mother's weak reply. "You have defeated me."

"Ada, I want you to be well, you know that, I-"

Ada's laugh sounded high and thin. "Like a caged bird," she said shrilly. "You can't even open the cage when the bird is dying."

"Ada!" came Lord King's hoarse voice. "Stop that. You are not dying. You are unwell, only."

Annabella didn't hear the remaining words, perhaps because they were too faint, or perhaps because they were drowned out by the thundering of blood in her own ears.

It was too much. Her passion for Henry, the strength that it had cost her to refuse him, the shock of learning of her mother's activities, and the idea that she... Annabella felt herself shutting down, closing in on herself, and found herself stumbling down the hall, down the stairs, and into the bright drawing room that faced the slope of the grounds.

She stood there a moment, her hands hanging uselessly at her sides, when the door opened behind her, and she turned to see her father in the doorway. She looked at his ashen face, and he looked over her red and swollen eyes. He closed the door behind him.

"How much did you hear?" he said softly.

He always knew.

"Is it true?" she said. "Is mother... is she... is she dying?"

Lord King sighed heavily, and walked to the cart that held his scotch. Annabella watched him in silence as he poured himself a drink. He walked to the fireplace, his hand clenched around the crystal glass.

"I don't know, Annabella," he said finally. "She's very ill. Apparently, she has been seeing a doctor for several months."

"And you didn't know?" Annabella said, remembering her mother's sudden strange illness the night of the Babbage's party.

"No," Lord King said sharply. He drank slowly from his scotch. "I knew she had been unwell, yes. I didn't know that it was anything that should give me cause for alarm."

"And... is it?" Annabella said.

Lord King looked up at his daughter. "Annabella, you don't need to concern yourself with-"

"Father!" snapped Annabella. "I am not a *child*! And even if I *were* a child, I already know enough to be shocked and afraid, but not enough to even

102

know how to *feel*. Now for God's sake, stop pretending that everything is well, and *tell* me!"

Lord King stared at his daughter as her words came out in a torrent. Annabella saw herself in his eyes, all her anger and frustration and grief sharpened and magnified.

Lord King turned away from her, and walked to the liquor cart. He poured her a small glass of scotch, and held it out to her.

Annabella stared at it, and up at her father.

"As long as we're breaking rules, you may as well have a drink," Lord King muttered. "Sit down, Annabella."

Annabella sat on the chaise-lounge, collapsing her heavy skirt and curling her legs beneath her. She cradled the precious drink carefully, afraid to drink it, but unwilling to put it down.

"The gambling," Annabella said. "What happened?"

"Charles Babbage told me a few days ago," Lord King said, sinking into the armchair on the other side of the fireplace. "She went to him in London with a proposal to create a program for the Engine to generate odds on the horses that she was betting on."

"Why?" Annabella returned. She took a sip of her glass, and nearly coughed as the searing liquid went down her throat. A pleasant warmth seeped through her limbs.

"You tell me," Lord King returned. "You're the analyst."

"No, that's not what I meant," Annabella said, shaking her head. "Of course the Engine can create odds if it has data, just as a human can, but if it's dealing with horses, it would have no way of accurately predicting the result of a race. I mean, why did she need the program?"

"Because she was in debt," returned her father. "Your mother has been gambling with men who can lose their entire fortune to gaming, which, happily, your mother cannot. But it meant that she was had run out of money."

"And sold her jewels to pay for it?" Annabella said, taking another sip of her scotch.

Lord King smiled grimly. "You have excellent hearing, my dear. Yes, she sold her jewelry. And was planning to win it all back using the Engine."

103

Annabella shook her head. Her mother had programmed the Engine before it was even built. How could she have such a flawed view of its capabilities?

"The money doesn't matter," Lord King said, staring into his glass. "If she had asked me to pay for it, I would have been angry, but not..."

He looked up at Annabella. "It's not the money. It's the company that she has decided to keep."

Annabella stared into her glass. "Father... is she dying?"

She looked up at her father, who was staring into the fire. "I don't know, Annabella," her father said hoarsely.

Annabella swirled the scotch in her glass, feeling certain that if her father had felt hopeful, he would have told her so. She felt a numbness creeping through her, an inability to acknowledge what she had heard in his voice.

"Now," her father said, "perhaps you will tell me why you've been crying."

"Father, it was -"

"I know it was not because of your mother," her father interrupted. "You have been crying for a long time."

Annabella focused her gaze on the swirling amber liquid in her glass. "Henry Babbage ... proposed to me this morning."

She looked up at her father. He registered no surprise, but he was frowning. "And?"

"I... I had to refuse him," Annabella choked out, hoping that the remaining tears wouldn't fall.

Her father's eyebrows raised in surprise. "Refuse him? I'm sorry, Annabella, I thought that you and he-"

Annabella blinked, and a tear rolled down her cheek, causing her father to stop. "Go on, Bella."

Annabella wiped away the tear with her hand. "He... he said that if we were married, that I... that I couldn't work anymore. On the Engine."

"But surely Henry would have allowed you, at home, to continue to contribute to his work," Lord King said.

Annabella let out a bitter laugh. "Yes, I'm sure I would be allowed to help with his work, but I couldn't do my own. It wouldn't be my *own* if I, if I-" Annabella stopped, as the tears came, the sobs threatening to overwhelm her.

Her father gazed at her in silence for a moment. "You want to be acknowledged for the work that you do on the Engine?" he finally said.

"I want to *share* it, Father," Annabella said, leaning towards her father's chair. "What good is science and mathematics and discovery if there is no one to tell, no one to learn from?"

Lord King nodded slowly. "I understand that, Bella." He sighed, and leaned forward towards his daughter. "But I think you would be mistaken not to give Henry another chance. A man will do a great deal to make the woman he loves happy. Henry would have seen that in time."

Annabella looked down. "He made his feelings clear to me."

Her father tilted his head as he looked at her. "It means that much to you, does it?"

"Oh, Father," Annabella murmured. A tear rolled off her face and into her glass of scotch. "It means everything. It means that I have a purpose."

"You would have had a purpose as Henry's wife," her father said gently.

"It would not have been enough, Father," Annabella murmured.

"Yes. I know all about that," her father returned bitterly.

XIV

Tis not too late to seek a newer world.

~Alfred, Lord Tennyson~

"What in God's name is wrong with you?"

Henry ran a hand through his hair, making it stand on end. It fit well with the rest of him. His eyes were hollow, the eyes of a man without enough sleep, and he knew that he had not shaved recently enough. In the ten days since he had left Ockham Park, he had felt himself in danger of unraveling completely.

He had finally had to give Brunel some explanation for why he was scattered, and why, more importantly, Annabella had yet to return to the works with him.

Evidently, the explanation had not been sufficient.

"There is nothing the matter with me, Mr. Brunel, I-"

"Incorrect, Babbage!" Brunel said, slamming his palm onto the desk. "You're telling me that you turned down a woman that you not only love, but who could have shared and understood all of your work? There is most definitely something wrong with you."

"That is *not* what I told you, Brunel," Henry snapped, turning towards Brunel's desk. "*She* refused *me*."

"Because you were stupid enough to deny her the chance to have some share in what you've worked on together! How could you possibly think that she would allow that?" Brunel said, jumping from his chair.

"Evidently you and she live in the same fantasy," Henry growled. "It is not possible for a man's wife to come to work with him, you know that as well as-"

"Why in the hell not?" Brunel returned. "It is only not *common* for a man's wife to have the ability to share his work with him, because we never *let* them! You have found a woman who can not only share it with you, but who is able to challenge your own ideas. Do you know how incomparably rare that is?"

106

Henry stared at Brunel, fuming. He no longer knew what he was angry about, whether it was Brunel's interest in his private life, or the fact that somewhere under his frustration, he knew that Brunel had a point.

"It's too late now," he said stiffly. "She refused me. It would be ungentlemanly to ask again."

Brunel looked at him steadily, with what appeared to be genuine sorrow. "Damn," he murmured softly. "So then... what's to become of your project?"

Henry swallowed. "That is your decision."

Brunel sighed. "Damn."

Annabella pulled on her gloves, pacing outside Brunel's office. The ground outside Brunel's office was frozen under her boots, and cracked as she paced back and forth. She had rehearsed what she would say many times. She hoped it would allow her to continue her work while minimizing the pain of seeing Henry. Yet every time she thought about it, she felt that she was asking too much. How could she ask to continue her work with Henry, without him there? Surely Henry had told Brunel something of what had happened – was she even welcome here anymore?

Her hands were becoming cramped with cold, and she was considering leaving, and returning later, when the door of his office swung open.

Annabella froze. Henry Babbage came down the first two steps with his head down, as he put on his hat. When he lifted his head, he stopped at the sight of her.

Annabella searched his face for the disdain she expected to see. It was not there. She began instead to see the real forms of his face: the stubble on his jaw, and the circles under his haunted eyes.

She knew she didn't look much better. Her cheeks were pink with cold, but she had been pale with lack of sleep for several days.

He took a step closer to her across the cold ground, ice crunching under his boots. "Miss King," he said, bowing stiffly and touching the brim of his hat.

"Mr. Babbage," Annabella replied with a brief nod of her head. To any other man, she would have offered her hand, but with Henry it implied an intimacy that was too painful for her to endure.

"I hope," Henry said, then stopped, and cleared his throat. "I hope your mother is well?"

Annabella swallowed. "She is better than she was over Christmas, thank you. We hope she will continue to improve."

Silence settled between them, as their breaths curled in the air. Henry pulled sharply on the wrists of his gloves, and looked like he was going to say more, then stopped.

"I ought to… I need to speak to Mr. Brunel." Annabella said, hoping that he would step aside to let her pass.

He did not. He continued to give her the same look, as if he were about to speak, but could not find the words.

"I must wish you good day, Mr. Babbage," she said, hating the formal sound of his name as it left her mouth. She lowered her eyes and brushed past him, so she did not have to see the affect her cold words had on him.

Annabella stepped into Brunel's office, and glanced past the entranceway to where Brunel sat behind his desk. His chin was dropped against his chest – he was not working, but seemed to be brooding over something.

"Mr. Brunel?" she said softly.

Brunel lifted his gaze, and his eyes softened. "My dear girl," he said, "tell me that you didn't run into that idiot Babbage when you came in?"

Annabella felt her resolve weakening as she held Brunel's gaze. She felt tears threatening her eyes, and fought them back. She was furious at her weakness, and at Henry for ruining this moment for her – a moment for her to ask for what he had denied her.

"Mr. Brunel, I'm here to ask you about the continuation of my project," Annabella said carefully. The words felt rehearsed even to her, but she sat herself in the chair opposite Brunel and willed her hands not to shake.

Brunel raised an eyebrow. "*Your* project?"

"Yes," she said quickly. "It is my project, and I can finish it."

Brunel stared at her. "Miss King, even with Henry's help, you were going to be hard pressed to finish the programming in time for-"

"The school," Annabella pressed on. "The school opens in two days' time. Their first project will be the tapestry program for the Exhibition."

"Annabella, I mean, Miss King, you cannot be serious," Brunel said, leaning forward to rest his hands on the desk. "Even you and Henry were struggling with the bloody thing – wait, tapestry? Wasn't it a music device?"

"Henry-" Annabella swallowed. "Mr. Babbage and I spoke about changing the codes to be patterns within a piece of fabric for the demonstration. It would be time-consuming to program, but repetitive. A perfect project for training new analysts. It would allow me to focus on the translator program."

Brunel drummed his fingers on the table, and gazed at her quietly for a moment. "Yes," he said eventually. "I see what you mean. All right, so you will use the existing room?"

"I need a larger one," Annabella said firmly. "To accommodate both the Engine and other students."

Brunel shook his head. "This is madness. But... as it happens, Mr. Babbage has offered to take over the building works of the *Great Eastern*, so it would seem you are my best option."

Henry had what? Having been ready to fight against him for the chance of keeping her project, Annabella stared at Brunel in shock. Her expression was not lost on him.

"I'm inexpressibly sorry, my dear Annabella," Brunel murmured. "For both you and that poor idiot who just left. I can't for the life of me understand him."

Annabella smiled sadly. "He can't change the world, Mr. Brunel."

"Utter bloody nonsense," Brunel spat. "If we don't change our world, I'm damned if I know who will."

XV

The busy have no time for tears.

~Lord Byron~

Annabella drew a shaking breath, and placed one hand on the door of the training room. On the other side of the door there was a hum that foretold a worryingly large amount of voices. Her students. Her new analysts. Men that were meant to trust her to teach them how to work this new machine.

This *was* madness. She had heard it so often in the past two days – in the flurry of preparing to open the Analysts' Institute – that she had begun to hear it her sleep. Her father had told her so at least five times when she had first explained the plan to him. She was almost beginning to believe him, but she knew that he didn't have the strength to deny her. Not when she was clearly increasingly unhappy.

Annabella tensed her hand, and pushed open the door.

Twenty pairs of eyes settled on her face, some scornfully, some curiously. They were all men. Most were dressed in rough brown and dark blue clothing. They were hands from the factory, mostly, but amongst them, she saw one or two who were meeker, who had clean white shirts on, who were unmistakably clerks. They too stared at her, and seemed to be looking past her, as though expecting someone else.

In the front of the crowd, she saw a most welcome and familiar face, and gave a small smile. Bentham smiled back at her.

"Good morning, gentlemen," she said.

Those who had not been staring at her before turned to stare now. Annabella swallowed.

"For those of you who do not know, my name is Miss King. I will begin by showing you the plan of the-"

"Where's Master Henry?" one of the men shouted.

Annabella focused her gaze on him, and forced herself not to glare. "He will not be joining us. I will be your teacher."

"*You?*" another voice returned from the back of the room. "I told you this was a joke, Bentham."

Bentham jumped to his feet, turning on the man, but Annabella placed a calming hand on his arm. She wove her way to the back of the room, feeling her thundering heart trying to claw its way out of her throat. She stood in front of the man who had spoken, and raised her head to look him in the eye. He was older than her, though not as old as her father. He wore an arrogant half-smile on his face.

She realized suddenly that her pounding heart wasn't fear – it was rage. Fury at being belittled and ignored, once again. If she wasn't prepared to accept that from Henry, she was *damned* if she would take it from this man.

"Tell me," she said, loudly enough for the room to hear, "What is your name?"

"Jameson, *Miss*," he replied sharply.

"Tell me then, Jameson," Annabella said, "what does the mill do?"

"The what, miss?"

"The mill," Annabella said, "in the Engine. You do know what a mill is, do you not? You do make Engines, do you not?"

"The mill's the bloody stack of cogs," returned Jameson.

"And how is the bloody stack of cogs in the mill," Annabella returned, eliciting a gasp from several of the men near her, "different from the bloody stack of cogs that makes up the store?"

Jameson scowled as her. "How in blazes should I know?"

"You should," Annabella returned, raising her voice, "because it is key to how the machine that *you* make works." She turned and looked at the rest of the men. "You don't know, Mr. Jameson, and I'll wager that most of the rest of you don't either. You make machines, and it's others that benefit from them. I know how to make the Engine work. I know how to make it *dance*," she said, feeling heat rushing to her cheeks, "and to make it do things that it wasn't even invented for. So you can either learn that from me, a *woman*, or you can march straight out the door."

By the time Annabella had reached the front of the room again, Jameson had left. All the other men had stayed.

January passed for Annabella in a blur of crunching cold and whirling numbers. The men she taught – the analysts, as she thought of them – worked away gruffly but diligently at what she taught them, giving her a grudging respect that she imagined came mostly from Bentham. She had heard an occasional critique flung her way and be met with a firm stare from the former factory hand, who seemed to see it as his duty to defend her.

The men were not overly polite, it was true, and didn't hesitate to contradict her, but they weren't patronizing. They expected her to contradict them in their mistakes and did the same to her – and taught her some colourful language in the process.

It was on a strangely warm morning in February, when Annabella was working on a series of punch cards that would weave curled patterns, that Annabella noticed two figures lurking in the doorway. Looking up at Bentham, she saw that he had noticed them as well.

"It's you they'll be wanting, miss," he said, nodding towards the door.

"You can finish punching this series?" Annabella asked as she pulled off her gloves. She had taken to wearing long leather gloves, that went nearly to her elbows, whenever she worked on pieces of the Engine.

"Right enough," Bentham said gruffly. Annabella grinned. *Right enough* meant that he could do it in his sleep.

Annabella walked past the rest of the analysts and made for the door. She stepped onto the outer walkway that circled the outside of the building.

Waiting on the walkway were two women. One was young, about her age, with transparent blond hair caught off her face with a band of grey cloth. The other was older, maybe her mother's age, with a messy knot of mousy brown hair. She was, Annabella realized, Brunel's housekeeper, Rosie Bearce. Both looked like they might bolt at any moment.

"Can I help you?" Annabella said as gently as she could, despite her impatience to return to her work.

Rosie opened her mouth, and then closed it again, as though unsure of what she wanted to say.

"We want to work for you," the younger woman said in a rush.

Annabella looked at the young woman. "What is your current employment?"

"I work for Mr. Brunel," replied the older woman. "She's a hand," she added, gesturing to the younger woman. A factory worker.

"And what is it that you want to do for me?" Annabella replied.

"I've heard," the young woman said, "They said... I've heard that you wouldn't turn women away."

Annabella smiled. "Not if they are worth it. Though I'll warn you, you'll have to do the job of three men to be considered worth it."

"Tain't any different than house work, then," Rosie said shortly.

Annabella raised her eyebrows. "Your names?"

"I'm Evy Hayward," replied the younger woman. "This is Rosie Bearce."

"And what can you do, Miss Hayward and Mrs. Bearce?" Annabella said, crossing her arm.

"I can do arithmetic," Evy began shyly.

"I have a machine that can do that," Annabella pointed out.

"I check things," Evy rushed on. "I can see if there's mistakes. Fix 'em."

Annabella turned to Rosie. "And you?"

"I weren't born yesterday," Rosie said, "but I've kept my place, whatever machine tried to take it. And I work for Mr. Brunel, which is no picnic."

Annabella felt a smile flicker on her face. "I'm sure it isn't."

She gazed at them both. Why not? They weren't so different from her, were they?

"You can have two weeks to try it. I'll decide then to keep you or not," Annabella replied.

Evy's face lit up, and Rosie nodded with satisfaction.

"You'll need to mend your clothes," Annabella added. "To make the sleeves tighter."

Evy and Rosie had been in the school a week when Annabella arrived home one Saturday afternoon, hot and tried, to find that she had a visitor in the drawing room.

Sarah came bursting into the hall as she came in from the street. Annabella had walked that day, and her close fitting green wool dress felt grey from the dust of the streets. She still had her long leather gloves in her hand, when she met Sarah's worried face.

"Miss, you must change!" Sarah whispered hurriedly. "Lord Blunt is in the drawing room, and it's you that he wants to see!"

Damn, Annabella groaned inwardly. She had a code she wanted to write out before she forgot it, for another series of woven patterns – she didn't have time for anyone else, and certainly not for Lord Blunt.

"I'll go straight in, Sarah," Annabella replied. "Give me a basin upstairs to wash in – I won't change."

"But you're in your-"

"My work clothes, yes," Annabella sighed. "Hopefully he'll decide to leave more quickly this way."

It was a few short moments later that she met Wilfrid Blunt's half sneer of a smile as she entered the drawing room. She vaguely considered the possibility of informing him that she did not have the time to see him, but couldn't bring himself to be quite so rude.

She held out her hand to him. "Mr. Blunt, how do you do?"

Blunt took her hand and pressed it lazily. "Miss King. A pleasure to see you as always." He took a seat, as though it were he, not her, who was welcoming a visitor into his own drawing room.

Annabella pressed her lips together, and took a seat opposite him. She considered ringing for a cup of tea – she needed one after her day – but she was already counting the length of time it would take for that to finish, and thought better of it. She didn't need a cup of tea that badly.

"I see you are still at your project," Blunt said with the same lazy arrogance he had used at Ockham Park. "How is it coming along?"

"Well," Annabella replied, unable to keep herself from talking about her beloved Engine, "The analysts have been learning quickly, and we've

114

developed a new code that makes the sort from the store to the mill smoother, so-"

"Hmm," said Blunt, and Annabella stopped.

She folded her hands in lap. What was the point? Blunt couldn't even fake interest in the Engine, and she wasn't about to fake interest in him.

She rose to her feet. "I'm afraid that you have been kept waiting for nothing, Mr. Blunt, but I have business that I need to attend to."

"Oh, but Miss King, I was enjoying your recount of-"

"No you weren't," Annabella said sharply. "You were barely staying awake for it. Now if you would be so kind as to excuse yourself - it has been a long day."

Annabella had the satisfaction of seeing Blunt's smirk slip into shock at being spoken to in such a way. *Good*, she thought bitterly. Maybe he'll leave.

But the smile returned – wider, and somehow strangely more delighted than before. Blunt rose to his feet. "You are quite right, Miss King – it was entirely rude of me. I confess that I don't entirely understand your mechanical talk. Perhaps we could do something we might both enjoy – a ride, perhaps?" he said, bowing slightly.

Annabella felt even more annoyed by his humility than by his arrogance. "I'm afraid I'm very busy, Mr. Blunt," she said. It took no effort for her to say – it was entirely true.

"One afternoon," Blunt wheedled. "For your health. You can spare that, surely?"

The last of the thin light was fading through the front windows as Annabella entered the house. Much as she hated admitting it, her ride with Lord Blunt had made her feel better. She smiled as she entered the house, at the thought that she would have preferred just her horse's company, rather than Blunt's. Still, it had got her out of the house, which she likely would not have done without him. She paused to glance into the drawing room.

Her father was sat in one of the drawing room chairs, staring in silence into a glass of what smelled like scotch. His necktie was loosened, and he looked lost in brooding thought.

"Good evening, father," Annabella said softly, her mouth feeling strangely dry.

Lord King glanced up, and offered a feeble smile. "Bella," he said, "will you come sit with me?"

"I've just come back from a ride," Annabella replied, motioning to her clothes. "Let me change, and I'll come back down."

"Yes," Lord King replied, his voice bewildered. "Of course."

Annabella moved to the stairs, and stopped. There was something in his voice that suggested to her that if she left him, he would not be there when she returned. She removed her riding coat and placed it with her hat and gloves on the hall table, and walked into the drawing room. She sat on the edge of a chair across from her father, and for a moment neither of them spoke.

"You were riding with Lord Blunt?" her father said finally. He didn't look up from his glass.

"Yes," Annabella said, "the weather was surprisingly fine."

"And how was Lord Blunt?" Lord King added, looking up at her and taking a drink.

Annabella looked at her father for a moment, trying to detect what it was he was really asking. "He was well. He has a very healthy opinion of himself, so I shouldn't think he could ever *not* be well."

Lord King smirked. "Indeed. And what are his intentions towards you, I wonder?"

Annabella frowned. Lord King was looking at his glass again, and Annabella wondered if she should even reply. "I don't know of any intentions at all," she said finally. "He invited me for a ride in the park. And I must say I do feel better for having gone."

Lord King looked up sharply. "I didn't know you were feeling ill."

"Not ill, Father," Annabella said wearily. "Just tired."

Lord King continued to look at her as if trying to determine whether or not she was telling the truth.

"How is Mother?" Annabella said finally.

Lord King swirled the glass he was holding. "It's a bad day," he said softly.

116

Annabella swallowed. A bad day meant pain, and fits of anger.

"You should spend more time with her, you know," Lord King said gently.

"Yes," Annabella said softly. "But I always feel like she doesn't want to see me."

It was more than that, of course. It was the feeling when she went to her mother's room, that she was intruding on someone she barely knew. She could never be sure which mother would greet her: the quiet invalid, the frantic, bitter one, or simply the woman in writhing, pacing pain. The worst was her mother as she had always been, hard and judgmental, holding in every agony by force of will.

Annabella clenched her hands together. "Have you heard anything from Byron?" she asked. She knew her father had written to her brother when her mother had first become seriously ill.

"No," Lord King replied, looking into his glass.

"No?" Annabella frowned. "But surely... the Navy must know where he is."

"I don't know, Annabella," Lord King murmured.

They both fell silent for a moment.

"Will you be riding with Lord Blunt again?" Lord King asked suddenly into the silence.

"I don't know," replied Annabella. "I don't know whether I want to."

XVI

Now hatred is by far the longest pleasure;
Men love in haste but they detest at leisure.

~Lord Byron~

Henry dragged himself up the stairs to his club. His head was throbbing, and he was looking forward to a moment's peace. His own rooms seemed solitary and confined, and his father's house demanded conversation of him; at the club, nothing was asked of him, and he could lose himself in the bustle of the talk around him, cocooned for a few hours away from the world.

By the time he reached the top of the stairs, he was already annoyed. Somehow, the voices inside the club grated on him, and as he stepped into the room, he realized why.

Standing at the far end of the bar, holding a drink in his hand, was Lord Blunt. He was speaking in an overloud voice to the men around him, boasting idiotically about his night with some actress.

Henry slid away from the entrance, hoping he hadn't been seen, and sank into one of the chairs. The laughter from the far end of the room was irritating, but mercifully distant. He ordered a scotch, rested his head back on the chair, and sighed.

It had been a monotonous day. He had spent most of it at the Millwall shipyard on the Thames, overseeing the progress of the *Great Eastern*. It was dull enough work that he almost wished he were back working on the Engine, but just the thought of working alongside Annabella made his head ache. He tried not to think of her, because it made him think of her icy words when he had last seen her, and how they had sliced into him.

There wasn't really much for him to see to at the shipyard, if he were honest. The mechanics were simply working through how to fix the problems with the double hull, when–

"Have you seen any more of that King girl?"

The voice came loud and clear across the room, hitting Henry like a hammer to the temple. He clenched his glass, and reminded himself not to be stupid.

"A great deal," came Blunt's lazy drawl. "She can't see enough of me, it seems. It's just a matter of asking."

Henry took a gulp of too much of his scotch. It scorched his throat and caused him to burst into a fit of coughing. He sat forward on his chair, and immediately regretted it, as he realized the other men could see him.

"Babbage!" one of the men next to Blunt, by the name of Sinclair, called out to him. "Come and join us!"

Damn, damn, damn. Henry cursed himself inwardly and swallowed against the burning in his throat. He stood and turned to face the men at the bar.

He was rewarded at least by the look of general displeasure on Blunt's face. *Good – so the feeling is mutual.* He walked slowly towards the group.

"Does she know about your little actress, Blunt?" a man standing across from Blunt asked flippantly.

Blunt smiled lazily at the man, pointedly ignoring Henry. "It hardly seems like good manners to tell a lady about such things, don't you think?"

"It's hardly good manners to do such things, let alone speak of them."

Henry felt the stares of all the men crank towards him, and realized that it was he who had spoken.

Blunt turned to face him. The arrogant smile was still in place, but his eyes were seething.

Sinclair gave an uneasy laugh. "The perfect angel, are you, Babbage?"

"We can't all be," said Blunt, attempting to regain control of the conversation. "We all have our little secrets, don't we, Babbage?"

"She doesn't," replied Henry without an ounce of humour.

"Of course *she* doesn't," replied Blunt with a sneer. "I don't attempt to model my behavior on that of a woman."

Henry took a sip of his drink. "Perhaps you should start. You might find you gain some honour by it."

119

The rest of the men looked between themselves uncomfortably. Henry felt heat rising under his collar.

"Honour," Blunt spat. "I suppose it was honour that took you to India, was it? Or was it honour that brought you home?"

"You speak of things you know nothing about," Henry said, his voice growling in anger.

Blunt smile. "You think so, do you? Well, educate us then. Tell us your tale of *honour*," Blunt said with a flippant sneer. "Which of your stories would you prefer to tell, Babbage? That of the tradesman, or that of the killer?"

"Blunt!" gasped Sinclair. "Henry was serving Queen and country."

Henry didn't reply. His head was reeling with the desire to throttle Lord Blunt, but his mind was returning obsessively to Annabella. He took a step towards Blunt.

"You are making a mistake if you think that Annabella will overlook your actions," Henry hissed softly. "She is not the weakling you think she is."

"Evidently not," Blunt murmured, a crooked smile on his face. "She sent you on your way soon enough, didn't she?"

Henry threw back the last of his scotch, and slammed the glass down on the bar. He turned on his heel and stalked out of the club.

Henry tore across the yard towards the building that housed Annabella's schoolroom. He hadn't dared to enter it before now – it somehow felt entirely hers, and he hadn't wanted to intrude. He didn't care now. He felt only an angry heat swelling in his throat, a desire to deny what was burning in his ears.

He couldn't believe it. Annabella, who had pushed him away, couldn't possibly be thinking of that arrogant brute as… He hated even to think of it.

He swung himself up the stairs and onto the platform outside the door. Peering in, he saw Bentham, and what he could only assume was Annabella.

He could hardly actually see her. She was wearing a dark pink dress, fitted the way they always were, with leather gloves pulled all the way up to

120

her elbows, and a heavy canvas apron. Her hair was piled away from her face, strapped under a pair of riveted goggles.

She looked like a blacksmith out at a ball.

Henry swung the door open without knocking.

Bentham looked up in surprise. "Master Henry."

Annabella pulled back the goggles, and rested them on her forehead. "Mr. Babbage," she said evenly. "Can I help you?"

"Bentham, would you kindly give myself and Miss King a moment?" Henry said stiffly, still standing in the doorway.

Bentham looked carefully from Henry to Annabella. Annabella gave a brief nod. Bentham tipped his cap at her, and quietly left the room.

"Once again, Mr. Babbage," Annabella said, pulling off her gloves, "can I help you?"

He opened his mouth to speak, and wondered where on earth he had planned to start.

"I hope you are well, Miss King," he said stiffly, trying to put his thoughts in order.

Annabella raised her eyebrows, and shifted her gloves to the other hand. "You are not here to perform niceties, Mr. Babbage. What is it that you want?"

"I have been speaking with Lord Blunt," Henry said, although *speaking* was perhaps too polite a word. "He has apparently become an intimate acquaintance of yours."

"Has he indeed," Annabella said, a small smile pulling at her lips.

Her smile made knots coil in Henry's chest. He couldn't decide whether it meant that it was not true, or… was that a fond smile?

"I see," Annabella said, pulling her gloves between her hands. "And what exactly is it that you want to discuss?"

"Why are you so often in his company?" Henry demanded, trying to calm the frantic beating of his heart.

Annabella stared at him. "I'm quite certain that that is absolutely no business of yours."

"Do you have any idea what kind of man he is?" Henry raced on, hating every word that came out of his mouth, knowing that jealousy rang in each one, even if they were true.

"Do *you*? And why on earth is that of any interest to you?" snapped Annabella, as she took a step towards him. "You are not my father. Who I choose to see, as an intimate acquaintance or not, is absolutely *not* your concern."

"Are you engaged to him?" Henry snapped out.

Annabella stared at him, clearly furious. Her cheeks had flushed scarlet, and her eyes snapped fire at him. "Did he tell you that?"

Henry didn't reply. He looked away, and ran his fingers through his hair.

"And what of it? Have you come to bring me to my senses?" Annabella replied, throwing her hands in the air.

"You can't marry him, Annabella." The words were out before he could stop them, before he could remember that he no longer had the right to use her first name.

Silence descended between them. Henry found that he was breathing hard.

"How *dare* you," she hissed. "You have no right to come here and tell me who I can or can't marry. You … you made your choice," she said softly.

"And you think Lord Blunt will make a different one?" Henry said with a hard laugh. "You think that that… *man*, who could not understand the half of what you're doing, would let you continue your work?"

"And what if he does?" Annabella retorted. "What if he wants badly enough to make me happy that he will let me have what I most need?"

Henry stepped forward quickly, until he was close to her, looking down into her face. Annabella took a step away from him, and Henry forced himself not to reach out and grab her arm.

"Make no mistake," he said in a tight voice, "Lord Blunt will *never* take on the opinion of the world for you. I may have hurt you, but I never lied to you."

Annabella looked up into Henry's face, and Henry saw her anger soften for just a moment. But then it was there again, hardened against him.

"I think you should leave," Annabella said softly.

"Just tell me," Henry breathed, not moving away from her, "are you engaged to him?"

Annabella glared at him. "I am not currently engaged to him, no."

Henry took a step away from her. He felt as though she had punched him in the chest. He didn't know what her words implied, and he suddenly couldn't bear to know. "I apologize for my intrusion, Miss King," he murmured. He turned away from her, his mind in a worse turmoil than when he had arrived, and left without another word.

"You're both daft."

Annabella looked over towards the door. She had been leaning on the Analytical Engine, trying to calm her shallow breathing after her encounter with Henry. She was still too angry to forgive him – angry that he could have given her the protection of his love, and had chosen not to. But she couldn't deny that part of her frantic breathing came from once again being so close to him; she wanted to sink into his arms and erase the sorrow that was evident in the worn lines of his face.

Bentham was leaning in the frame of the door, his arms crossed over his chest. To Annabella's shock, he had an amused smile on his face.

"I beg your pardon?" she said, turning to him and planting her fist firmly on her hip.

Bentham waved away her indignation. "None of your high and mightiness, Miss. I said, you're both daft."

Annabella considered calling him out on the impropriety of his comment, but thought better of it. This was what she wanted, wasn't it? To be treated equally?

"And why, pray tell, are we both daft?" she said with a resigned sigh.

Bentham's smile widened. "Because you both love each other more than the Earth under your feet, and you can't so much as say so."

Annabella flushed scarlet. "Bentham! Were you listening at the door?"

Bentham shrugged. "Didn't have to be at the door, Miss. We could hear you and Master Henry out in the yard."

We. Dammit. "Since you heard everything anyway, you will know that Henry – I mean, Mr. Babbage does not have the feelings for me that you suggest. Maybe he did once, but-"

"I did hear some rubbish about him making his choice. I suppose he told you that you couldn't work no more, did he?" Bentham muttered, walking across to the machine.

"How did you – never mind, as you heard, you're wrong about him," Annabella replied in exasperation.

"I ain't wrong. As usual," Bentham replied shortly, picking up a stack of cards. "He loves you truly, and every day that he ain't with you is making him a desperate man."

Annabella offered no reply. She didn't like the idea that Henry still held feelings for her. It would be too easy to give up everything she had struggled for, to give in to her own longing to be with him. Even as she wanted to, she knew it wouldn't be the same. It wouldn't be the two of them with their heads bent over punch cards and algorithms; it would be him gone away to work, and her left at home.

"You might think these cards are enough, Miss," Bentham said softly. He placed his hand on the Engine. "That *she's* enough. But she's made of metal, Miss. She's never going to be enough comfort for you."

Annabella looked up at him. "Is she enough comfort for you?"

"No," Bentham replied shortly. "But my wife died three years past."

Annabella stared at Bentham in shock, and realized how little she knew about him. She knew his first name was John, but only because she had had to complete some papers for him, and she had had to ask. She realized looking at him now that his care worn face belied his age – he likely wasn't any older than Henry. If his wife had died three years ago… then they couldn't have been married long.

"What was her name?" Annabella said.

Bentham gave a sad smile. "Margaret," he said. He looked at the ground in silence for a moment, and then back at her. "The Engine's all I have. It ain't all you have, Miss."

"It isn't that, Bentham," Annabella replied softly, turning and looking at the towers of cogs, the heavily greased wheels. "I feel like… if I weren't

124

working on her, there would be a piece of me missing." She turned to look at Bentham.

His smile was gone, and was replaced by only a sad gaze. "If I'm any judge, Miss, a piece of you is already missing."

Annabella shook her head. "Let's get back to work, Bentham."

XVII

Since thou art Being and Breath
And what thou art may never be destroyed.

~Emily Brontë~

It was only a week later that Annabella found herself forced to keep an engagement to go riding with Lord Blunt. She found she had a sudden strong desire to refuse, and instead of lying to herself, she admitted to herself that it was because of what Henry had said.

She *did* know what kind of man Blunt was. Even while trying to court her – or whatever it was that he was trying to do – he still managed to flaunt his arrogance and ignorance. Annabella found it easier on most occasions to just let him talk, and let her mind drift. She couldn't think of a good reason for refusing their already made plans, but she knew that this would be the last time she would ride with him. Whatever his intentions were, she didn't need them.

Even without Henry's outburst, she could well imagine that Lord Blunt couldn't be trusted to respect her or her work if they had been married. She had never really considered the possibility of marrying him, which left the troubling possibility that she had seen so much of him merely to annoy Henry.

Annabella laced up her riding boots, her corsets digging into her ribs as she did so. Sarah stood nervously by her. Annabella had finally insisted that she couldn't very well be considered any kind of professional if she couldn't put on her own shoes, even if it admittedly make her very short of breath.

Lord Blunt met her in the drawing room with the same drawling drivel as always, and they went to collect their horses.

London was hesitantly allowing daffodils to bloom in some of the parks, and was even considering the possibility of leaves. It was still chilly, but the clear day made for a brisk and welcome ride through Hyde Park. She never mentioned it to Lord Blunt, but Annabella consistently chose Hyde Park because of the looming building that she could see gradually taking shape beyond the trees.

The Crystal Palace, they were calling it. It was, astonishingly, nearly finished, though it was only a few months ago that it had been merely a dream of the Prince Consort's. It looked to Annabella like something between a palace and a giant greenhouse, its great iron frame draped in a glittering robe of glass. Through the panes she could see the branches of enormous trees, already set into place so that they would be in full foliage in time for the Exhibition. A giant greenhouse, that could grow not only enormous plants, but machines of all kinds.

It should have been deeply exciting. She should have been thrilled, chattering to her companion about the Exhibition itself, about the Engine, about their exhibit. But she wasn't. The companion was all wrong, and all she felt was tired. She needed to finish the project, but she was exhausted at the mere thought of it.

Lord Blunt had been talking all that time, and he had drawn his horse closer to hers as he had spoken. She had hardly noticed him, until he caught the reins of her horse.

"Lord Blunt?" Annabella blinked in surprise.

"I asked if you wanted to stop to look at the Exhibition for a moment," Lord Blunt said, evidently for the second time, an edge of annoyance in his voice.

"Well I don't," replied Annabella. On seeing the surprise on Lord Blunt's face, she sighed, and gentled her reply to, "I'm quite tired, Lord Blunt. I think it's time for us to return home."

"Of course," Lord Blunt replied, in a voice that Annabella assumed was intended to be gallant. "I can lead your horse if you like."

"That will hardly be necessary," Annabella replied. She twitched the reins out of his hands, and turned her horse's head back the way they had come. Lord Blunt was left with no choice but to follow.

The ride back to Annabella's house was quiet, because Annabella made it so by riding slightly ahead of Blunt. Their horses rounded into the courtyard of her father's house, and Annabella slid from the saddle, not waiting for Blunt to offer his help.

"I'm sorry that you were too tired to enjoy this ride, Miss King," Lord Blunt said, sliding off his own horse. "Perhaps the next one will be-"

"Thank you, Lord Blunt, but there will not be a next one," Annabella said, her firmness surprising even her.

It certainly surprised Lord Blunt. "I beg your pardon, but whatever do you mean?"

Annabella resisted the temptation to roll her eyes as she handed her reins to the older groom, who led her horse away to the stables. The reaction was so typical of Blunt, so filled with assumption. As if it were simply impossible that she wouldn't want to see him again.

Annabella began pulling off her gloves, and walking towards the house. "I have enjoyed our rides, Lord Blunt, and they have provided me with much needed fresh air. But I do not wish to arrange another, thank you."

Blunt stepped in front of her, and Annabella stopped. His face was becoming red, in the effort to keep his voice smooth and controlled. "My dear Miss King, I have enjoyed your company, and I would-"

Annabella laughed, astonishing both herself and Blunt by doing so. "My company? How could you possibly know what my company is like? I have spoken barely two words together when we have been out, and the only company that you have enjoyed is your own."

Blunt swallowed. "Miss King, pardon me, I did not mean to give offence."

Weariness began to settle through Annabella. The last thing that she wanted was to explain her heart to Lord Blunt. "Lord Blunt, if you please, I am quite tired, and I –"

"Then I am not to see you again?" Lord Blunt said, moving to step in front of her again.

"That you will see me again, I have no doubt," Annabella said. "But I decline your invitation to ride again, thank you."

Blunt's mouth twisted into an ugly sneer. "You have led me to believe that my attentions were welcome. That you welcomed, and I dare say expected, more."

128

"How so?" Annabella snapped, becoming impatient and cold standing in the courtyard. "You never asked my thoughts, how could you possibly presume to know them?"

"Is this because of that self-righteous engineer?" Blunt said, stepping closer. "Was he filling your head again with some nonsense about your genius?"

Annabella blinked, finding herself surprised at Blunt's sudden sneer. "I hardly need him for that."

"What did Babbage say to you?" Blunt demanded.

Well, well, Annabella thought. She wondered what Henry had said to Blunt – or what he had overheard – that had provoked Blunt's reaction. She narrowed her eyes at Blunt. "Why? What ought he have told me, Lord Blunt?"

Blunt pressed his lips together, and said nothing.

"Whether you believe it or not, Lord Blunt, I am capable of thoughts and preferences of my own. They have nothing to do with Mr. Babbage. Now kindly stand aside."

Lord Blunt didn't move, but instead glared down at her, his anger plain on his face. "You are honestly choosing him over me?"

Annabella stared at him. "I am not making a choice of one man over the other. I am deciding that I no longer wish to continue keeping your company."

"You are a spoilt fool," he hissed at her. "You'll never get a husband by being so obstinate."

Annabella grinned. "How *very* liberating."

She moved to pass him, and he grabbed her upper arm and pulled her to face him.

"Let go of me," she said, her voice low.

Lord Blunt gripped her arm tighter. "He is nothing. An upstart mechanic with blood on his hands. An imperialist thug who-"

"You know nothing about him," Annabella burst out before she could stop herself. She could feel heat flooding into her cheeks; she hated how the sneer in Blunt's voice affected her, how deeply his words cut into her.

Blunt laughed, a sardonic laugh as irritating as his insolent voice. "How completely perfect. The daughter of the Earl of Lovelace coupling with the *inventor's* son. Does your poor father know?" he said, his voice mocking.

Annabella lifted her chin, and glared at Blunt. "I'm beginning to worry about your hearing, Lord Blunt. There is nothing for my father to know. The fact that I have refused you does not mean I am in love with Henry Babbage," she said, trying to keep her gaze proud and firm, even as her voice hitched on saying his name, even as her chest contracted around the thought of him.

Blunt gave an ugly smile. "Are you telling me that *he*, a tradesman, a soldier, a man with no title, has won your poor little heart?"

Her own determination had surprised her, but she suddenly wanted to weep, as her fury began to leave her, replaced with weary sorrow, and the realization of how much Blunt's insults about Henry had bruised her. She could still feel her cheeks hot from the emotions that raged in her, of anger, of pride, and of fierce, protective love.

It didn't matter; she didn't need Henry's word for it that Blunt was an arrogant ass. The fact that he had been surprised by her rejection of him should come as no surprise, and left her with no regrets.

"There is nothing poor or little about my heart," Annabella snapped in fury. "I do not have to answer your assumptions."

She tried to pull away from him, but instead he yanked her around and gripped both of her arms in his hands.

"You will let go of me," Annabella said, glaring up at him. His face was flushed, his amusement gone.

"You would choose his world," Blunt spat, "a world of machines and industry, over mine?"

"His world is *my* world," Annabella said, her emotions spilling over, unprotected, in her words. "If you had listened to me for even a moment, you would know that the world of Engines is the one I live in now, the only one that gives me joy."

"What, your mechanical plaything?" Blunt sneered in disbelief.

"It is not a toy," Annabella said fiercely. "It is my future, and it will shortly also be yours."

130

"I doubt it," Blunt said with a smile.

"Then you will be left behind," Annabella said. She wrenched her shoulders out of Lord Blunt's grasp, and pushed him away from her. She straightened her sleeves, and glared at his startled face. "Now get out of my way."

Somewhat to her surprise, he did. She stalked past him into the house, and slammed the door behind her without saying goodbye.

XVIII

To have the sense of creative activity is the great happiness
and the great proof of being alive.

~Lord Byron~

Annabella sank into a chair behind the table that had somehow become her desk. It had been week since she had last seen Blunt, for what she hoped was the last time. It had been strangely restful: no Blunt, no Henry, no outbursts between her mother and father. She had tried to see her mother in the morning, when she thought she might be well enough rested. Ada had refused to see her.

Instead of being the dutiful daughter, she was here, with the Analytical Engine looming over her, in a space that was her own. In a world where nothing else seemed quite right, having a place to go where she was valued and content seemed worth clinging to.

She felt strongly that there must be something that she should be doing, but allowed herself to simply lean back in her chair and close her eyes. The analysts had left for lunch, leaving her to wait for hers to be brought over from the inn. Even quiet, the school seemed to hum with the energy of sums and codes and patterns. She heaved a sigh of relief, and let the tension in her neck uncurl itself for a moment.

She wasn't sure how long she had sat there when the door opened. Annabella looked up, to see a young man bearing a tray with tea and a lunch of bread and cheese and meat. Behind him, in the doorway, was Charles Babbage.

"Mr. Babbage!" Annabella cried, the words sounding strange in her mouth. She felt oddly guilty at having been so relaxed. She paid the young man from the inn hastily, and he placed the tray quietly on the desk and left.

"I beg your pardon for interrupting your lunch, Miss King," Charles Babbage said gravely.

"No, it's a pleasure to see you, Mr. Babbage," Annabella rushed to assure him, and found to her surprise that she meant it. He was a familiar face, one associated with the Engine without strain or heartache. "Will you join me?"

"I will not, but please, eat," Charles Babbage said, seating himself across from her.

"What can I do for you?" Annabella said as she poured herself a cup of tea.

"I have heard some news about your mother," Babbage said.

Annabella paused with her teacup half raised. "I'm sorry, about-"

"Her health, my dear," Charles Babbage said gravely, saving her the trouble of guessing.

Annabella put down her cup. "Yes. Did my father tell you?"

Charles nodded. "I have known your father a long time, my dear, and your mother... even longer. And I... I have known illness of that kind myself."

Annabella nodded, looking at her tea, thinking of Babbage's wife and daughter Georgiana. She had never known Babbage's wife, but Georgiana, who had been a few years older than her, had died only recently. She thought for a moment to correct him, to tell him that her mother was only ill, and not dying, but didn't.

"I've come to ask you not to stop your work."

Annabella looked up at Babbage, her eyes wide with surprise, but he continued. "I know what you must think. That such a request is callous, and insensitive to the pain that your family must be feeling. But I make it as much for your mother as for the rest of us. The Engines – they would not have been possible without her work. She is a part of them, but you are making them greater than she ever imagined. You are continuing her work."

Annabella silently met Babbage's gaze, and held it for a moment before replying. "Mr. Babbage, my father told me once that you did not publish my mother's work under her name because she was a woman. That you thought the Engine would not receive its funds if you did. Is that true?"

Real sadness flowed across Charles Babbage's face. "It is true that I thought those things, yes. Whether or not the Engine would have received its funds with her name on her work is something that we will never know."

"Do you think you were wrong?" Annabella pressed.

Charles Babbage did not answer immediately, and instead looked at her quietly. "There is no way for me to know. Our world is moving too fast for us to spend much time regretting our past ideas. If you judge me today for what I thought then, you will most certainly find me guilty." Charles Babbage paused for a moment. "The same may be true of my son."

Annabella's stomach lurched, and the question was on her lips before she could stop it. "How do you mean?"

"Henry did not tell me what passed between you and him at Ockham Park," Charles Babbage said softly. "But I have gathered since that he made a decision he regrets. Hopefully there will be time for him to change his mind. And for you to change yours."

Annabella swallowed the lump in her throat. It was strange to think of either her or Henry actually acknowledging that they had made a mistake, when they had only been cold or angry at each other since it had happened.

"Do you have enough options for your display for the Exhibition?"

Annabella placed her teacup down, and managed a coherent answer. "We, yes, we have. I was just speaking with one of my analysts before lunch, and she was telling me that all our variables total up to three thousand."

Charles Babbage nodded his approval. "How convertible are the programs? To other applications, I mean?"

"I would say about eighty to ninety percent of it, though I would have to check the numbers," Annabella replied. "It's only the output, really, that is not interchangeable with other tasks. Everything else is numbers, as you know."

"And you're prepared and able to explain that to anyone who should ask at the Exhibition?" Charles demanded.

"Of course," Annabella said, rather more sharply than she meant to.

"Indeed," Babbage said with a small smile. He rose to his feet. "You have a glorious task ahead of you, Miss King. I hope that you will pursue it."

134

Annabella rose to her feet. She extended her hand to him, and he shook it firmly. "I hadn't considered any other option, Mr. Babbage."

Annabella sat on the end of her bed as the day drew to a close. Her room had just enough light still filtering through the windows to see by. She had just sat down on the bed and begun to take off her boots when there was a gentle knock at the door.

"Come in," she called, and Sarah gently opened the door, holding a lamp in her hand. The orange light cast across Sarah's features showed a worried face.

"Miss, I didn't know you were back, otherwise I would have-"

"It's all right, Sarah," Annabella said. She pulled off her second boot, and threw it on the floor. "I only just returned."

Sarah lit the other lamps in the room, and set hers down on a table. "Miss,..." she said softly. "There must be,... is there anything..." She straightened, and smoothed her apron. "What can I get for you, Miss?"

Annabella tried to be practical. She was aching and hungry, and knew it was likely that her father had told the servants not to serve supper. "Perhaps I could have something to eat, Sarah?"

"Of course Miss!" Sarah said, wringing her hands together. "Fresh bread from this morning, and stew."

"Please bring them up. And a pot of tea," Annabella added. "And Sarah?"

Sarah turned back from the door to look at her, her eyes bright.

"When you return with the food..." It had been such a long week, with so much on her mind, with no one to talk to... "would you stay a while with me? I could use someone to talk to."

Sarah smiled. "Of course, Miss."

"I don't understand, Miss."

Sarah was sitting in a chair in Annabella's room, at Annabella's insistence. Somewhat to Sarah's horror, Annabella had pressed her to accept a cup of tea of her own. Annabella was on her bed, changed into a nightgown and a warm robe, with her tea and dinner on a tray next to her.

She had just finished explaining to Sarah her week: Henry's outburst, which had necessitated explaining his earlier proposal, her ride with Blunt, and her refusal of him. They had not yet spoken of her mother, and they were both, for the moment, content to leave it that way.

"What part?" Annabella said, cradling the cup of tea in her hands.

"Your refusal of Mister Henry," Sarah said, her hands tentatively holding the saucer of her teacup. "You love him, and he loves you, and he wants to take care of you, and you won't marry him because he won't let you *work*?"

Annabella grinned. Put in those words, and coming from her tired, overworked maid, it did sound silly.

"I know," she said instead. "But this work... it's become a part of me. I have a purpose now, something that fires my mind. I can teach others to see the things that I see, and to have that taken away from me, by the very person who gave it me..." Annabella held the cup against her chest, and swallowed hard. "I can't, Sarah."

Sarah nodded slowly. "It's strange. Being rich should give you everything you want. But then you, and Lady King..." Sarah sat up suddenly, almost spilling her tea. "I'm sorry, Miss, I didn't mean to-"

Annabella waved wearily. "What were you going to say about me and my mother, Sarah?" she said, swallowing the lump that formed in her throat.

"I was just thinking that for you, and her... it isn't enough to be looked after," Sarah said softly.

"No," Annabella replied. "Children are looked after."

Sarah was silent for a moment. "Could I learn to be an analyst?"

Annabella looked up, feeling warm inside. "Would you want to, Sarah?"

Sarah smiled sheepishly. "I just... when I was helping you to work on the Engine, when it was just us two, you used to show me how the cards worked, and how you wrote the programs in. I still remember how, and I thought maybe-"

"I'd like that," Annabella said, with a smile. Not a sad one, for once, but a genuine, eager smile.

Sarah bit her lip. "Only, I'm not sure how I would manage it, Miss, not with putting in a full day of work, of course, and I-"

"You wouldn't," Annabella said hurriedly. "Of course you can't. I'll arrange it, Sarah. I'll get you enough time to learn." It had suddenly become very important her to that Sarah come with her, that she have the same chance to learn as Evy and Rosie. She frowned. "Still, it will mean a lot of work for you."

"I don't mind work, Miss," Sarah returned.

"No. Of course you don't," Annabella said with a grin.

XIX

Sad Patience, too near neighbour to despair.

~Matthew Arnold~

Annabella stood up from where she was bent over a table in the training room. She looked about the increasing crowded room that served as her school for analysts. A number of men were working at the tables strewn around the room, some completing punch cards, some completing code in notebooks. Evy Hayward and Rosie Bearce were feeding punch cards into the Engine, Evy talking softly as she did so, Rosie as always focused and dedicated to her work. They had both worked out just fine as analysts. Rosie was quiet but hardworking, while Evy often answered for them both. She was tentative, but clever.

At a desk near the door, Bentham was bent over Sarah's shoulder, showing her patterns on a range of punch cards, explaining to her the input of the machine. Annabella hadn't asked permission from her father or mother; no one was keen to disturb Lord and Lady King just at the moment, Annabella included.

Sarah was frowning carefully at the cards on the table before her, but Bentham, Annabella noticed, was looking not at the cards, but at Sarah. True, Bentham knew the program better than anyone, except maybe for Annabella herself, but there was something more.

Annabella shook her head, and let the thought slide away. She pulled on her gloves, and walked to Evy and Rosie.

"Did the last run work?" she asked.

"Almost, Miss," Evy replied. "There was a catch in the tenth and twentieth row. We're checking if that was the loom rather than the Engine by running it unattached," she added, gesturing to the disconnected loom.

Annabella nodded. The loom that they had connected to the Analytical Engine, that would receive the output and translate it into fibers, was far from perfect. It was old and unreliable, and more than once what had seemed like a problem in their program had been fixed by adjusting the output on the loom itself. Two catches, though, so evenly spaced, sounded more like the Engine.

"How many have we run so far?" Annabella asked, glancing up at the cog towers of the Mill.

"Well, getting on about fifty patterns, Miss, not counting variables for colour and size, so on about three thousand, give or take?" Evy replied, pulling the crank to restart the Engine.

Annabella blinked. The massive amount of variables in the Engine still never failed to stagger her. She waited until the Engine came to the end of its run before she spoke again. "Three thousand that *worked*?" she said.

Evy gave a slow grin. "Of course three thousand that worked. You think I'd've moved on to three thousand and one if the rest of them hadn't?"

Annabella grinned. "No, of course not. Carry on."

The morning wore quickly away, and at one o'clock Annabella sent the analysts off for their lunch. It was a cold day, but windy and clear. Most took it outside in the yard, but she saw some of them leave the yard for the small patch of park near the river.

"Miss?"

Annabella looked up to see Sarah standing shyly next to her.

"Was there anything you needed, Miss? Only, some of the analysts were going to take lunch in the park, and I was-"

"No, of course, Sarah," Annabella interrupted her. How often did Sarah see people who didn't work for her parents? Never? "Of course, please join them."

Annabella watched with something very like envy as Sarah gathered up her bonnet and basket of lunch, and followed Bentham out the door. She looked back at her work as the analysts filed out of the room, and it became quiet.

"You all right, Miss?"

Annabella raised her head, and found herself meeting the soft and whimsical gaze of Evy Hayward. The young woman was looking at her with genuine concern.

"I… yes, Evy, thank you for asking," Annabella said, swallowing hard and forcing a smile.

"It's only… I don't mean to be rude, Miss, but I had heard that your mother was sick, and I…" Evy stopped, frowning, looking like she wanted to say more.

Annabella sat back in her chair. "Do you have any family, Evy?"

Evy shrugged with a sad smile. "Da died when I was little, and I nursed Mama last spring when she passed. I have a sister, but she…" Evy's sympathetic face suddenly fell, with an emotion that Annabella couldn't identify. "She's married. I don't see her much."

Annabella looked down at the table, unsure of how to continue. She felt callous, wrapped in her own sorrow, while this young woman was willing to sympathize with her.

"It's only a stepping stone, miss," Evy said gently.

"What is, Evy?" Annabella said, wearily raising her head.

"This life," Evy murmured. "That's what my mama told me. It's only a stepping stone to the other side, where we'll find peace."

Annabella looked at Evy, and managed a thin smile. She wished that she could have the same faith that she saw in Evy's face – simple and unquestioning, faith that made it all bearable. But she didn't.

"Can I get you something to eat, Miss?" Evy said.

Annabella blinked. "Thank you, yes, Evy. And some tea from the inn across the way, if you would be so kind."

Evy gave her a final smile and dropped into a small curtsy, before leaving the room.

"Father?" Annabella called as she entered the house.

There was no response. That was usual, these days. Annabella rarely saw her parents. Instead, she saw the quantities of doctors that filtered in and out of the house at all hours. She walked up to her room, where Sarah had left a bowl of warm water on her nightstand to wash after her walk back from the works. Sarah had insisted on leaving before her, to ensure that she could at least complete her duties as Annabella's maid before Annabella arrived home. Annabella wasn't quite sure how Sarah managed it all.

Annabella pulled off her dusty clothes and laid them over a chair. Over the whirlwind of the past few weeks, there had been strangely little time for her to consider her mother's illness. Annabella had fallen into a vigorous routine that filled her thoughts completely, that left no room for grief. She ate breakfast in her room each day, and walked to the works, letting the bustle of the London streets, the dirt, the carriages, the workers walking to warehouses swallow up her thoughts. She took her lunch in the school room, sheltered and alone. At the end of the day was another walk, to buy her time, to exhaust her thoroughly so that sleep would take her. She ate by herself once more, often in her room. Sarah would stay with her when she wanted a companion, and would speak mostly of the school, and increasingly, Annabella had noticed, of Bentham.

Annabella splashed water on her face. She felt more free than lonely. There were no expectations on her, no dinners, no balls, nothing that would interrupt the rapidly increasing pace of progress towards the Exhibition. Her dress for the Exhibition had been delivered that week. It was silver and close fitting like her other work dresses, though the dressmaker had decided to add flowing, feathery decorations to the tight sleeves.

Annabella had just put on her clean clothes when a gentle knock on the door announced Sarah. She entered, smiling, with a pot of tea and a meal on the tray.

"A night in, Miss?" Sarah said, placing the tray on the table.

Annabella smiled. "As usual, I suppose-"

"That's not true!"

Annabella and Sarah both froze. The shrieked, wailing voice had come from along the hall. It could only have been her mother's voice.

"Sarah," Annabella said slowly and carefully. "I think it would be best for you to return to the kitchen this evening. A night in for you as well."

"Yes Miss," Sarah whispered, quietly leaving the room.

Annabella left her dinner on her table and put a shawl around her shoulders. She padded gently down the hall in her stocking feet, and assumed her familiar position of listening outside her mother's room.

"…cannot understand, Ada, is how a woman of your intellectual capacity could be so utterly foolish," came her father's voice, in a low growl.

"What do you know of my intellectual capacity," returned her mother's bitter voice.

Annabella pressed her forehead against the door. With everything else going on, what could it possibly be this time?

"I cannot condone or take responsibility for such reckless behavior," Lord King said, evidently trying to remain reasonable and calm.

Ada King gave a high pitched laugh. "Cannot take responsibility for me? You own me, you fool, you-"

"Do not make this into *my* scandal, Ada!" Lord King barked. "I have given you every liberty within my power to give, and you have taken every advantage of it! Even after Christmas, when we spoke of it, you still-"

"I'm dying!" Annabella backed away from the door as Ada's voice came through it in a sob. "What does it matter now?"

Annabella registered no shock at her mother's words. She didn't wonder at not feeling more grief in the face of her mother's revelation; she wondered at the fact that she hadn't felt more before now. She must have already known.

There was silence on the other side of the door, aside from a soft weeping, and the rasping of Ada's breath.

"Ada," came Lord King's voice. It was gentler now, but still the voice that he might use to a child he was punishing. "There is no action that we take in our lives that is without consequence. The consequence of your most recent action is that your visitors will be restricted while you are ill."

"No!" Annabella all but gasped at the frantic shriek that was her mother's reply. "Why in God's name would you? You cannot-"

"You lost two thousand pounds gambling on a *horse*, Ada. A bet that you could not have placed yourself. I don't know who placed it for you, or who sold the diamonds to pay for it, but I will not allow you to do so again."

"William, please," Ada's sobs came through the door.

"No, Ada," Lord King returned, gently. "You will have Annabella, and myself, and anyone else may visit while we are there."

There was no reply. Annabella held her breath at the door, waiting for her mother's protest, but none came.

Lord King's footsteps sounded in the direction of the door. Annabella stepped back from it just as the door swung open, and glanced up into her father's face. He looked at her, and didn't speak.

142

"Is it true?" Annabella said finally. "Is Mother dying?"

His face was etched with utter exhaustion, and when he spoke, his voice was hoarse, but strangely emotionless.

"Yes. Your mother is dying."

There was no hesitation, no attempt to deny it. There was no change in his demeanour after saying it, as if he had been repeating it in his own mind over and over.

"The doctor wasn't sure how long she would last," her father went on mechanically. "He has left her something for the pain."

He turned and walked down the hall to, Annabella could only assume, his study and a glass of scotch.

He had left the door open.

Annabella stood staring at it, and swallowed hard. She stepped quickly into her mother's bedroom, for the first time in months.

It was gradual, but what hit her first was the smell. There was the smell of something metallic, which Annabella thought might be blood. There was the papery cloth smell of bandages, a pleasant but musty kind of smell. Underneath it, came a sticky, almost sweet smell that Annabella remembered from when she had had fever as a child – laudanum.

Annabella stepped further into the room, blinking, after the darkness of the hall, in the light of a single gas lamp, and rounded the corner of the heavily draped bed.

Her mother lay on the bed, her dark hair flung across the pillow. She was desperately, achingly thin, with dark circles under her closed eyes. Her nightdress was rolled up to show one of her forearms, where a bandage covered a wound. Annabella glanced at the table beside the bed, at the bowl that still showed the stains of rivulets of blood. Ada's surgeon was bleeding her; Annabella did not know why. She thought of the surgeons coming in and out of the house, and wondered how often it happened.

Ada moaned, and thrashed in what seemed to be a light and restless sleep. Annabella glanced again at the table, and saw the bottle of laudanum, the alcohol drenched opium that had given her such fitful sleep as a child.

"No…" Ada moaned slowly. "No… no!"

Annabella stepped back from the bed, troubled by her mother's agitation. What should she do? Was her father not going to return?

"No! Don't take him from me. No!"

Annabella sat down on the bed carefully, reaching past her mother's flailing arms, and pulled her mother to her.

Ada's hands went to her clothing, and caught her shawl in grasping fingers. Annabella wrapped her mother against her chest, and began to rock her gently. Ada began to sob, violent sobs at first, mixed with mingled cries, and then gradually gentler and softer ones, until her body went limp in Annabella's arms.

Annabella cradled her mother's thin, frail body as the sobs ebbed away, and waited for her breathing to become regular and quiet, even though it was shallow. She lowered her gently back to the bed.

Annabella made sure that her mother's bandage was still in place, and tucked the covers around her. She pulled Ada's long hair off her face, and laid it across the pillow. It was only then that she started to cry.

XX

These beauteous forms,
Through a long absence, have not been to me
As is a landscape to a blind man's eye:
But oft, in lonely rooms, and 'mid the din
Of towns and cities, I have owed to them
In hours of weariness, sensations sweet...

~William Wordsworth~

Henry stepped into the Crystal Palace, the home of the Great Exhibition, and felt his gaze be drawn upward to the soaring structure. He had no justifiable reason for feeling the way that he did, but he had the sense that all his current misery was tied up in this place. He glared resentfully up at its spider-wed iron frame and scintillating glass ceiling, and down its central nave. The Crystal Palace was massive, a cross between a cathedral and a train station, teeming with displays, crammed to bursting with people and things. In the entranceway, an enormous black hulk, a twenty-four ton chunk of coal, caused throngs of people to stream around it, like water splitting around a rock in a river.

He hadn't seen Annabella, except from a distance, since his outburst in the schoolroom. His father had told him, of course, how ill her mother was, which only made him feel worse. Had she known that her mother was ill even then? And then for her to endure, to be able to work when he had abandoned their goal— it all made his woes seem insignificant.

Henry walked down through the central nave, surrounded by people eager to see the displays of the Exhibition. The displays here were relatively small —all the heavy machinery displays were at the far end, where they could be hooked into sources of power, steam, gas, and for a rare display, electricity. The crowd was evidently delighted by all it saw – clothes and musical instruments of all kinds, clocks that seemed to do everything except actually give the time, hats for every possible reason and of every possible design.

Henry knew that the building had been Paxton's design, and that the concept of the Exhibition had been that of the Prince Consort; and yet somehow, as he walked through the displays of ingenuity for the sake of ingenuity, Henry couldn't help but feel that it was all pure Brunel. Henry could practically hear the older man banging on about progress, and the rapid advances into the modern world. Brunel's love of ingenuity was not just his business; it was his one true passion. Henry wondered whether that wasn't the real reason why Brunel had taken on building his father's Engine. Not because he felt he could profit by it – but because he loved it for its own sake, and believed in it when few others could.

Henry reached the north-west axis of the Crystal Palace, and looked up at where the Analytical Engine display was to be. He couldn't see Annabella anywhere – all he saw was a wooden structure, and what looked, to him, like the back of an Engine. It had a cover, that showed no moving parts. It was often the side that faced the public in Brunel's many train stations, but Henry couldn't determine why it would be facing the public now. Wasn't Brunel's very intention that everyone be able to *see* the workings of the Engine? And where was the loom? Or bells, or whatever Annabella had finally decided would demonstrate the Engine? He smothered his frustration, and made his way close to the front of the crowd, as Brunel stepped to the stage.

Brunel wore a dull silver waistcoat under his customary dark jacket, and had the beginnings of a manic grin on his face. He spread his arms wide and began to speak.

"Ladies and Gentlemen!" His voice boomed over the crowd, and their voices hushed slightly.

"Welcome, to the Great Exhibition of the Works of Industry of all Nations!" Brunel cried, gesturing around the soaring Crystal Palace with a great sweep of his arm. "You have seen, no doubt, miraculously things here today – miraculous, but nevertheless created by the hand of Man, and not the hand of God! And now, you stand before the truest and greatest work of industry here – the one that may *control all the others*!"

146

A murmur ran through the crowd, and Henry smiled despite himself. Brunel was a great engineer, but this was what he did best – making people believe, making them follow him into what was, to most, impossible. He would have made a very fine preacher.

"Now, as some of you may be aware, the invention that you are about to witness is the work of one Mr. Charles Babbage, and has for years been the force behind our trains, our navigation, and our mathematics. But today, you will all become aware of the infinite possibilities that the Analytical Engine can offered to each man – and each woman."

A soft murmur went through the crowd, accompanied by a small chorus of laughter.

"For what you will see today cannot be said to be the product of one man's work," Brunel continued. "It is instead due to the imagination of many men, and many women - " more laughter from the crowd. " – that this Engine was not only created, but is able to do more than ever before conceived. What you will see today, ladies and gentlemen, is only the beginning. And it is you who will determine its future."

A hush fell over the crowd, and Henry felt his skin prickle. Something about Brunel's words felt truly, terrifyingly, real.

"Ladies and Gentlemen, allow me to present to you, the *Steel Lady*, and her finest analyst, *Miss Annabella King*!"

Brunel stepped to one side as the wooden structure gave a thunderous groan. There was the sound of grinding gears and a shriek of releasing steam. And the Analytical Engine began to turn.

Gasps rang up from the crowd, and although he knew what it was, Henry found himself riveted by the spectacle. There had to be a railway turntable in the wooden stage, normally used to turn several tons worth of locomotive, now groaning as it turned the compact weight of the Analytical Engine. As it swung ponderously slowly, the front of the Engine came into view, and Henry's sharp intake of breath joined the gasps of the crowd.

The Analytical Engine *gleamed*. The structure of the Engine had been wrapped in a curving cage of what Henry presumed to be steel, polished and sweeping around the towers of cogs. The store towers reflected the light, encased with glass panels. Light danced across the bare metal of the mill towers. This Analytical Engine, this Steel Lady, as Brunel had called it, looked like the glittering offspring of the Crystal Palace that surrounded it.

The first impression was so overpowering that for a moment even Henry didn't notice the loom that sat in front of the Engine, and it took another second for him to see the tiny figure that was utterly dwarfed by the massive display. *Annabella.*

She was wearing a shimmering silver gown, worn straight and close to her body like all her work dresses. The arms of the dress were straight, with small floating pieces of gauze attached at the wrists. Her hair was piled back on her head, and spilled down her neck in thick dark curls. She wore her goggles on her head, and a fixed, polite smile on her face.

She was *exhausted.* He was some distance away, and yet Henry could see the lack of colour in her cheeks, the dark hollows under her eyes. Her expression was strained. It couldn't just be the work, Henry felt sure; he had worked long hours with Annabella on the Engine, and she had always been engaged and passionate about what she was doing. Here, she looked close to collapsing.

Brunel had begun to speak again, but Henry wasn't listening. Annabella had been scanning the crowd as she stood next to the Engine, and her eyes were now locked on him.

When the turntable had first begun to turn, the nerves in Annabella's stomach had vanished, replaced with a strange, singing numbness as she came around to face the crowd. At first, the crowd had been a swimming mass of colours, but it had gradually resolved itself into upturned faces. Many of them looked shocked, many more looked amused. Some were whispering to others, looking not at the Engine, but at her. Annabella felt keenly conscience that the faces that looked the most affronted by her very presence were those of the women. Which made a kind of sense, if she thought about it. She tried not to.

Her eyes scanned towards the front rows of the crowd, down the left side of the stage. Her scanning stopped, and her stomach lurched as her eyes came to rest on a man standing two rows back, looking hungrily up at the stage.

148

Henry. His eyes were fixed on the stage, but they didn't look particularly pleased to see her. His face was grim, his jaw set. He was carefully and neatly put together, but he looked pale and unhappy. Annabella couldn't tell what he was thinking, but whatever it was, it wasn't bringing him a great deal of joy.

"… infinite possibilities!"

Annabella jumped, and pulled down her goggles. She probably didn't need them, but it made her feel more like she was actually working, and less like she was a magician's assistant. She briefly wished that she had her work gloves.

She stepped up to the Engine, and began to feed the cards. She had done it so many times before that she didn't need a list of codes to tell her what to input; it was as if the codes were words to her, as simple as asking politely. She put in her request, and pulled the crank.

A gasp rose from the crowd as the Engine thundered into life, its cogs spinning as the mill was turned by its steam powered driver. The loom in front of the Engine began to clatter back and forth, weaving out the pattern that she had designed for it. It was a simple enough pattern of woven diamonds on a bottle green background – it would have made Henry a very nice waistcoat, Annabella thought, before she could stop herself.

"I know what you're thinking!" Babbage called out over the clamour of the various machines. "How is this innovation? How is this invention? Surely this is just another loom, and you've seen enough of those in this Great Exhibition to last you a lifetime!" The crowd laughed, but remained riveted by the noise of the Engine. "Looms take time, ladies and gentlemen – time to set and to design. Mr. Jacquard's loom might be able to weave a picture of the man himself, but can Mr. Jacquard's loom change to suit your tastes?" Brunel lifted the small piece of cloth that the loom had managed to finish. "Shall we make our pattern smaller or larger, ladies and gentlemen? Smaller or larger?"

Of the cries that rang out from the crowd, "larger" seemed to be the preferred alteration. "Larger it is!" cried Brunel. "Miss King, if you wouldn't mind?"

Annabella turned back to the Engine with a smile. Codes flowed from her fingers as she slid the cards into place. The Engine slowed, taking in the new instructions, but didn't stop. The mill spun, and a moment later, the new pattern began to form on the loom. The same diamonds, the same pattern. Only larger now. More dark threads selected, less of the lovely bottle green in the background.

It took a few moments for the loom to produce a piece of fabric large enough for Brunel to show the crowd, but once he did, the crowd responded with eager applause.

"But wait!" Brunel began.

Annabella stepped up to the loom, and began to quickly detach it from the Engine.

"What if you are a clerk? An insurance man? An accountant? What good is a loom to you?"

Annabella folded back the arms of the loom, made sure it was self-contained, and stepped back to stand against the Engine.

"The Analytical Engine, ladies and gentlemen, is not a loom – it is a machine for everything and for everyone."

The turntable groaned again, and even though she knew it was going to happen, Annabella still jumped when the outer turntable began to turn at her feet, while she and the Engine remained motionless. Maybe the idea that she was a magician's assistant was not too far off; she herself was amazed at the illusion, at the speed at which Brunel's men had loaded the new display, and she smiled as the rotary printing press spun slowly around into her view.

The level of chatter rose in the crowd again, and Annabella watched carefully as the turntable brought the press close to her. Before the turntable had fully stopped, she stepped carefully over to the outer ring, her dress whisking around her.

She heard the excited murmur of the crowd as she detached the arms that connected the press to the Engine. Brunel was rattling off the potential uses for the printer – printing out navigation charts, calculated tables, tallying customer orders – and Annabella attached the arms to the mill and snapped them into place. She began to turn the cogs, setting the Engine for the demonstration piece – a simple railway timetable. She rested her left hand on its frame, and pulled the crank to set it in motion again.

She moved to turn away from the Engine, and found herself yanked back towards it, facing the whirling cogs inside the mill. She looked down at her left hand, and realized what was wrong.

The feathery decorations on her sleeve had become caught in one of the cogs in the mill. The heavy machine was twisting and pulling her sleeve into the cog, taking her hand with it.

Something was wrong. Henry felt his chest clench as Annabella jerked back towards the Engine. She wasn't visible to the whole crowd – she was mostly hidden behind the press - but she was visible to him, from where he stood to one side. Her left arm was bent at a strange angle, and as she began to pull on it, Henry realized why.

Her hand was caught in the Engine. No, not her hand – her sleeve, those stupid decorative sleeves. And if her hand wasn't already caught – Henry assumed from the lack of screams that it wasn't yet – it soon would be.

Henry began to push at the men and women in the two rows in front of him, who only protested with "I beg your pardon, sir!" but didn't budge. The wooden stage loomed high and large before them, and Henry began to fight his way around the side, looking for the flight of stairs, his eyes riveted on Annabella.

She was tugging on her sleeve, her other hand now braced against the frame of the Engine. He couldn't see her eyes behind her goggles, but her mouth was set in a thin line of concentration. Her shoulders were tense, and her body was straining, hoping for something to give.

Annabella's pulse pounded in her ears, louder than the Engine. She couldn't hear Brunel, couldn't hear the crowd anymore. She could only see the cogs, could only see the angle that they were spinning at. She only had a second to realize what was about to happen, before it did.

She slammed her right hand against the Engine to push herself away. The cog jerked back, ready for the next variable, and then spun into the space where her fingers were. She couldn't curl her hand away any further. The sleeve ripped as the teeth of the cog snapped into place, taking the first knuckle of her little finger with it.

151

Henry had reached the stairs and had launched himself two steps up when Annabella jerked back, her hand free, and turned to the side to face him. She pulled her goggles back onto her forehead, facing him with startled and frightened eyes. Her left hand hung at her side, the sleeve torn partway up her arm, blood dripping off her fingers. Her fingers. Henry's mind tried to understand what he was seeing.

Annabella expected to scream, but no air came. She resisted the urge to sob with relief. Pain began to sing up her hand, and she didn't dare look down at the state of it. She tried to wiggle her fingers, and agony lanced through her hand. Stars blinked in front of her face.

As the world shifted into focus, she pulled her goggles back onto her forehead, and her eyes locked with Henry's. He was frozen on the stairs, his own breathing fast, his eyes wide and his face pale. He was looking at her, waiting for something, waiting to know what to do.

Annabella nodded slowly, and Henry stepped down to the bottom of the stairs, but didn't turn to leave. Annabella stepped close to the printing press to wrap what remained of her sleeve around her injured hand. She could feel the blood pounding in her finger.

Brunel had not stopped his explanation, and the Engine had not stopped its demonstration. Hooked into the press, it was retrieving the instructions for the railway timetable, and when it was set, the press began to print them. As it was too loud for a moment to continue to speak, Brunel turned to face Annabella.

He frowned at the look on her face, and then glanced down at her hand. The blood had soaked into the fabric, and his eyes widened when he saw it. He took a swift step towards her, and motioned for her to stay behind the press. She rested her injured hand at the back of the printing press, plastered a smile on her face, and willed it all to be over. She felt sweat beginning to prickle along her neck.

The printing press finished, and the Engine left out a sigh of steam.

"And here you have it, ladies and gentlemen!" Brunel called, lifting the piece of paper from the press. A loud applause hit Annabella like a wave,

152

and she fought the urge to close her eyes. "An Engine adapted to any task! An Engine for everyone! An Engine that can do anything!"

He stepped close to Annabella, and took her right hand in his. They bowed together to the crowd – *again the magician's assistant, only I didn't quite get sawed in half,* Annabella thought bleakly – and Brunel leaned to her ear to speak to her.

"Stay on the outer wheel," he said gently. His voice was tight. "I'll send you around."

"Miss Annabella King, ladies and gentlemen!" Brunel called out. "Save your questions, please!"

Annabella saw Brunel wave to one of the turntable operators, and forced a smile as the turntable lurched into life. She held herself upright and trembling, until she felt herself to be in the shadow of the Engine. She sagged against the printing press.

The turntable spun to a stop behind the Engine, at the top of a ramp. At the bottom of it, Henry Babbage was waiting for her.

XXI

The will to neither strive nor cry,
The power to feel with others give!
Calm calm me more! Nor let me die
Before I have begun to live.

~Matthew Arnold~

Damn, Annabella thought as she looked at Henry's taught face. *I will not, I will **not** fall into his awaiting arms.*

The thought was quickly drowned out by a fierce stab of pain from her hand. She took one teetering step towards the ramp, her legs feeling like water, and stopped to steady herself.

Henry took a step towards her, and Annabella held up a hand to stop him. Henry's face went rigid at the sight of her injured hand. She shuffled down the ramp, and very nearly collapsed against the back wall of the Crystal Palace. Henry was at her side, a hand on her elbow, his body shielding her from view.

"Annabella," came his hushed whisper close to her head. Annabella took a deep breath, trying to calm herself down. She unwittingly drew in the smell of him, the smell of leather and rosemary soap and wool. It was both soothing and unsettling.

"What happened?" His voice came out sounding hoarse, and she tried to move away from him. He backed away, but reached for her hand.

He unwrapped the small piece of fabric from it, and drew in a sharp, hissed breath. She looked down at her own hand.

Her little finger ended at the first knuckle. Beyond that she could see a mass of blood, and could make out the white shards of her remaining bone.

"Oh," she whimpered. Henry gripped her wrist in his hand, and fumbled for his pocket-handkerchief. He let go of her hand for a moment, and her finger spurted blood.

"Oh God," she gasped. She felt panic rising, felt it squeezing around her throat, but couldn't stop it. She felt the sobs beginning to rise.

154

Henry roughly tied the handkerchief around her finger. He took her by the shoulders. "Annabella," he said firmly. "Annabella, look at me."

Before she could answer, Brunel appeared around the Engine on the stage, and nearly leapt down the ramp.

"How is she? Why is she still here? You need to get her out of here and get her home, and-"

Henry rounded on Brunel, still holding one of Annabella's shoulders. "What in God's name happened up there?"

"I didn't see it, Henry!" Brunel sounded anguished, as he tired to look at Annabella's injury. "My dear, how is your-"

"How could you let her wear those ridiculous sleeves?" Henry demanded. "They could have-"

"Oh *dammit*, Henry, I'm still *here*!" Annabella gasped, pulling her shoulder out of his grasp. "Do not speak over me as if I were a child." The protest held less affect when she sniffed back tears and had to pause to gasp for breath. "And Mr. Brunel is not in the habit of choosing my clothes. I can make that decision on my own."

"Annabella, please," Henry said, reaching out for her. "Let's get you out of here, you need-"

"Do not presume to tell me what-" She cried out in pain, curling her hand into her body, and moaned. Henry's arm went around her back, holding her protectively.

"For God's sake, stop fighting me, Annabella," Henry whispered. He lifted his head and spoke to Brunel. "We need to get her to a surgeon."

Annabella whimpered, and leaned into Henry.

"Your apartments are the closest, Henry," Brunel said. "Take her there, and I will go for a surgeon. And then your father, my dear."

Annabella looked up at Brunel. He looked stricken at her pain, and like he was about to say more, but he instead turned abruptly to leave.

"Can you walk?" Henry said. He slid his arm around her waist, and put her uninjured arm over his neck.

"I didn't crush my foot," Annabella said, looking up at him. His face was drawn and pale. Annabella sighed.

"I believe I can walk. But I will need your help."

They spoke little on the short ride to Henry's apartments, as Brunel's carriage lurched slowly through the jam of carriages and carts. Henry sat beside her in stiff silence, looking down at her hand occasionally. Annabella felt the world around her growing fuzzy and unfocused, but she wasn't aware of how much until she felt Henry shaking her shoulders to wake her.

"Annabella!" he said sharply. "Stay awake!"

"Why?" Annabella tried to say, but it came out as something more like "whuh?"

"You're losing blood; you're going to start to feel faint. You need to stay awake."

"Can't." Annabella mumbled, and slumped against Henry's shoulder.

No, no, no, damn damn!

Henry lifted Annabella from his shoulder, and her head lolled back against the side of the carriage. Her face was white and beaded with perspiration. She was trying to open her eyes, without succeeding.

Henry tried to breathe less frantically. Tried to convince himself that she was merely injured, that she would be all right, that a surgeon was coming who would care for her. He was tearing himself apart inside, trying to find a way that he might have prevented this.

The carriage rolled to stop in front of his home, and he gave a final, futile attempt to shake Annabella awake. Her head dropped forward onto his shoulder, and he took the opportunity to cradle her into him, the silver silk of her dress slipping under his hands. He lifted her awkwardly from the carriage; she cried out, but didn't wake. He staggered up the stairs of his house, and kicked at the door until it opened. Tom Adams, his single permanent servant, stood in the doorway, and stared at them.

"Adams, Miss King is injured," Henry said, in what he knew was more of a bark, as he stepped in the house. "Has the surgeon arrived?"

"Surgeon, sir?" Adams replied, frowning at Annabella.

"I'll take that as a no, then," Henry said as he leaned against one wall. "I'm taking her to the front bedroom. Bring me spirits, bandages, and a bowl. And two glasses," he added as an after thought.

156

By the time Henry had made it up the stairs of his home, his arms were aching, and he was panting. He nudged open the door of the front bedroom. It was rarely occupied; it was plain white with an occasional ornament in blue. It looked like an infirmary room.

Henry lowered Annabella to the small bed, and stood up, stretching his back. He looked down at her, and saw with a lurch of his stomach that she was breathing in fast, shallow breaths. She moaned, and shifted her head on the bed.

Now what? He didn't have a permanent maid. There was no one there who could help her out of her clothes, and she couldn't draw more than a shallow breath because her corset was tight around her. Could he wait, and send for her servant?

He sat on the bed beside her, looking down at her, listening to her shallow, rasping breathing. He finally lifted her from the bed, and shook her gently. She moaned again, and her eyes opened slowly.

"Annabella," he said holding his voice steady, trying to look her in the eyes. "You need to loosen your clothing. So you can breathe. Can you do that?"

Annabella looked at him, and frowned. "My hand," she said.

"Yes, your hand is injured," Henry said, with strained patience, "but you need -"

"No," Annabella said breathlessly. "I can't. Because of my hand."

Dammit. Henry drew a slow breath. "Will you… can I… will you let me help you?" He felt his face going scarlet, and told himself not to be an idiot.

"Yes. Please," Annabella said, gulping back tears.

Henry held her upright, and shifted around to sit behind her. He pushed aside her hair, and cursed under his breath. Her dress had what seemed to be an infinite number of buttons down the back. With shaking hands, he began to unbutton the back of her dress, as the door opened, and Tom Adams stepped into the room carrying a tray, and froze at the right of them.

Henry might have laughed if he hadn't felt like he was about to be sick. "The tray next to the bed, Adams," Henry said. "And tell me when the surgeon arrives. Or Lord King," he added. *Who I hope like hell will be here soon.*

"Yes, sir," Adams said. He walked in, the glasses clattering on the tray as his hands shook, and placed it next to the bed. He stepped tentatively away and closed the door behind him.

"Henry?"

Henry jumped, his hands still trying to undo the buttons. "Yes, Annabella?"

"What will happen to my hand?"

Henry stared at the curls of hair trailing on the back of her neck. "I... I don't know, Annabella. I'm sure the surgeon will know."

"Will I..."

He heard her start to sob, saw it shaking the back of her shoulders, and felt his heart twist.

He didn't know what to say. He had seen enough damaged and shattered limbs, had seen enough amputations, to know their consequences. He had known soldiers in India who had lost their leg to a foot injury, who had died from an injured hand. He had watched more than one of his men become infected and diseased, from the smallest of wounds. When he had been shot, he had spent a week with a wound in his shoulder, delirious from fever, the heat smothering him, before an Indian servant had doused him in cold water and washed the wound in alcohol. He was lucky that his heart hadn't stopped in the process.

It wasn't that he didn't know; it was that he did know, and didn't want to tell her.

"Please, Annabella. Just rest. I'll help you, and then..."

Another of the buttons popped away, revealing her cream white chemise underneath.

Henry swallowed, and closed the last button that he had opened. This wasn't right. He didn't want to admit that he had ever imagined a situation in which he would be undoing her clothing, but if he had, this wasn't it. He couldn't be the one to help her, not with what he felt.

"Here," he said, and pulled her towards the pillows. He laid her gently back down, and stood to pull his jacket off.

158

He rolled back his sleeves, and sat down next to her. "If you would let me see your hand?"

Annabella held out her left hand, looking groggy and confused. Henry began to unwind the handkerchief from Annabella's hand with tense and clumsy hands. The fabric of the handkerchief came away with flaking blood, and revealed the damage to Annabella's finger. Henry wondered bleakly how much longer the Analytical Engine would have needed in order to remove Annabella's whole hand.

"Mr. Babbage?" Annabella said softly.

Henry lifted his head to meet her tearful gaze, as he realized he had been staring at her injury. He reached for the bottle of cheap spirits on the tray.

"It's Henry," he said, more roughly than he meant to, as he held Annabella's hand over the bowl on the tray.

"I don't think that that level of familiarity is-"

Annabella was cut off by her own cry of pain as he poured the alcohol over her wound, washing away the fresh blood that had begun to flow. Fresh tears streamed down her face.

"-is appropriate. Anymore," Annabella choked out, as Henry dabbed at the wound with a bandage.

"You'll always be Annabella," Henry said, lifting his eyes to look at her. He coughed, and put down the bandage. He poured a glass of scotch, and handed it to Annabella. "Drink this. The surgeon should be here soon. You need to rest until then."

"What will he do?" Annabella said, taking the glass.

Henry looked up at her, his face pained. "I don't know," he said. He hoped it didn't show in his eyes that he absolutely did.

"I can't close the wound with the bone exposed. I will need to remove the bone down to the knuckle."

Henry leaned against the mantle in his front room and willed himself not to be sick. The surgeon stood near the door, next to Lord King, who was still wearing his coat and hat. Brunel stood in the middle of the room.

"Where can it be done?" Lord King said. His voice was rough and low.

"Here, if the gentleman has no objections," the surgeon said, looking in Henry's direction. "It would be best if she were not moved."

Henry nodded hastily. "Of course. If Lord King permits it."

Lord King nodded. "Her mother is very ill. If it can be done here, it would be less of a disturbance."

Anger flared in Henry at the suggestion that Annabella's welfare was a disturbance, but he smothered it. Of course Lord King had to think of his wife.

"She would be best kept here when it's done," the surgeon added. "Is that possible?"

"Of course. As long as she needs," Henry said, feeling his throat constrict.

"Shall I send to your house for her clothes?" Brunel said to Lord King.

"Yes, if you would be so good," Lord King said, "and tell Sarah she's to come now, as soon as she can."

Brunel nodded. He picked up his hat, and cast a look in Henry's direction that Henry tried to ignore. He left the room.

"I will need you both to help me," the surgeon said, as he removed his coat.

"Help you, sir?" Lord King said, setting down his own hat. Henry closed his eyes, dreading the response that he knew would come.

"I need you both to hold her steady while I work," the surgeon replied, gesturing with his head towards the stairs.

Hold her down, Henry thought, clenching his fists. *You need us to hold her down while you remove her finger.*

"Yes, yes," Lord King said with a cough. "We will come." Henry only nodded.

"Do you have something to calm her?" the surgeon asked as they followed him up the stairs. "Laudanum?"

"No," Henry replied. "I don't keep laudanum."

160

He hadn't kept any in the house since those first few months of his return from India. It was too easy to take, and to take a lot, when the nightmares came. The drug didn't so much dull pain as mask it. Henry had spent enough nights thrashing in his sleep to know that it didn't matter what the pain, laudanum would push it away – and send along a host of demons instead.

The surgeon looked at him as though he were quite strange. "I have chloroform, but it may not agree with her."

"No," Lord King said quickly. "No chloroform."

The surgeon looked back at Henry. "Well?"

"She had a glass of scotch earlier," Henry replied, as they reached the door.

"Fine, she can have another then," the surgeon replied, and pushed the door open.

Annabella was still on the bed, cradling her bandaged hand. She looked up at them with red eyes as they entered. Fear flickered across her face.

"Father?" she said, and swallowed.

"Yes my dear," Lord King said, taking a few slow steps forward. "We are here to help the surgeon."

Annabella's eyes flickered back to the surgeon. "What does he… what ..?"

"I need to finish the amputation before I can close it, my child," the surgeon said.

Annabella's mouth trembled. "You need to cut off the bone?" she said, her voice flat.

The surgeon blinked. "No. I will…" He cleared his throat. "I will remove the flesh and dislocate your final knuckle. It… would be better if you didn't watch."

Henry wouldn't have thought that Annabella could become paler than she was, until she did. He was worried for a moment that she might faint, but she only nodded. "Yes," she said, "I understand."

She looked up, and met Henry's eyes. He felt hollow. He reached for a glass and the bottle of scotch.

161

"Here," he said, pouring her a glass, and handing it to her. "Drink it all."

Annabella looked at it, and swallowed the liquid, coughing as she finished it. She handed the glass back to Henry.

"Lord King, you here, if you please," said the surgeon, setting his case down, and gesturing to Annabella's right hand. "And Mr. Babbage, on her left hand, if you please. Oh, and you may need this."

Henry turned to the surgeon, who handed him a thick leather strap. Henry swallowed, and placed his knee next to Annabella's side on the bed. Her eyes met his. They were wide and frightened.

"If you would extend her left arm, Mr. Babbage," the surgeon said.

Henry did so, and looked over at Lord King. The older man was staring at him, clearly not sure of what he should do.

"You will need to hold her shoulder and upper arm," Henry said, "and lean your weight onto them."

"You've done this before, have you?" Lord King said in a voice that shook ever so slightly.

"A few times," Henry admitted. He turned to look at Annabella.

"Henry," she whispered, as he took hold of her shoulder and arm, and leaned over her.

"It will be all right, Annabella," he said, trying to mean it.

"Hold her," was all the surgeon said.

Annabella gritted her teeth suddenly, and Henry could feel her shoulder strain under his hands. Her neck arched backwards, her eyes wide and frightened and fighting against unshed tears. Her whimpers and her rasping breath escaped her grinding teeth.

Henry tensed his hands, and leaned his weight against her. He suddenly missed the aching sorrow that he normally felt for her, that he had felt only hours before. It had been replaced by the feeling that his chest was on fire.

"Right," the surgeon said.

The sounds fell fast on Henry's ears, tripping over each other. There was a cracking noise, and then Annabella screamed.

162

She tried to wrench her shoulder against Henry's hand, and he held her against the bed. He was squeezing her upper arm hard enough to bruise it, and he could still feel her fighting against him.

Annabella wrenched the other way, and thrashed out of her father's grip. Henry let go of her shoulder and grabbed her other arm, pining her to the bed. She screamed again, and began to sob.

"Stop, please!" Her sobs came thick and fast, making her gulp for air, as she struggled in his grip. Henry forced himself to breathe, and tried to tell himself that she was fighting the pain, not him. It didn't stop his heart from breaking, but he told himself it anyway.

"Henry." She was crying out through gritted teeth, but he could still make out the words. "Please…"

Memories of blood and screams and gunfire lashed out at him. Hot, sickening images, ones that hadn't returned in years, suddenly wrapped themselves around everything that he could see and hear. Henry closed his eyes, and wrenched his face away from her, begging in his heart for it to be over.

There was a terrible popping noise, and another sharp scream, whether of pain or panic, Henry didn't know. Annabella's right arm slipped from under his grasp, and her hand swung up and struck his face, raking her nails across his cheek.

"King, dammit, help me!" Henry barked out. Lord King grabbed Annabella's other arm, freeing up Henry's hand. He held her pinned to the bed with one hand, and grabbed the leather strap with the other.

"Annabella! Here, please, bite this," he said, pressing the leather strap into her mouth. She bit it, and her next scream was muffled as it came straining through her teeth. He wrapped one hand under her head, holding on to her. She strained again, rolling her cheek against his hand, her skin hot to his touch.

He had lied to Lord King. He had never done this before. Yes, he had held soldiers down while their limbs were amputated – whole limbs, not just fingers - but he had never felt like this. His heart was pounding so hard that he could hear feel it in his throat. Every one of her screams tore through his ears, and he could feel his strength being sapped out of him as he watched her suffer. It was as though his own hands were torturing her.

Suddenly, it was over. Annabella's neck relaxed in his hand, and her head lolled back against the pillows, as she whimpered softly. The surgeon was stitching the finger, and then bandaging it.

Henry let go of her arm, and cradled her head in one hand while he caressed her cheek with the other. He felt worn out, like he could collapse there beside her.

"Mr. Babbage?" said the surgeon. He sounded far away.

Henry knew he should move. Lord King was there. This was his daughter. He needed to let go of her. Stand up. Leave.

"Leave them be a moment," he heard Lord King say. He heard footsteps leaving the room.

"Is he her fiancé?" he heard the surgeon say, as the door closed.

Henry almost laughed. He lifted Annabella's arm so that her injured hand was across her chest, and stretched himself out next to her. Her breathing was slowing now, and her eyes were closed. Her dress had slipped from her shoulder, and he could see the beginnings of bruises. Bruises that his hands had left.

"Forgive me," he choked out. He reached out to touch her cheek, and felt a ragged gasp escape from his lungs. The burning in his chest hadn't subsided; instead, it had worked its way into his throat. He might have been relieved that it was over, he might have felt the crushing self-reproach that he had ever let any harm come to her. He hardly knew what he felt.

He brushed a wisp of hair from her face. Tears stung the scratches on his face, and dropped onto the pillow next to her.

XXII

Ah, love, let us be true
To one another! for the world, which seems
To lie before us like a land of dreams,
So various, so beautiful, so new,
Hath really neither joy, nor love, nor light,
Nor certitude, nor peace, nor help for pain…

~Matthew Arnold~

Annabella woke, and everything hurt. She moved her hand, and yelped at the pain she found there. She reached carefully to touch the lines of bruises on her uppers arms. Her head was throbbing.

She tried to piece together the previous day. She knew her father had been there, but she couldn't quite remember why.

A sudden memory flashed over her. *Henry.* He was holding her, squeezing her arms until they hurt, anguish plainly etched in every angle of his face. There was pain firing through her hand, and she was thrashing, swinging her hand at Henry, scratching his skin.

And then, someone's tears. Maybe hers. Maybe his.

Annabella cried out, and sat up, and instantly regretted it. Her head whirled, and the room faded from focus.

"Miss? Miss!" A warm voice that she recognized as Sarah's called to her. She felt Sarah's hand on her arm.

"Yes, Sarah, yes, I'm all right," she said, as she breathed slowly. She squeezed her eyes shut, and begged the room to slow down.

She drew a breath and slowly opened her eyes. Sarah was leaning over her, frowning, her eyes concerned.

"Miss, hadn't you better lie down?" she said gently.

"No, Sarah, thank you," Annabella said. "Help me get up, please."

"Miss, I don't think that would be-"

"If you don't help me up, I will get up myself, Sarah. And I will likely end up collapsed on the floor." Annabella said, trying to make her voice sound like she meant it. "Please tell me that I have some clothes."

Annabella walked slowly into the front room of Henry's home, a heavy, masculine room with mahogany furnishing. She was leaning heavily on Sarah's hand, trying to ignore the throbbing in her own. She still felt lightheaded, but was determined to find him.

From the door, Annabella could see a fern in a glass case near the window, and a paneled wall with a small fireplace. On either side of the fireplace were framed etchings of industrial scenes – a trestle bridge in one, and a mill yard in another.

Henry sat in a dark red leather chair, his back to them, looking out of the window. There was an uneaten breakfast of bread and butter on a tray beside him, and his hand was gripped around what looked like a cup of coffee. He was wearing his waistcoat, and a shirt with the sleeves rolled back. Annabella thought she saw blood on one of the cuffs. He hadn't changed his clothes, then. He almost certainly hadn't slept.

"Henry?"

He jumped when she spoke, and managed to not spill coffee all over himself. He set it down on the table, and rose hastily to his feet. There were three raw red lines down his left cheek.

"Annabella," he said. His voice sounded hoarse.

"Sarah," Annabella said, still looking at Henry, "Could you ask Adams to get me something to eat?"

Sarah hesitated only a moment, before she placed Annabella's hand on the back of the red chair. She left the room.

"Henry, your face-" Annabella stepped forward, but stopped when Henry stepped away.

Henry coughed. "Won't you sit down?"

Annabella sat. Henry did not.

"Miss King," he said, pacing towards the window.

"Not Annabella?" she said softly.

166

Henry ran a hand through his hair. "I need to apologize for my behavior yesterday. Some of my actions-"

"Were necessary under the circumstances," Annabella supplied. She didn't want him to go on.

"I,.... Annabella, I know that you... that your arms are injured... and I..." He stopped as his face flushed, and ran his hand through his hair again.

"I was frightened," Annabella said softly, "when you had to hold me to-" She swallowed, as agony scrolled across Henry's face. "But I know that... you had to. And you must know it too." She held up her bandaged hand.

The colour drained from Henry's face. "Annabella-"

"And you did it well. Much better than my father did," she added with a smile.

Henry did not smile. He looked utterly miserable. "That brings me no comfort."

She cleared her throat. "Does the Analytical Engine have a shut off to its steam?"

Henry blinked. "A shut off?"

"Yes," Annabella said. "For situations like this. Or when you burned your arm."

"No," Henry said slowly. "As a matter of fact, now that you say it, I don't think I've ever seen an engine – of any kind – that did."

"Hmm," Annabella said. "We should speak to your father about that." She looked up at Henry, trying to read his thoughts.

Henry didn't reply to Annabella's remark about his father, but instead sat down across from her. He felt a number of replies crowd into his mind. How if she had worn her working gloves, there would have been nothing to be caught in the Engine. How if she hadn't tried to do two different adaptations of the same program in the same demonstration, the machine would have run more smoothly. The thought that fought for supremacy was simply how, if he had had the power to do so, he could have stopped her. If she had been his wife, and belonged to him, he could have stopped her, and kept her safe, and it wouldn't be wringing his heart to see her in pain.

167

He didn't say it. He had learned better. That was her whole point, wasn't it? That if he could have stopped her, and had, he would be snuffing out who she was, who she needed to be.

They sat together in silence for a moment, before Annabella gave a short laugh. "If Brunel were here, he would tell us that this is the cost of progress."

Henry snorted. "I don't care to pay the cost of his progress."

"I do," Annabella said quietly. Henry flicked his eyes at her. "It is a sacrifice, but also an honour to be a part of such a machine."

"How can you-" Henry flared, and then drew in a sharp breath. "My father wouldn't see it that way."

"My mother would," Annabella bit out.

"Annabella-" Henry said, getting to his feet, trying to stop her words.

"And I don't believe that you see it any differently," Annabella said, her voice becoming high and thin.

"Annabella, please stay calm, you-"

"You're not above risking you life for your country, for a cause you don't even agree with," she pressed, sitting forward in her chair.

"That's not the same," Henry growled, turning away from her, his right hand laced through his hair, his left jammed into his pocket.

"But imagine what we could do," Annabella rushed on, ignoring his reply, "if we all thought it was worth the while to risk the same for invention, for science. For progress."

"Stop it, Annabella," Henry snapped, rounding on her. "You already know that I want the same things as you do. I'm.. I'm not beyond giving my whole life to them," he added, feeling his throat constrict.

"Then why is it different for me?" Annabella returned, her voice rising. "Why is my decision of what I'm willing to risk different from yours?"

"Because I can't-" Henry all but shouted, and then stopped suddenly, breathing hard as he tried to regain his composure. "Because I can't *lose you*," he said hoarsely.

He looked away for a moment, wondering how much he could say, how much he had to say. He paced across the room, and took her uninjured hand in his.

168

"It isn't because you're a woman," he said, staring at their hands. "I am not the hypocrite that you believe me to be. It fills me with anguish to see you hurt. In any way. And last night…"

He lifted his eyes up to meet Annabella's soft, sad gaze.

"Last night it tortured me to see you hurt," he finished, around the ache in his throat. "To be the one to hurt you."

"Henry," Annabella said. "I can be hurt without leaving my home, simply by watching…" Annabella swallowed, and it took Henry a moment to realize that she was thinking of her mother. "Mathematics and science will not solve everything, I know that. But at least it gives me purpose. It gives me a choice. And the choice I have made may ask sacrifices of me." She hesitated, and met his eyes. "As it already has."

Henry looked down at their clasped hands again. It felt familiar, and right. There seemed nothing out of place in being with her, her dressed for her work and him with his sleeves rolled back, just as they had been together before. Henry fought down the need to pull her to her feet, to pull her into his arms – because that was what had ruined it all, wasn't it? Wouldn't she be with him even now, working by his side, if he hadn't fallen in love with her?

For a moment, neither spoke. The honesty that had passed between them seemed too heavy to break. Henry let go of Annabella's hand. He was trembling inside at how much he had said, and how much more he wished he could say.

Instead he said, "Perhaps I should take you home.

Annabella hesitated before replying. "Yes. I think that would be best."

XXIII

It is desirable to guard against the possibility of exaggerated ideas that might arise as to the powers of the Analytical Engine. In considering any new subject, there is frequently a tendency, first, to *overrate* what we find to be already interesting or remarkable; and, secondly, by a sort of natural reaction, to *undervalue* the true state of the case, when we do discover that our notions have surpassed those that were really tenable.

~Ada King, Countess of Lovelace~

"Thank God," Brunel exhaled, as he sank into one of the overstuffed chairs at Henry's club. "Now this is civilized."

Henry couldn't help but smile. He understood how Brunel felt; it was as though the demonstration of the Analytical Engine had opened a floodgate, full of people who hadn't known, until a month ago, that there was anything missing in their lives, but who were now absolutely certain that they needed one of these contraptions.

Annabella's injury was not public knowledge. He had barely seen Annabella since the night of the demonstration, and then only from afar, rushing into the schoolroom, or leaving the yard. She always had gloves pulled over her hands. Henry could only imagine the agony it would have been to put them on.

He was constantly reminded of her. She was everywhere for him now, as London rushed to copy not her mind, but her look. Henry had been walking passed Selfridges only the week before, and had looked up into one of the large paned windows. It had taken him a moment to decide what was strange about the display, but by then he had also seen the sign in the window: *"Available to be tailored immediately, the King dress – as seen at the Great Exhibition! Soon available in Analytical fabrics!"*

The dressmaker's dummy in the window was dressed in what seemed to be a copy, in blue linen, of Annabella's dress. The arms were tight and closely tailored, and included, Henry had noticed with a lump in his throat, the fringes along the wrists that had caused Annabella's injury. Images of her had swirled past him as he continued walking – the Exhibition, the many hours they had spent together while she had worn such a dress, and back further, to the first time that she had come to the works, and had come out of Brunel's office with her skirts over her arm. In spite of his agitation, it had brought a small smile to his face.

"Back to the works for the afternoon?" Henry asked, over the glass of his ale.

Brunel nodded. "I'll hand the requests over to Miss King in their broad form. There's enough department stores with the same requests that she should be able to make a program to suit them all."

"So what is it the department stores want, by and large?" Henry asked.

"Flexibility," Brunel replied with a grin. "The ability to have the newest patterns faster than any of the others. Though with them all ordering Engines, I don't see quite how that will work."

"So it was the loom, then?" Henry frowned. "None of the other applications sold?"

"The loom had inherent visibility, which is what the stores want in these new pane-window stores," Brunel pointed out. "But there are other orders. Firms, banks,
insurance companies… less visible, but able to see the profit in having an Engine as a computer instead of a human."

Henry's thoughts shifted to his conversation with Annabella about the livelihoods the Engine would take, but said nothing about it.

"She's also well. In case you don't get around to asking," Brunel added, raising an eyebrow over his ale.

Henry fixed Brunel with a glare, and then sighed. He wished it could be enough that she was well, instead of still feeling so desperately that he needed to see her. "I would thank you, but I have a feeling you weren't trying to be helpful."

"I was, in fact," Brunel replied sharply. "You can't go on like this forever."

Henry ignored Brunel's last comment. It was not a line of conversation that he wanted to pursue. "Is she still…?" Henry paused. "Is she still working? I thought with her hand,…and that her mother was quite ill."

Brunel shrugged, a resigned shrug. "Nothing has changed, that I know of. I know that Lord King has been spending a great deal of time with the Royal Society. Gets them both out from under foot, I imagine."

Henry could imagine as well. He barely remembered his mother's illness, but he had been twelve when his sister Georgiana died. It wasn't the sickroom he had wanted to escape, so much as the faces of those around it – particularly his father's, and the emotions of resignation and penetrating grief that fought for control of him. Getting out of the house had felt like a breath of freedom.

"What happened, at your home?" Brunel said.

Henry stared into his ale. "The doctor removed her finger down to her first knuckle. You know that already."

"What happened with you?" Brunel pressed.

Henry was quiet, staring at the table. The scratches on his face had healed, and Brunel had been patient enough not to mention them when he turned up at work with them. "I held her while he did so it. With Lord King."

He hadn't seen Lord King since the night of Annabella's injury. He vaguely knew that he should talk to the man, but couldn't think what he would say.

He looked up, and Brunel was nodding. "Oh. I see."

Henry swallowed a mouthful of ale. The memory of it still made his chest hurt.

"She misses you, if you ask me," Brunel commented.

"I didn't."

"She may even need you," Brunel continued, his voice kind.

Henry stared in his glass, and spoke softly. "I doubt it."

"Mother?"

Annabella gently pushed open the door of Ada's room with her elbow, carefully gripping a tray in her hands. She had met Sarah on the stairs carrying up the tray of soup and tea, and had carefully taken it from her. She

172

was learning to balance things with her injured hand, and her other fingers compensated reasonably well.

Ada's room was largely unchanged since Annabella had last been there. The blood-stained bowl was still beside the bed, as were the bottles of laudanum – more than one now – and the bandages. Her mother was sitting up in bed, a book held in limp hands, clearly not reading it. She looked up as Annabella came in.

"Annabella," she said.

Annabella blinked. Her mother's voice was the softest that she had ever heard her use, wispy, and almost gentle. Annabella walked carefully into the room, and set the tray of food on the table beside the bed.

"Good evening, Mother," she said, forcing her voice up beyond a whisper. She picked up the mahogany bed tray from beside the bed, and set it across her mother's lap, its feet on the bed sheets. "Sarah has sent up some soup and tea. What would you like first?"

Ada gave a bitter laugh. "Laudanum," she said without hesitation.

Annabella looked from the tray to her mother. "Don't you think you had better eat something first?"

Ada closed her eyes and shook her head. "If I don't take the laudanum, I won't be able to eat."

Annabella had a feeling that her mother was stretching the truth, but she took one of the small crystal glasses from the side of the bed, and picked up the bottle.

"To the edge of the etching," Ada said.

"Don't you have anything to measure it?" Annabella asked.

"That is a measure," Ada snapped. "I'll do it if you'd rather not."

By way of reply, Annabella poured out the requested amount, and handed it to her mother. Ada drank it quickly, set the glass down on the bed tray, and leaned back with a sigh.

"I see your disapproval, my Bella," she said. "You'll see. One day, when life hands you more than you can bear..."

Annabella collected the glass, and put it beside the bed. She thought of her finger, curled into her palm where her mother couldn't see it. It hurt every day, more or less. Some days she was sure that it was still there, and it had surprised her when she had gone to play the violin and had not been able to. There were moments in the training centre, if someone bumped her or she pushed a card in wrong, when pain would fire through her whole hand, so sharply that she saw spots in front of her vision.

She had never taken anything for her pain. So far, it was not more than she could bear.

Annabella placed the bowl of soup on the bed tray, and turned to pour two cups of tea. Steam rose from the thin porcelain pot, and Annabella breathed in the rich smell of the Darjeeling. Annabella handed her mother a cup of tea and sat down in the upholstered whicker chair next to her mother's bed, her hands cradled around the fragrant cup of tea.

Her mother gave her glance that plainly said *You're staying?* but said nothing. For a moment neither of them spoke, while Ada ate slowly, and Annabella relished a moment of peace and quiet, however tinged with sickness and weariness it was.

"I saw one of your dresses in the *Ladies World Journal* yesterday," Ada said, placing the spoon on the tray and turning to face Annabella.

Annabella was astonished to see a small smile on her mother's face. "My dresses?" she said. "Oh, my work dresses. Yes," Annabella grinned, "I saw one in Selfridges last week."

"You've created quite a stir with those dresses," Ada said. Her voice was becoming slower and softer, and Annabella wondered whether it was the laudanum taking effect.

"I hope to change more than dresses, Mama," Annabella smiled.

"You have, my Bella."

Annabella curled herself in tighter on herself, feeling strange and out of place. Her mother hadn't called her Bella for years.

Ada's eyes closed, and her head drooped against the pillow. Annabella placed her cup down on the table, and moved to take the bed tray away. As she picked it up, her mother reached for her wrist, and pulled herself up slightly, very nearly knocking the dishes onto her lap.

"If John calls, you will let him in, won't you?"

Annabella looked at her mother's face, the eyes half closed, her hair spilling back behind her, her face flushed. She twisted her wrist, and her mother's hand fell limply away.

"John, Mama?"

"If he calls, you will let him in? You won't turn him away?"

Annabella lifted the tray from her mother's lap. "It's all right, Mama," was all she could think to say. "He hasn't called."

"No," murmured Ada. "Of course."

Annabella put the tray down next to the bed, and collected the dishes. As an after thought, she reached out to remove the book that still lay on the sheets, and flipped to the first page. The title was written in old, ornate writing: *On the Economy of Machinery and Manufactures. By Charles Babbage.*

On the front page was an inscription scrawled in tight, neat handwriting:

> *To My Enchantress of Numbers,*
>> *For your perusal. Of possible use for the construction of our Engine, I think. Would be happy to hear your thoughts on the matter.*
>> *With regards,*
>> *C. Babbage*

XXIV

Light flows our war of mocking words, and yet,
Behold, with tears mine eyes are wet!
I feel a nameless sadness o'er me roll.

~Matthew Arnold~

"Who do you think?"

Bentham glanced up at Annabella, and rubbed the edge of his jaw. It was a close, hot day, pushing towards the end of July, with thunderclouds showing in the west. The training room was stifling, and sweat showed along the edge of the strong worker's neck.. Annabella looked out the small windows in the direction of the thunderclouds, feeling the back of her dress clinging to her. She would be grateful for the rain.

"Evy and Rosie would be best for it," Bentham said, looking over the orders for a dress pattern from the larger department stores.

"Because they're women?"Annabella said sharply.

Bentham snorted. "You think so little of me, Miss? No – because it's complicated, lots of variables, and they see this kind of variable better than the others. Anyway, they're likely to enjoy it."

Annabella grinned. "Good. Put them in the lead of it, with Matthews and Ashburn helping them."

Bentham smiled. "Ashburn will be a'right. Matthews isn't going to like answering to a lady. Present company excepted."

"How unfortunate for him," Annabella replied lightly. She began to pull her work gloves off her hands. "If there's nothing else…?" she asked, raising an eyebrow at Bentham.

Bentham shook his head. "Just punching work at the moment, Miss." His expression softened. "You go and tend to your mother, Miss. I'll let you know if there's aught you're needed for."

Annabella looked up at him, and gave a small, sad smile. She left the training room, making her way out of the yard.

There was more of a breeze in the streets, but there was also the clustered stench of a million different smells: food going rapidly bad in the heat, the close sweat of thousands of bodies tramping through the streets, the hay and fodder from the horses being churned into a fine, choking dust. Annabella took as many side streets as she could to make her way home – the smells were stranger, but at least there were fewer of them. She made her way quickly, eager for a wash and a cool, clean dress.

Bancroft opened the door when she arrived at the house, and she smiled a greeting at him – but he didn't smile back. His face was pinched and his brows knit together.

She was about to ask him what was wrong, when she glanced through the entryway, and saw a case standing in the hall. She frowned as she realized that it was her father's.

It was then that she heard the voices, raised as always and coming closer. Bancroft slipped away behind her, leaving her gazing up the stairs as the words became more distinct.

"… nothing further to say on the matter, Ada," Lord King's voice came from one of the rooms in the house.

"You can't, William!" Ada's voice. Hysterical. *Sobbing*. "Please. I was honest with you-"

"*Now*," Lord King snapped back. "You were honest only now, and the Lord knows why."

"I cannot take it to the grave with me, William!" Sound of footsteps. "No! Please, come back."

"You are beyond my reach, Ada, if you were ever in it," came Lord King's resigned voice, as two figured appeared at the top of the stairs.

Her father was wearing a dark suit and a travelling coat – he had his hat in his hand. Her mother was behind him, wearing only a nightdress, her dark hair in a loose braid over her shoulder. She was gripping Lord King's arm in her thin, frail hands.

"Let me go, Ada," Lord King said firmly. "Before you hurt yourself."

"You can't leave," sobbed Ada. "Don't, you-"

Lord King pushed his wife's hand away, and Ada fell to her knees on the landing. Lord King paused, and began to reach for her. He stopped abruptly, turned, and came down the stairs towards Annabella. He glanced up at her, before he brushed past her.

"Bancroft!" he called through the house. "Deliver my case to the station, if you please!" He made his way to the back of the house, towards the stables.

"Father!" Annabella called, running towards him. He didn't slow down, and walked out into the courtyard at the back of the house. The sky had turned a dark charcoal colour, and large drops were beginning to splatter on the paving stones.

"Father, wait!" Annabella said, moving in front of him. He moved to get past her, and she planted her hand on his chest. "Where are you going?"

Lord King pushed her hand away. "Ockham Park," he said, walking past her towards the stable of his horse.

"Ockham?" Annabella followed him, bewildered. "Why? When will you be returning?"

"I have no plans to return at the moment," Lord King said roughly, as he reached the stable door.

"Father!" cried Annabella, reaching to stop his hand from opening the door.

"It is not your concern, Annabella!" her father said, his voice rising as he turned to face her.

"It is my concern! Mama is *dying*," Annabella choked out. "Where can you possibly need to go?"

Lord King paused, his hand on the handle of the stable. "Away," he said, his voice small. "I cannot tell you why." He pushed the stable door open, and stepped inside. The groom was already holding the bridle of his horse.

"No," Annabella said hoarsely. She stepped forward, and grabbed the horse's bridle. She rounded to face her father. "No. I don't accept that."

"Let go of my horse, Annabella," Lord King said, his voice angry, but his eyes full of pain.

"No! You can't simply walk away, and leave me with Mama while she is so sick, and-"

178

"There are people to care for her, Annabella-"

"There is no one to care for *me*!" Annabella cried, jumping back from her father as he reached for the bridle of the horse. The horse paced and pulled back in surprise. "What do you mean for me to do while she's ill?"

"I cannot stay," Lord King whispered. "She has brought me more pain, more shame than you can know..." He shook his head, snatched the reins from Annabella's hands, and led the horse out of the stable.

"The gambling?" Annabella called, following him into the yard.

"Lower your voice, Annabella!" Lord King hissed in return. The rain was coming down fast now, in heavy drops.

Annabella ran to catch him. "What does that matter now?"

Lord King turned to look at her. "There is more-" he began, and then stopped. He swung himself onto his horse. Water was already coursing down his travelling coat, beading on the fabric.

He gave her a last sad look, and urged his horse forward. It bolted out of the yard, and her father was gone.

"Father!" Annabella cried after him. She felt small and stupid, and soaked to the skin. She shivered, and ran across the yard to the house.

Sarah was in the hall as she came in, and looked at her, her eyes wide. "I can draw you a bath, Miss, if you-"

"Where is Mama?" Annabella bit out, wiping raindrops out of her eyes.

"I took her to bed, Miss," Sarah said, her voice uncertain. "I thought-"

"Yes, thank you," Annabella said, walking past Sarah and heading up the stairs as quickly as her heavy clothes would allow. She pushed hard against her mother's door, and threw it open.

Her mother was lying on the bed, curled around herself, crying quietly. Annabella walked around to the side of the bed to face her. Her mother was biting her lip, tears rolling down her face.

"Why?" Annabella demanded.

"Annabella-" Ada said weakly.

"Why did he leave?" Annabella pressed. "What did you do?"

"Why do you assume that I did anything?" Ada cried, pushing herself up in the bed.

It fills me with anguish to see you hurt. In any way. "Because Father wouldn't have left you now without a reason."

Ada fell back against the bed, and reached out one hand for the bottle of laudanum on the table. Annabella snatched it away.

"Annabella!" Ada wailed, reaching towards her.

"No," Annabella said, her fear and frustration replaced with anger. "Tell me first."

"It was John," Ada sobbed out.

Annabella blinked. "John?"

Ada nodded. "John Crosse. He and I, we have... had an affair."

Annabella felt like the floor was crumbling away under her feet. She wasn't sure what she had expected, but it wasn't this.

John Crosse. Andrew Crosse's son, who had spent Christmas with them. John Crosse, who was nearly the same age as his father's wife. It suddenly made sense to Annabella why Ada loathed Cornelia Crosse. It wasn't simple contempt – it was jealousy. Because of John.

Annabella gripped her hand around the bottle of laudanum. "I... for how long?"

Ada sniffed. "Two years."

She wasn't sure how, but somehow Annabella had expected something recent, something tied to her mother's illness, as if everything that was damaging was one and the same. Instead, to know that it had been so long...

The name spun in her head. John Crosse. Arrogant and handsome... and a reckless gambler.

"And I suppose that he placed your bet for you as well?" Annabella said bitterly.

Ada's eyes widened. "I just wanted-"

"And you told Father?" Annabella said slowly.

Ada nodded. "Annabella-"

"How *could* you?" Annabella said, angry tears rising in her eyes. "How could you dream of betraying-"

"Don't!" Ada snarled out. "You will not talk to me of betrayal. You will not judge me, when you have taken my place in everything I wanted!"

180

"I have *earned* that place!" Annabella snapped.

"By doing what?" Ada cried out. "You only work on the Engine because Babbage's son is in love with you. You have earned *nothing* – you haven't given a fraction's worth of the effort to the Engine that I did!"

Annabella tried to remember the last time that she had struggled to breathe as much as she was now. She could only liken it to losing her finger. Because that was what this was – it was her mother tearing away a part of her, leaving her raw and bleeding and screaming inside. And it occurred to her that it was as senseless as the crushing Engine. Ada was lashing out at anyone in her path - Annabella simply happened to be in the way.

"That," Annabella said, drawing a shaking breath, "is *not* true, and you know it. And if you paid attention to anything aside from your own misery, you would know that I refused Henry Babbage months ago." Annabella swallowed, her voice sounding like a hoarse whisper to her own ears. "Because he *wouldn't* let me work on the Engine as his wife."

Annabella watched surprise flicker across the anger on her mother's face, and realized with a stabbing sadness that this could well be the first that her mother had heard of it. "I have earned my right by what I gave up for it. And I haven't squandered it by gaming and dallying with-"

Ada laughed bitterly. "Neither had I, when I was a child like you. Given time, you will be bitter and alone like I am, and will turn to anything that will-"

"No I will not!" Annabella all but shouted. "I will not waste the chance to prove to everyone that they are wrong, that I am not weak willed and impulsive. As you have."

Ada sagged back against the pillows, and she stretched out a hand to her daughter. "Annabella, the laudanum, please."

Disgusted, furious, and shivering wet, Annabella threw the bottle of laudanum onto her mother's bed, and stalked out of the room.

July gave way to August with a fury. Rain swept through the city, turning the streets into a churning swamp. Wooden and dirt roads, badly in need of paving stones, had become a vicious mix of mud, sawdust, hay, and animal waste. The water that should have swept the city clean only became trapped in the muddy streets. Annabella lifted her skirts up as high as was decent as she walked, feeling the wet beginning to seep into her boots. She thought for not the first time that she should have taken the carriage. But the walk gave her a chance to think, to form her words carefully. The driving wind and rain made her feel awake.

She had barely spoken to her mother since her father had left. She knew it was selfish of her, and that her mother needed her, but somehow, she couldn't see her in the same light as before. It was as if Ada's place as her mother was inseparable from her place as her father's wife. Annabella no longer knew what to think of her own mother. In the end, none of her musings had really contributed to her decision; it had been made for her, as soon as her father had left for Ockham.

Annabella entered the yard of Brunel's Engine Works, and glanced around at the various buildings. Her eyes lingered on the training room. She wanted to go in, only to oversee, to ensure that everything was going as planned. She didn't. Bentham was inside, so everything was running smoothly, or she would have been told. Besides, she knew that if she went inside, she would linger, distracted from what she had really come to do, hiding from where she really needed to be.

Annabella let her skirts drop onto the wet paving stones of the yard, and turned wearily towards Brunel's office.

The small room looked as it always had. Brunel sat at his desk, hunched over his work. He wore spectacles, close to the end of his nose, that Annabella had never seen before. He looked older. He looked up as she entered.

"Miss King, my dear," he said, motioning to the chair in front of his desk. He glanced at her bonnet and cape, shimmering with water, and frowned. "Don't tell me you walked here?"

Annabella nodded, and sat herself opposite him. "I needed the fresh air."

"Can I get you anything? I can send someone for a cup of tea, or something stronger?" he said, beginning to stand.

Annabella shook her head, and waved for him to sit down. "No, please. I won't be here long, I'm afraid." She looked at her hands, and then back up at Brunel's questioning gaze.

"I need some time off," she said, feeling silly even as she said it. "To care for my mother."

Brunel nodded almost imperceptibly, his eyes soft and sad. "Of course-"

"Bentham can take care of most matters, and the assignments have already been given for the department stores, so it should simply be a matter of the analysts completing their sequences," Annabella continued, hoping that she sounded professional.

"Of course," Brunel said, assuming the same tone. "If there is something that they cannot solve-"

"They may contact me," Annabella replied. "Sarah will continue to train as an analyst, so she can update me on the progress of the projects, and if there is anything urgent, send Bentham."

Brunel frowned. "You don't need your maid to assist you in caring for your mother?"

Annabella's mind flicked to the many long, dull hours while her mother flitted in and out of sleep, laudanum induced or otherwise, and shook her head. "The house is full of servants, Mr. Brunel. My mother's maid has taken on some of Sarah's duties. We can manage without her."

Brunel nodded. "Thank you for coming to speak to me. You must have known that it was not necessary."

Annabella swallowed. She did know, and the thought that she could come and go and not be missed frustrated her. "There is one more thing."

Brunel raised an eyebrow.

"When I return to train the analysts, I would like to be paid."

Brunel's shock registered only subtlety on his face. His lips parted, and his eyes widened slightly, but within a second he coughed and cleared his throat, and leaned his hands forward on his desk.

"May I ask why, Miss King?" he asked.

"I work for you," Annabella said, forcing out her words, as she convinced herself that she was not asking for anything unreasonable. "My work is, I think, valuable. I should therefore be paid."

Brunel leaned back in his chair. "But of course you should, Miss King. We will discuss terms on your return, yes?"

Annabella nodded, swallowing hard. "Thank you, Mr. Brunel," she said, gathering her skirts, and standing to leave. "I ought to be getting back, I-"

"Annabella."

Annabella looked up at Brunel's face. The employer's keen look had faded, the professional edge had ebbed away, and he was looking at her with sadness and fondness.

"You do know that you are valued here. You do know that, my dear?" Brunel said, leaning forward.

Annabella felt a lump well up in her throat. She was suddenly conscience of how much she owed to Brunel for his trust in her. She felt her mother's words, vicious and illogical as they were, stab at her, undermining everything that she had worked for.

"You have always made me feel so, sir," she said softly.

Brunel rose to his feet, and stepped around his desk. He took one of her elbows in his hand, and turned her to face him.

"You must know, my dear Miss King, how much you have accomplished here," he said. "We have come so much further than we could ever have done without you."

"Mr. Brunel," she whispered. "I'm just an analyst."

Brunel stared at her, as though not understanding what she had said. "Just an analyst?"

Annabella nodded. "I write algorithms, I punch cards, I create codes. That's all. An analyst."

Brunel laughed. It was a short, sharp laugh, that nevertheless left a lingering grin on his face. "My dear, you sell yourself utterly short, and I hope you will work on that before we negotiate the terms of your employment. You are an analyst," he said firmly, "with everything that that implies. The Mr. Babbages, junior and senior, are just inventors, with everything that that

184

implies." He paused, and gave a small smile. "I am just an engineer, but look at what that means, Annabella! We all of us imagine more than is there. You write codes you say, and punch cards, but you couldn't see the codes if you couldn't also see the possible."

Annabella opened her mouth to speak, but the rawness of the back of her throat wouldn't let her. Brunel gave her a small smile, and squeezed her elbow.

"I know you'll be back, Miss King. And when you are, I know you'll be worth every penny."

XXV

Friendship may, and often does, grow into love,
but love never subsides into friendship.

~Lord Byron~

Henry slid off his horse, and handed the reins to a young boy who
waited on the street. He tossed him a coin, and the boy tipped a sopping wet
cap at him.

He turned, and hesitated in front of the door of the imposing cream
coloured house. He took a step back into the rainy street, water dripping off
his face and coat. He gripped the leather folder of papers that he held in his
hand, and looked at the door again.

It had seemed like such a good idea when he had first said it.
Bentham had been bent over a series of codes when Henry had arrived at the
works, and was frowning and rubbing his forehead. He was now in practice
the foreman of Annabella's training institute, and he was sufficiently
competent at it that Henry had been surprised to see him puzzled.

"Something the matter, Bentham?" he had asked.

"I'm sure Miss had an idea of what she was about, but for the life of
me I can't see how to work this into the order," Bentham had muttered by
way of reply. He had looked up at Henry at that moment. "Evy and Rosie
couldn't make head nor tail of it, and I'm not sure if it's because Miss made a
mistake, or we did."

Something in Henry's chest had twitched, at the realization that *Miss*
could only be one person. "Can't you send home the codes with Sarah and ask
her?"

Bentham had shrugged. "I would, Master, but Miss Sarah" – Henry
wasn't sure if he'd imagined it, but he thought the man's voice grew gentler at
the mention of her name – "didn't come in today. I think Miss's mother was
took quite ill."

Henry had nodded. "I'll take them."

186

Just like that. A foolish, utterly mad suggestion, now that he was stood in front of her door. She was already away from her work, worried no doubt about her mother. What right had he to intrude on her?

He took one step back, then one firm step forward, and knocked on the door. His heart beat painfully fast, until the butler, Bancroft, opened the door.

"Sir?" the butler said, stiffly, but not impolitely.

Damn. Henry realized that he had been hoping that Sarah would open the door. It would have been so much easier to simply hand the papers off to the maid, to give to Annabella. He swallowed now.

"Is… is Miss King home, Bancroft? Would she speak to me? I have a message from Mr. Bentham," he said, sounding more pleading than he wanted to.

"This way, if you please, sir," Bancroft said, allowing Henry to follow him into the front drawing room. He took Henry's wet coat, and left Henry alone in the room with a bow.

Henry paced the room, looking around at the furnishings but not seeing them. He wondered for a moment whether it would be enough to leave the papers with Bancroft, and was considering leaving when the door opened.

Annabella stepped through, and gave him a small smile. She had on one of her close fitting work dress, in an apple green linen, with an apron tied over the skirt. Her hair was gathered firmly back at the base of her neck in a simple knot. He knew she was tired, in the paleness of her face and darkness of her eyes, but in some ways, she seemed relaxed, as if she were beyond exhaustion.

More importantly, she looked like she might be genuinely glad to see him.

"Mr. Babbage," she said softly, her voice imparting an intimacy to his formal name. She held out her hand, and he squeezed it, feeling the strength in her thin fingers. He could feel a warm flush rising under his collar.

"Miss King," Henry said with a nod.

"Forgive my appearance," she continued, dropping his hand. "You find me as a nursemaid today, I'm afraid."

Henry winced at her apology, knowing that it implied a distance that he did not feel. It also made him painfully aware of how he looked. His boots were muddy up to his ankles, his hair and face wet from the rain. He could feel the dampness in the shoulders of his jacket. "Forgive me, I did not mean to intrude, but I-"

"It is not an intrusion," Annabella said, her voice sounding more like herself. "A change of scene would be most appreciated. Shall I have some tea brought up for us?"

Henry nodded wordlessly. He felt keenly that he didn't belong here, but at Annabella's invitation, took a seat on one of the stuffed chairs.

"Your mother is..." he started to say. *Well, I hope*, he had been intending to add, when he knew it was not true. "How is your mother? Is she comfortable?"

Annabella looked up at him, from the place she had taken on the edge of the ottoman. "In a manner of speaking. She takes medication frequently for her pain."

Henry had a clear sense of what that meant. If there were anything that could be done for Lady King's pain, it would be through laudanum. It would mean that she was not comfortable; she was either in pain, or delirious from the drug.

"Was there... something in particular that you wanted?" Annabella asked, smoothing her apron.

"Oh, yes!" Henry said, feeling stupid as he reached for the leather folder that he had placed on the table. "Bentham has run into a catch, sorry, not a catch in the machine, but a problem. He thought it might be in your instructions or in their codes."

He handed her the folder, and Annabella took it with a frown. She opened the front cover, and gazed intently at it. Henry waited in silence, waited while the tea was brought in and set on the table, waited while she flipped through several of the pages.

"Yes of course!" she burst out suddenly, with what seemed to be real excitement. "It's both, actually. One of their branches won't work unless it runs through my earlier algorithm, which I didn't put into both parts of the code." Annabella got to her feet, and collected a pencil from the desk on the

188

far wall. She returned to the ottoman, still talking. "I thought I would be running this code myself, so I didn't make it clear."

She wrote for only a moment, and scanned over the page. "That should do it," she said, handing the folder back to him. She tucked the pencil into the knot of her hair, as she did when she was working, and Henry felt the ghost of a smile on his lips.

"Tea, Mr. Babbage?" she said, bending over the table.

Call me Henry. Henry, please. "If you please," he said stiffly. He watched in rapt silence as she lifted the turquoise porcelain teapot, and poured it into the cups. He knew he was staring at the shape of her hands, the blunted, scarred end of her injured finger, her wrists, and wished that he didn't miss the sight of her as desperately as he did.

Annabella handed him a teacup.

"Is your father well?" he said, as he looked up. "It's been a long time since I-"

Henry stopped speaking, as he registered the look on Annabella's face. Her lower lip was pulled in, and she was looking down at her teacup. "I'm sorry Anna- that is, Miss King, I didn't mean to-"

"No, it's all right," Annabella said, raising her eyes and giving him a tight smile. "It's been a long time since you've seen my father, you were going to say. It's been a long time since I've seen him too."

Henry frowned. "I don't understand."

"He has been at Ockham Park this past month or so," Annabella said. Her tone shifted between making it sound entirely normal, and registering her underlying anger.

"This past month? But your mother-" Henry said gently.

"Is desperately ill, yes," Annabella bit out. "Is... dying."

Henry cupped his hands around his teacup and watched Annabella's eyes become bright with tears. The temptation gnawed at him to reach out and take her hand, but instead he just looked at her, not knowing what to say. He couldn't think of a single reason why Lord King would have left. No reason seemed good enough.

"Forgive me, Mr. Babbage," Annabella said, setting her teacup down abruptly. "You didn't come here to listen to my family's struggles."

189

"I am happy to listen to yours," Henry said before he could stop himself.

Annabella flushed but didn't acknowledge his comment. "And you? I hope you are well."

Henry looked up at her, and saw, to his surprise, more than politeness behind her words. She was holding her teacup cradled in her lap, looking at him with a frown of what looked to be real concern.

"I..."

What could he tell her that would be true? He couldn't tell her that since he had gone back to working in the Engine factory, more than once in the past month he had looked up, looking to ask her a question, expecting her to be there, and she hadn't been. That he worked longer, because going home was too quiet, too empty. That he avoided his club, because seeing Blunt there would have reminded him of her in the cruelest possible way.

"I am well enough," he said, and hoped he had managed to make it sound true.

She raised an eyebrow. "You're a terrible liar, Hen– Mr. Babbage. I presume Brunel has already told you that you're working yourself to death?"

Henry managed a grin. "Only about once a day, yes. Though he barely leaves the works himself."

Annabella smiled, and took a sip of her tea. "I can understand that. I miss it."

Henry looked down at his tea, and up at her again. "You will be returning, won't you?" He hadn't meant for the words to sound as entirely full of longing as they did, but he didn't regret saying them.

Annabella glanced at him in surprise, and sat with her lips parted for a moment. "I hope so," she said finally. She looked at him for a moment, and then back at her hands.

He pushed back the hope that bloomed in him. It was a luxury he couldn't afford. "Miss King, forgive me, I have taken too much of your time, I should-"

"Mr. Babbage?"

Henry paused, still in his chair.

190

"If you have the time in your afternoon, would you be so good as to escort me on a short ride? I know it's raining, and I wouldn't trouble you, it's only that I don't leave the house very often, and mother will be asleep, and I-"

"Yes. Yes of course," Henry blurted out. "When would you like to go?" He was suddenly aware that the joy flooding through him must have been visible on his face. He suddenly didn't care.

"Now, if it's convenient," Annabella said, getting to her feet. There were the edges of a smile tugging at her mouth. "I'll be dressed in just a few minutes."

"Now, of course, yes," Henry said. He rose to his feet, and they stood for one tremulous moment without speaking. Annabella smiled at him, and left the room, untying her apron strings as she went.

Henry watched her go, and walked to the doorway of the drawing room. He leaned against the frame of the doorway, and let an irresistible grin split his face.

Henry sailed up the stairs of his club. His hands were cold, but his face felt warm, and he couldn't suppress the smile that flitted about his mouth. He knew it made him look like a mad idiot, but he couldn't stop it.

The afternoon with Annabella had been blissful. It had rained heavily, and when he had returned Annabella to her home, her hair was curling in damp wisps within her bonnet. There was colour in her face, even as the rainwater had dripped down her face.

He had been about to leave, when she had rested a hand on his upper arm, as he stood one step down from her at her front door. "Come ride with me again, if you please," she had said gently.

He had taken her hand in his, and pressed her gloved fingers. "Of course," he had said with a smile.

Henry swung onto the top floor of the club with a final massive stride. He had spent the afternoon with Annabella. She had been pleased to see him. And she had asked him to return.

He strode to the bar at the back of the club, shrugging out of the shoulders of his jacket as he did so. Short as the ride had been, he could feel the soreness creeping into his muscles, and a familiar burn along the scar of his once injured shoulder. He was not so different from Annabella – it had been too long since he had been out of doors, since he had exercised at all. Well, now he had an all too welcome excuse.

He deposited his jacket on one of the leather armchairs near the bar, and ordered a glass of scotch. He was lifting it from the bar when he heard a familiar and obnoxious voice.

"Babbage! What the devil are you doing here?"

The tension that the ride had eased out of him coiled back into his shoulders, and he tried to look relaxed as he took a sip of his drink. Slowly, with an exaggerated casualness he did not feel, he turned.

"Blunt," he said. "How lovely to see you." He was lying, but the slightly off-kilter grin on his face was genuine.

Blunt was walking towards him, none too steadily. He sneered at him, as usual. "What are you so damned happy about?" he demanded.

"More than you, apparently," Henry replied, raising his eyebrows and his glass, and taking a slow drink.

Now that Blunt was close to him, Henry could smell the gin fumes off of him, wafting over the much more pleasant smell of his scotch. Blunt's eyes were flickering and unfocused, trying to glare at Henry without succeeding. His lurching idiocy had attracted attention from the other members of the club, and there were enough of them there, close to supper, that Henry could feel their many eyes on the pair of them.

"That Miss King finally stooped to take you, has she?" Blunt slurred, grabbing onto the closest chair for support.

It annoyed Henry that Blunt had even guessed that his joy was because of Annabella, but he calmly took another sip of his drink. "If she had, you'd be the last man alive I'd share it with," he said.

"Ha!" Blunt said with a smirk. "I guess she needed someone to run to after I rejected her."

Fury bubbled in the back of Henry's throat, but he pushed it down with a deep breath and a mouthful of scotch. He knew it was stupid and antagonistic, but he took a step towards Blunt. "Miss Annabella King doesn't *need anyone* to run to. And I doubt very much that it was *you* that rejected *her.*"

192

He saw anger flash in Blunt's eyes, vague and unfocused. "And why do you doubt that? What the hell do you know about it?"

Henry grinned. "I know *her*. I know that she would see through you in an instant, that she would see that compared to her, you are a vacant fool."

Blunt stepped forward, and grabbed the lapel of Henry's waistcoat. Henry's grin widened. Blunt was trying to be intimidating, but he was no match for Henry, and was drunk besides.

"What did you tell her, you upstart?" Blunt growled.

Henry actually laughed, and took a sip of his scotch. "What did I need to tell her? She already knew that you couldn't understand the half of who she is and what she does."

"I don't see you fairing any better, Babbage. Maybe she doesn't want a man with blood on his hands," Blunt said, tightening his grip.

"Could be," replied Henry, setting his glass down on the bar behind him. "Though in your case, it's more likely that she doesn't want a man who is a ignorant coward."

Henry had seen the punch coming before Blunt even raised his arm; he could see the anger rising in his eyes, the need to lash out at him. It had given Henry time enough to set his drink down before the punch came. Blunt was also, stupidly, punching with his left hand; he swung it wide and slammed it against the wooden pillar of the bar.

Blunt yelped in pain, and let go of Henry's waistcoat. Henry grinned and pushed himself free of the bar. Blunt wheeled on him, his fists raised in a mockery of a boxing stance.

"What is your plan, Blunt?" Henry called to him, his hands relaxed at his side.

"I intend to teach you a lesson, *tradesman*," snapped Blunt.

Henry grinned. "To know my place, *my Lord*? And how do you intend to do that?"

"I was taught to box, peasant. Because I'm a *gentleman*," Blunt said, and lunged at Henry.

Blunt's movements would have been slow and awkward even while sober, but drunk, they were pitiable. Henry caught one of his arms, and twisted it behind him. He caught Blunt's feet in a kick, and threw him to the floor.

"Pathetic, Blunt. If you were less of a gentleman, you might be more useful," he said with a grin.

"Come back here, Babbage!" Blunt said, staggering to his feet, as Henry turned and bent to pick up his jacket from the chair next to them.

"Don't be an idiot, Blunt," a voice called from one of the onlookers. Henry didn't see who it was.

"Come here and fight, if that's all you know how to do," Blunt yelled. "Fight for your little whore of an analyst, if she's so-"

Henry flashed up from collecting his jacket, swung, and cracked his fist into Blunt's jaw. He had the momentum of his whole frame on his side, and Blunt went careening back and fell against a chair. Henry was across to him in two strides, and seized his necktie in his fist. Anger hummed through him as he hauled Blunt to his feet.

"If she's so *what*?" Henry snarled.

Blunt gave a nasty grin. "Touched a nerve, did I, Babbage?" he slurred. The side of his face was starting to swell. "Rushing to her rescue, *again*? Didn't do you much good at Ockham Park last winter, did it?"

Henry glared at Blunt, his heart hammering in his ears. He wanted to tell Blunt everything that scorched through his mind, of how much Annabella was worth fighting for. It occurred to him that he hadn't known how much himself.

No, that wasn't right. He had known it; he just hadn't considered that fighting might mean something other than using his fists. That bravery might mean something aside from facing gunfire. He had been unable, unwilling to face the disdain of the society in order to let Annabella work, and be who she was. How could he have been such a fool? It hit him suddenly that bravery was what he felt now – absolutely not giving a damn what anyone else thought of the woman that he loved. Fighting could mean stepping back, and waiting, and hoping that he hadn't squandered his only chance.

And it could mean the patience to endure his own aching heart, even in the face of an idiot like Blunt.

194

He let go of Blunt's tie, and pushed him away. Blunt stumbled, his grin slipping. He looked at Henry in confusion and anger.

"Keep her then," he growled. "She's not worth having anyway. She would rather lower herself to your level, than keep to her own. She's not *normal*."

Something in the way Blunt said it, something in the bitterness of defeat in his voice, made a flutter of hope unfold in Henry's chest. He gave a wry smile as he pulled on his jacket. "Oh, I know," he said. "In fact, I'm counting on it."

Murmurs followed him as he walked out of the club, adrenaline and scotch buzzing in his system. He paused on the stairs, and grinned to himself.

His knuckles hurt from punching Blunt's jaw.

The memory of Annabella's smile that afternoon warmed his heart.

It had been a good day.

XXVI

Remember me when I am gone away,
Gone far away into the silent land;
When you can no more hold me by the hand,
Nor I half turn to go, yet turning stay.

~Christina Rossetti~

Annabella had just left her mother's room when Bancroft told her that there was a gentleman to see her. Annabella felt the flutter in her chest, and began to untie the strings of her apron. She considered putting on her riding clothes, but thought it better to walk down and greet him first.

She had been riding with Henry twice since he had first brought her the work problems. On one occasion he had brought her messages from the work, simple things that didn't really need her help, but that she poured over. She loved the work for its own sake, but also for its messenger. She felt less alone, less cut off from the outside, and cherished the few small hours that she could spend in his company. They were quiet hours, mostly, whether because of his shyness, or from her need for peaceful solace, she wasn't sure.

She tried not to think beyond the present moment. The wounds of their past were still with her, and she felt them more keenly when she wasn't working on the Engine. It seemed impossible that she had denied him, when what she had denied him *for* was so far away. She tried not to wonder whether she hadn't made a mistake in the choice she had made all those months ago. She enjoyed being near him. For now, that was enough.

She came down the stairs, and turned into the drawing room where he usually waited for her. "Mr. Babbage, I think we should-" She stopped, as the man in the room turned to face her.

It was not Henry. It was John Crosse. He looked older then when she had last seen him. There were circles under his blue eyes, and he wore dark stumble on his jaw. He was still standing in his riding coat and boots, and was holding his hat in his hand.

"Miss King!" he all but gasped. "I asked to be shown up at once, but your butler-"

"Told you to wait. Yes, obviously," Annabella said stiffly. Why was he here? Obviously she knew why, but why now? Why had he waited until now? "Can I get you some tea, Mr. Crosse?"

Crosse frowned. "No, I... that is, no thank you, I only wanted..." he swallowed, and stared at the floor. "I wish to see your mother."

Annabella waited just half a second before responding. "I'm sorry, Mr. Crosse. My mother, as I'm sure you know, is very ill, and is only seeing her family. She is not taking visitors."

"No, I'm not..." Crosse's cheeks coloured. "I'm not a visitor."

"Really?" Annabella said mildly, folding her hands in front of her skirt. This was her father's house. Even gone, it was his. This man did not belong here. "You certainly aren't family."

"Annabella, I-"

"My name is Miss King, Mr. Crosse," Annabella said sharply. With all that she had to bear already, she was not about to let Crosse treat her as a child.

Crosse looked up, startled, and seemed to reassess her. "Miss King, I'm afraid you don't understand, I-"

"No, Mr. Crosse, it is you that does not understand." Annabella felt suddenly weary instead of angry, and was surprised that her voice held any firmness at all. "I know about your affair with my mother. You think that it gives you the right to see her now. It does not."

Crosse stared at her, stunned and pale. He swallowed hard twice before speaking. "I don't know by what right you stand between me and-"

"By the right of the last person standing," Annabella snapped, more harshly than she meant to. "My father is not at home. My mother is ill. I am the last voice to say what is appropriate in this house, and I am telling you that you will not visit my mother."

She could see Crosse growing frantic, his breath quickening and his eyes scanning her face. She tried to keep her expression neutral.

"Miss King," breathed Crosse. "Please. I... I must see her."

Annabella lifted her chin. "Good day, Mr. Crosse."

Crosse opened his mouth as if he were about to speak, and then closed it. He tipped his hat to her, and left.

Annabella let out a heavy sigh, and turned to pace the drawing room. Her thoughts were at war with each other. On the one hand, the propriety seemed obvious; her mother's lover was not welcome in her father's house. Even in his absence. End of discussion.

And yet, the logic of that position had begun to weaken even as she had asserted it. Her father owned everything in the house, even when he wasn't there. Including her mother. Including her. And that, a quiet voice hissed in her own mind, was unspeakably wrong. He could abandon them, could abandon her to face all his burdens, and he still owned them both. He ought to have forfeited that right when he had decided that he couldn't bear to be under the same roof as her mother.

Even if she had not felt her bitterness towards her father eating away at her resolve, she recognized what she had seen in John Crosse's face, and what she had heard in his voice. The love that bordered on despair. The longing to be by that love's side, even when all hope was gone. She had heard it in her own voice often enough.

Had seen it in Henry's eyes, on more than one occasion.

"Dammit," she muttered to herself. She dashed out the door.

"Mr. Crosse!"

He had not gone far. He turned at the sound of his name, and rushed back towards the house.

"Miss King?"

Annabella looked down at him from the top step. "She is dying, Mr. Crosse."

Crosse flinched, and nodded quickly. "I know. That's why I must see her."

Annabella waited for only a moment. "I will give you a half hour. Then you must leave. And if you upset her, I will call the servants to remove you."

Crosse's shoulders sagged with relief. "Thank God. My dear child-"

"I am not a child," Annabella said. "Thank God if you must. Come with me."

198

***

Annabella sat with a cold cup of tea in her hands. Crosse had left, exactly half an hour after she had let him into her mother's room. That had been an hour ago. She should go up and see her mother. She really should.

She still wasn't sure that she had done the right thing. Crosse's presence had unsettled her, but he was so unlike himself, unlike any way that she had seen him before. His self-assurance was gone, and he had been genuinely, grovelingly grateful.

She lifted her head, and set the teacup down on the table.

She left the room, and walked slowly up the staircase, and looked at the house around her. It felt like a cage, with frantic birds flapping inside it. Going out riding with Henry hadn't made it better. It had made it worse. She wanted fresh air, and the sounds of Engines and punch cards, and the chatter of her analysts' voices. Even as she longed for it, she felt guilty for wanting to leave.

She pushed open her mother's door. To her surprise, her mother was awake, and sitting up in her bed, gazing out the window.

"Mother?" she said tentatively. She almost wanted to be told to leave.

"Annabella," Ada said softly. "Will you come in?"

Annabella hesitated before slowly entering the room, and taking her seat next to the bed.

"John was here to see me," Ada said softly, as though she were not quite talking to Annabella.

"Yes. I know," Annabella said, looking at her lap.

"You let him in?" Ada asked.

Annabella looked up. Her mother's voice had a pleading quality to it. "Yes."

"I thought you might turn him away if he came," Ada said.

"I thought I would too," Annabella admitted. "It didn't seem right for him to be here in Father's house."

"And why didn't you?" Ada asked.

Annabella fell silent for a moment. "Because Father isn't here," she said finally. "And he truly seemed to care for you. And if Father won't be here to love you, then maybe he can be."

The words stuck in her throat. They were true, but it didn't make them easier to say.

"Thank you, my Bella," Ada said softly. She looked closely at her daughter. "You look tired."

Annabella almost laughed. Both at the simplicity of the statement, and at the fact that after all that had happened over the past few months, her mother had only seemed to notice now.

"Yes," was all she said.

"Has Henry been to see you?" her mother said.

Annabella couldn't help it; a small smile graced her lips. "Yes. He and I have been riding together this past week."

Ada nodded. "Good. Good."

Annabella thought she was finished speaking, when she suddenly said. "He's a good man, Bella. A kinder man than his father."

Annabella looked up with a jerk. She wouldn't have thought that her mother had a formed opinion of Henry, and as for Charles Babbage…

"What happened between you and Mr. Babbage, Mother? When you helped on the publication of the *Notes*," Annabella said.

"Helped," Ada returned softly. She smiled, a smile that held no humour in it. "The *Notes* of the Engine were my work. It was Charles who helped me."

Annabella frowned. It was a story she had heard before, often told in anger and raised voices, but never one that she had heard told quietly and calmly.

"Then why…?" Annabella murmured.

Ada turned and looked past Annabella at the window, and for a moment, Annabella was certain that she wasn't about to offer any further explanation. Then she spoke softly.

"I offered to translate Menabrea's work from the French for Charles. Menabrea had written an article on the design and proposed construction of the Engine, and I was working on a version in English."

"To what end?" Annabella interrupted.

Her mother glanced at her. "Mr. Babbage was having difficulty convincing Parliament and the Royal Society to continue funding the construction of the machine. He thought that if I translated the article, he would have something to show to them on the importance of the Engine."

"But your work is not only a translation," Annabella said, frowning. "The *Notes* ..."

"Yes," Ada said, nodding. "I found as I read Menabrea's work that not only were some ideas obscure – incomprehensible, almost – but he had left many areas of speculation unexplored. The *Notes* that followed were not only for clarity, but also to explore the algorithm that could lead to the most complete possible program."

"And they were published," Annabella said.

Ada sat silently for a moment, gazing out the window.

"The *Notes* were published with an introduction from Charles Babbage," Ada said. Her voice had grown tight, as if speaking had become an effort. "It was assumed that the *Notes* were written by Mr. Babbage himself."

There was silence in the room for a moment, and it was Annabella who finally spoke.

"Didn't Mr. Babbage correct them? Or Father would have, surely?"

Ada shook her head. "Parliament relented almost immediately. The Engine was built, and the investors were immediately interested. Your father and Mr. Babbage...they both told me that it wouldn't do to risk the continued success of the Engine. They felt – both of them – that revealing the true author of the program of the Engine would jeopardize its construction. The Engine had yet to be built. I didn't... there didn't seem to be anything left to do. They assured me... that there would be another time."

Annabella squeezed her hands around her teacup.

"And indeed there is," Ada said. She looked at Annabella, and met her daughter's gaze. "There is another time for an analyst. Just not for me."

"Mama-"

"I'm glad it was you, Bella. If it couldn't be me, then I'm glad it was you."

Annabella swallowed hard. "I won't waste it, Mama."

"No," Ada said softly. "I know you won't."

XXVII

Be near me when my light is low,
When the blood creeps, and the nerves prick
And tingle; and the heart is sick,
And all the wheels of Being slow.

~Alfred, Lord Tennyson~

"Is your father not yet returned from Ockham?"

Annabella glanced sideways at Henry, and shook her head. Their horses were walking slowly down her street, their hooves kicking up dust and hay. It had been dry for many days, and the dirt was caked over the cobbled street in flakes that broke under the horses' feet.

"I have no way of knowing when he will return," Annabella said, trying to keep anger out of her voice.

"You must be…" Henry coughed. "It must be lonely to be with just your mother, when she is so ill."

"She has been a little better of late," Annabella replied, surprised at finding that it was true. "It has given me a chance to speak to her often."

In fact, she had come to appreciate the hours when her mother was awake instead of dreading them. Her mother had begun to ask Annabella to show her the plans and designs for some of the Engine programs, and had discussed some of the algorithms that had caused problems in the Engine in its early days. Annabella had even gone so far as to run some patterns on the Analytical Engine in the house, and had returned later to discuss the results with her mother. Ada had different ideas than Annabella, but her basic understanding of the Engine was intact, and she could easily grasp the changes that the Engine had undergone. Annabella found herself enjoying discussing the Engine with her mother, and also regretting that she had never done so before.

They were coming to the yard of Annabella's house, and Henry slid off his horse, and took the reins of her horse. He offered her his other hand to help her down, and she leaned a hand on his shoulder, and eased herself to the ground.

She looked up at him. He still looked tired, but happier than he had been. She wondered if she looked the same.

"Thank you for accompanying me," she said. She flushed as she realized that her hand had lingered on his shoulder, and quickly removed it. The groom walked towards them from the stables, and Henry handed the reins of her horse to him.

Henry gave a small smile, and took her gloved hand in his. "It is my pleasure. I will call on you again?"

"Yes. Please do," Annabella said.

Henry let go of her hand, and swung himself back onto his horse. He smiled down at her, and nudged his horse forward and out of the yard at a swift walk.

Annabella watched him go wistfully. He had work to do, of course. She wished she did.

As she turned towards the house, another man walked into the yard, and she saw Bancroft come out of the house to meet him, as though he had been waiting for him. The man walked with a case next to him.

Her heart clenched. It was the doctor. He didn't pause to speak to Bancroft, but instead walked straight into the house.

Bancroft saw her, and seemed to sag with relief. "Miss King, thank God! I was about to send a servant out for you."

"What has happened?" she said, as she walked hurriedly to the house.

"It's your mother, Miss," Bancroft said. "She's... she's taken very ill, Miss."

Annabella's mouth went dry. "I'll go to her. Is Jenny with her?"

"Of course, Miss," Bancroft nodded.

"Can you send for Sarah?" Annabella said as she walked into the house. "She'll be at the works."

Annabella didn't wait for a reply, and hurried up the stairs, just in time to see the doctor enter her mother's room. Without waiting to take off her riding clothes, she followed the doctor into the room.

She heard her mother before she saw her. She was crying out sporadically, her cries followed by the soft, murmuring sounds of her voice. Jenny was on one side of her bed, holding Ada's hand and looking stricken with fear. The doctor was standing on the other, opening his case.

"Doctor?" Annabella said. She had seen him before, but couldn't remember his name.

He looked up, and nodded grimly.

Annabella walked into the room, and looked at her mother, who had seemed so well when she had seen her that morning. She was ash pale, glistening with sweat, and twitching back and forth in her bed.

"She has a fever, Miss King," said the doctor. "I'm afraid…" He shook his head.

Jenny let out a sob. Annabella swallowed back the lump in her own throat.

"How soon?" she said quickly, forcing herself to ask.

"Soon." the doctor said. "Change your clothes. I'll call if you're needed."

Annabella turned and rushed from the room. Her heart pounded as she fought herself out of her constricting riding clothes, and back into a green dress. Without Sarah, she couldn't reach the top buttons to do them up, but she left them open and hurried back down the hall.

The doctor had placed a cloth across Ada's forehead. He was holding her wrist, and looking at his watch. He looked up at Annabella as she entered, and his expression was bleak.

He stepped out of the way as Annabella stepped next to the bed, and sank to her knees. She took Ada's hand in both of hers, and looked across the bed at Jenny. The maid nodded, and rose to her feet and left the room.

"Mama?" she whispered.

"John…" said Ada.

"No, Mama, it's me, it's Bella," Annabella said, trying to make her voice stronger. "The doctor is here."

"He's here," Ada murmured, her eyelids fluttering, staring at the canopy of the bed. "He's brought me flowers. Metal flowers."

"Mama?" Annabella said, squeezing her hand.

"It's weaving. It's weaving numbers," Ada said, twitching to her side.

Annabella swallowed, fighting down tears. This couldn't be. It was as though her mother were already gone, and what remained in this bed were only a faint echo of her.

"Tell William that we're nearly done. The Engine. It's done." Ada's eyes were open now, and she was gazing straight at the canopy of the bed.

Annabella gulped down a sob, and pressed her cheek against her mother's hand.

"John!"

Annabella twitched awake, and looked around. She had fallen asleep in the chair by her mother's bed. The room had grown darker, and she couldn't see the doctor or Jenny anywhere in the room. Sarah was in the chair by the fire, and she looked like she too had been awoken by Ada's cry.

Annabella looked at Ada. Her mother was straining to lift her head, and was breathing fast and shallow.

"John... he's gone, John... William's gone," Ada muttered, falling back to the pillows.

Annabella knelt on the ground next to her mother's bed. "Mama? Ada?" Annabella said, pressing her mother's hand.

Her mother's hand strained in her grasp, and gripped onto her fingers. Annabella watched as pain twitched across her mother's face.

"Bella, is John there?" Her mother opened her eyes, staring wildly around the room.

Annabella swallowed. "Yes, Mama, he's here."

Ada fell back against the pillows. "I'm glad it's you, Bella..."

Her eyes closed, and her hand went limp in Annabella's.

Annabella sat forward, her chest aching, and touched her mother's face. "Mama?"

There was no response. She could not see her mother's chest moving with her breath. Not letting go her mother's hand, she snatched a mirror from the bedside, and held it over Ada's mouth. It remained clear and free of fog, reflecting back Ada's grey face.

206

"Mama," she whispered. She sank to her knees next to her mother's bed.

"Miss," came Sarah's gentle voice. "Miss, come away. She's past help." Sarah's voice broke on her final words.

Annabella's pulse pounded in her head as she reached out and shook Ada's hand. Her mother's head lolled to one side.

"Mama!"

XXVIII

I sometimes hold it half a sin
To put in words the grief I feel;
For words, like Nature, half reveal
And half conceal the Soul within.

~Alfred, Lord Tennyson~

"Still the same mayhem, then?" Charles Babbage said.

Henry leaned back in a chair in his father's drawing room, as Charles Babbage passed him a glass of scotch. It was a welcome pause; the Exhibition was drawing to a close, and it seemed to him that he had hardly slept since Annabella's demonstration. The investors occupied much of his time; some were well aware of the Engine's role, while others only thinly grasped the concept of what it could do. Everyone seemed to want one.

Henry nodded. "Successful mayhem, though. Brunel was right, as usual," Henry said with a rueful smile.

"Do they truly understand its function, these investors?" Charles asked.

"Not in the slightest," Henry replied, "but that seems to be the point. They understand its applications, and if that can benefit them, what else do they need to know?"

Charles Babbage sighed, and took a sip of his scotch. Henry was about to continue, when there was a knock at the door.

"Excuse me, sir," said his father's butler, Hawkes, when he entered. "There is a Miss Sarah here to see you. She says she has come from Lord King's house, sir, and she must speak with you urgently."

"Send her in then," Charles replied.

Henry put down his glass, and leaned forward. Sarah? Annabella's maid, the one who had become an analyst? Why would she be there?

Sarah hurried quickly into the room, and dropped into a speedy curtsy. She raised her head to look up at them, and Henry's pulse quickened in alarm. Her face was red, and her eyes were large and frightened.

"My dear girl," Charles said gently, "What is-"

"It's Lady King, sir," Sarah burst out, trembling on the edge of tears, "she's passed, sir."

Charles' glass clattered to the table by his side. Henry looked at his father in alarm, at the colour draining from his face, and felt something twist inside of him. He knew that his father was feeling the loss of his great protégée, while Henry's sudden lurch of pain was for Annabella rather than for himself. He had seen her only the day before, when they had been riding. When had her mother worsened?

"Thank you for coming to tell us, my dear, I-" Charles managed.

"No, you don't understand, sir," Sarah burst on, tears in her eyes. "It's Miss King, Miss Anna."

"What of Miss King?" Henry returned before his father could speak.

"She's all on her own, sir," Sarah replied, twisting her apron.

"But surely Lord King-" began Charles.

"Lord King is at Ockham Park, and hasn't been home almost since the Exhibition," Sarah sobbed, "and she... oh sir!" Sarah gasped. She set her gaze on Henry. "She's in such a state, I didn't know who to call, but I thought of you, sir, and I-"

"Yes, my dear, of course," Charles said, on his feet. "Go to the kitchen and have something to calm yourself while-"

"I must get back, sir, but you will come?" Sarah pressed, her eyes red.

"Yes," Henry said, on his feet, "we will follow you."

Sarah gave a weak smile, and was about to leave the room, when Henry followed her to the door.

"Sarah," he said in a hushed voice. "How... how is she?"

Sarah looked at him, anguish evident in her face. "I've never seen her like this, sir. It's like she isn't even there. She ... she needs you, sir." She looked up at Henry until he gave a brief nod. She dropped a curtsy, and hurried away.

"We?" Charles said with raised eyebrows as the door closed.

"Of course," Henry said, remaining at the door.

"Henry," Charles said, gently and calmly. "Are you sure you ought to be the one to go to Annabella?"

Henry paused with his hand on the doorknob. "Why would I not be?" Henry said, trying to make his voice neutral, and utterly failing. He couldn't be sure whether he wanted to go to her because of her anguish or because of his own inability to be idle while she was in pain.

"Because you are hardly a disinterested friend," his father replied bluntly.

Henry turned to face his father, trying to read his face. He had scarcely spoken to his father about Annabella. At first it had been too painful, and now he felt that his moments with her were a secret not to be shared, but to be treasured alone. He wondered if Brunel had told him.

Henry turned to look at the door, his eyes lowered. "What I feel for Annabella is irrelevant."

"You are not her protector, Henry," Charles said gently.

"I don't care," Henry replied firmly, his hand still on the door, his back to his father. "I don't care that it is unseemly for me to storm into her house, and I don't care that I have no right to bear her sorrow with her. I *do* bear it, and if I can give her any measure of comfort in her grief, I will be there to deliver it to her."

Charles said nothing for a moment, and then called, "Hawkes? Hail us a cab, please, quickly."

The hansom cab had barely stopped when Henry bounded out of it, followed rather more slowly by his father. He hurried up the stairs, and only had to knock once before Sarah let him in.

The house was eerily still. Henry felt his heartbeat like thundering machinery in his ears, compared to the unwavering stillness of the house. Sarah beckoned to them with a nod of her head, and they followed her up the stairs.

As they had reached the landing, Henry began to smell it. The creeping, chemical smell that was the mark of every sickroom he had ever known. It hit his mind as the smell of his mother's room when he was young. It was the smell of Georgiana's room, smells that should have brought healing and comfort that were instead only associated with death.

A man stepped out into the hall, carrying a medical case. He looked up at them, and extended his hand. "Gentlemen," he said, "Mr. Babbage and Mr. Henry Babbage, I believe? Thank you for coming."

"Where is Miss King?" Charles said softly.

"Lady King passed only a few hours ago," the doctor said, "I haven't been able to convince the poor girl to leave her side. You might have more success, I hope."

The doctor turned to Henry. "If you manage to get Miss King to leave, let me give you something to help her sleep."

Henry nodded, and followed his father into the room.

The smell so overpowered his senses and his memories that at first Henry barely saw the two figures in the room. As his eyes adjusted to the low lights of the two solitary oil lamps, he saw the figure on the bed.

Ada King lay with her head to one side, one hand on the top of the covers, utterly still. Her face was thin and ash-white, and her dark hair was coiled down one shoulder. Henry swallowed hard; she didn't exactly look at peace, but she was free from pain, at least.

He heard a small whimper coming from the side of the bed, and as Charles Babbage sat down next to the bed and took Ada's hand, Henry walked around to the other side.

Crumpled on the floor next to the bed, her hands covering Ada's other hand and her dark hair thrown across the sheets, was Annabella. She was curled around the crushed green cotton of her skirt, and looked like an exhausted and frightened child. Henry stared at her, the sight of her wringing his heart. How long had she been there? When had she last slept?

Henry crouched down next to her. "Annabella?"

She didn't lift her head to look at him, but simply uttered a low moan of "No...."

He moved closer to her, and began to gently disengage her hands from Ada's. "Annabella..."

"No!" Her cry was a fierce wail, and her hands gripped her mother's firmly. She raised her head to look at Henry, but he was sure that she wasn't seeing him. Her eyes were red with crying, and seemed to look straight through him.

"Mama," she whimpered softly, pulling Ada's unresisting hand to hers and resting her cheek on it.

Henry knelt behind her, and reached around her to take hold of her forearms. "Annabella, come with me, you must-"

"No," Annabella said hoarsely. Her exhausted voice bordered on delirium. "I can't leave Mama. Papa has already left her, and if I don't stay,…"

She didn't resist him as he gently pulled her away from her mother. She whimpered only, "Mama, no," as her hands slid from her mother's. She fell back against him, as though she had only been held in place by her grip on Ada.

She felt limp and hollow in his arms, as though every fiber of her body snapped. She drew a single shaking breath, and the sobs began, racking her whole body, until it was not enough for Henry to simply cradle her in his lap. Instead, he pulled her fiercely against his chest, and shut his eyes as he felt her body tremble against him. Her hands gripped fistfuls of his shirt and waistcoat, as if she were holding on with the last of her strength. Her agony overwhelmed him, and he felt his own breath becoming fast and ragged. He stroked her hair, trying, for both their sake's, to calm her hysterical sobs. He looked up at his father.

Charles Babbage had not moved since he had taken Ada's hand, and seemed not to notice Henry and Annabella at all. His eyes were on Ada, on her still and lifeless face, and there were silent tears in his eyes. Henry clutched Annabella against him, as it dawned on him that of those in the room, not even Annabella had known Ada better than his father had. She was the child that his mind would have hoped to have; to him she was still the Enchantress of Numbers, the young woman who had wandered into his workshop and understood his work as no one else had ever done. To him, she was always Ada Byron, the one who had given the Analytical Engine its first chance. And she, like Georgiana, like Henry's mother, like so many other gentle lights in his life, had just flickered out.

"Father," Henry whispered. "Does Lord King know?"

212

"No," said Charles Babbage, in a surprisingly calm, clear voice, his eyes never leaving Ada's face. "I must go to Ockham Park and tell him myself. You will stay here with Annabella."

"Father, I-" Henry gulped out.

"You were right, Henry. She needs you. Even if she doesn't want you, she needs you. Take her to get some rest," Charles said, still holding Ada's hand.

"But Father, will you-"

"Go to Ockham, yes," Charles said softly. "Just… give me one more moment."

Henry rose slowly to his feet, drawing Annabella with him. She swayed against him, and he wrapped one arm around her waist. She didn't resist, but leaned her head against his shoulder.

Henry turned and looked back at his father. The inventor of the Analytical Engine had not moved, his eyes still resting on the unmoving face of his friend and student.

"Henry?" Annabella said groggily, as they reached her room. She sounded surprised, as though she had only just realized he was there.

"Yes, Annabella," he said gently as Sarah opened the room, and led them in. He guided her to the bed, and eased her gently down to sit on the edge of it. She looked at him groggily as he stood up and turned to Sarah.

"Sarah," Henry whispered, pulling off his jacket and putting it over a chair. "Get her into bed. I will return in a moment."

Henry went downstairs and asked another housemaid to send a message to his home to send over a bag with some clothes. As he started up the stairs again, the doctor stopped him.

"Well done, sir," the doctor whispered. "I'll be back in the morning. In the meantime, if she has difficulty sleeping, four drops should do," he said, placing a small brown bottle in Henry's hand.

Henry turned it over in his hand. Laudanum. He thanked the doctor, and hoped like hell that he wouldn't have to use it.

He hurried up the stairs, and heard the soft cries even before he opened the door. Sarah had managed to convince Annabella to get dressed for

213

bed, but Annabella was sitting up in her bed, vigorously shaking her head, pushing away Sarah's efforts to coax her to sleep.

"Miss, please, you need rest-"

"*No*, Sarah!" Annabella wailed, her tears starting again. "She's all alone, I can't leave her…"

"Sarah, it's all right, you can leave us now," Henry said gently, placing the bottle of laudanum on the table.

Sarah let go of Annabella, and walked to him. She looked at him with fear and uncertainty.

"She needs sleep," she whispered.

"How long has she been with her mother?" Henry whispered in return.

"Lady King took a turn for the worst yesterday, and since then…" Sarah shook her head. "She's barely eaten anything. She just stayed by Lady King's bed."

Henry nodded. "Go get some rest, Sarah. I'll stay with her." Sarah nodded, and left the room.

Annabella moved to get up, and Henry took a quick stride over to the bed, and caught her hand.

"It's all right, Annabella, lie still," he said as gently as he could manage, his heart beating in his throat.

"I can't," moaned Annabella, grabbing his arm and pulling herself onto her knees on the bed. "My mother-"

"My father is with her, Annabella," Henry said, standing by the bed and gently taking hold of her shoulders. Her skin felt warm through the cotton of her nightgown, but she shivered as he touched her.

"Your father…" She looked up at him, as if seeing him again for the first time. "Henry," she murmured, "You're here." She reached up and touched his cheek.

"Yes, Annabella," Henry whispered, resisting the urge to pull himself away from her, "I'm here."

"But my mother…" Annabella frowned, and let her hand fall, as though she were reaching for a memory that was out of her grasp.

214

"My father is with her. It's all right, you can sleep now," Henry said gently, brushing her hair off her face.

Annabella reached up, and touched the tips of her fingers to his lips. His breath caught. His logical mind railed at him to stop, to let go of her, to leave. It cried at him that nothing had changed, that she was not his to comfort. He felt everything that was logical and rational crumbling under him. All he could see was her, red-eyed and raw and trusting, and all he wanted was to pull her close and never let go.

Henry turned his face away, his heart hammering, and swallowed. "Annabella," he said hoarsely, "you need to sleep now."

Annabella shook her head wearily. "I can't sleep, Henry," she murmured.

"You must try, Annabella," Henry said, gently easing her to the bed. "The doctor gave me something to help you."

Annabella shook her head on the pillow. "No, I can't," she protested. She tried to push herself up, and Henry sat down next to her.

He wasn't sure if it was her or him who moved, but he found that she was wrapped in his arms. One of her hands gripped the lapel of his waistcoat, while the other rested against his neck. Without thinking, he slid his arm around her back, supporting her wilted frame, and cradling her neck in his hand.

"*Please*, Annabella," Henry begged, "You are exhausted. You need sleep."

"I *can't*," Annabella insisted.

As much as he didn't want to, Henry turned to look at the bottle of laudanum. If he simply walked away, would Annabella sleep? Or would he simply leave her to her own hysteria? If he stayed, could he do her any good, or would he only torture himself in watching her suffering?

With one hand, Henry reached for the bottle of laudanum on the table, and fumbled off the dropper filled with the clear liquid. He held the dropper out to her.

"Annabella," he said, trying to steady his voice, "please. Take this. It will help you sleep, and-"

"Will you stay, Henry?" Annabella said in a voice that was nearly a sob.

"Yes, Annabella, I'll stay with you," he whispered. "Here," he said, gently offering her the dropper of laudanum. She took it between her fingers and moved it to her lips, and he carefully measured four drops into her mouth, which she swallowed with a cough. Her head dropped forward, her hand still holding a fistful of the fabric of his waistcoat.

He put the dropper on the table, and turned back to her. "There, now I-"

Annabella lifted her head, and pulled him sharply down towards her, and kissed him. The sharp bitterness of the laudanum hit his mouth. His mind screamed at him. This was wrong. Every moment of this was a betrayal of her when she was most vulnerable. His body clung to her, unwilling to listen, unwilling to let her go. He tightened his grip on her back, holding her against him, and lifted her jaw in his other hand. He could feel the warmth of her shaking hands through his shirt. She felt tense in his arms, like the string of an instrument pulled tight and ready to break.

Her hands released him, and her body relaxed against him. Her mouth fell away from his, and her head dropped against his chest. For just a moment, he held her there, her head nestled against his shoulder, his cheek resting on her hair. His breathing was fast and painful, and although the idea of letting go made him ache inside, he lowered her sleeping form to her bed.

He stood up, stoppered the bottle of laudanum, and all but staggered away from the bed. He could feel the residual taste of the laudanum making his head fuzzy. He eased himself into the chair where he had thrown his jacket, and prepared for a long night.

Morning light slanted through the windows, and broke Henry's restless sleep. Annabella had slept the fitful, delirious sleep that laudanum gave, crying out in the night, but she was quiet now, her arms thrown across her bedspread. Henry gathered his jacket, and quietly left the room.

As he opened the door, he heard the soft clinking of dishes in one of the rooms downstairs, and wondered if his father had returned so soon.

Pulling his jacket on over his aching back, he wandered down the stairs and into the drawing room.

Brunel was sat at a small breakfast table that had been laid with a meal, and glanced up as Henry walked in.

"Dear God, Henry, you look like hell," Brunel muttered.

Despite how he felt, Henry managed a smile. "A pleasure to see you as always, Isambard," he returned, as he sank into one of the chairs at the table.

Brunel had already rung the bell, and when the servant entered gave the short order of "Coffee for this one."

"How is she?" Brunel asked.

Henry folded his hands in front of him and stared at them. "I don't even know how to answer that." He looked up at Brunel. "How did you come to be here?"

"Your father sent word to me. He thought you shouldn't be left alone," Brunel said with a sip of his coffee.

"I'm quite all right," Henry replied.

"You look about as far from all right as any man I've ever seen," Brunel replied with his typical brusque manner.

"I haven't slept much," Henry replied, reaching for a piece of toast.

"Henry," Brunel said, with such serious kindness that Henry looked up at him. "This is only the last event in your recent misery. How long do you plan to spend like this?"

"Like what?" Henry said, and took a resentful bite of his toast.

"How long do you plan to spend pretending that she means nothing to you?" Brunel asked.

Henry lifted his head, surprised that even Brunel would be so blunt. His mind was still full of the night before, of the taste of Annabella's kiss, a kiss stolen from her in a time of grief. He didn't need Brunel to add to his guilt. "I have never pretended that," he replied.

Brunel rolled his eyes. "Fine, then do you intend to conceal it from her forever?"

Henry glared at him. "That is not your-"

217

"Do not tell me that it is not my concern," Brunel snapped, before Henry could finish. "I have spent too many months witnessing your abject misery for it not to be my concern. The heart can bend a great deal before it breaks, but it is not invincible. Neither are you."

Henry opened his mouth, and then closed it again. He glared at the table. "I have not concealed it," he replied softly. "I asked. I was refused."

"Henry," Brunel muttered, looking at him with real sadness. "After everything that has passed? Has nothing changed? You're barely the same man. And she sure as hell isn't the same woman."

Henry blinked. It was true, now that he thought of it. After all that Annabella had endured, all that she had done, she was not the woman she had been those many months ago. She was stronger. Sadder. And he ached more than ever to be with her.

He sighed. "I haven't given up," he said, and found to his surprise that it was true. "If I were to... ask again, it wouldn't be now. It couldn't be, with her mother. There will be another time."

"Mr. Brunel?"

Both men glanced up, and proceeded to scramble to their feet.

Framed in the doorway, holding onto one edge of it for support, was Annabella. She was consumed by the ruffles of a long silver nightgown, her dark, loose hair the only thing that kept her from looking like a ghost. Her eyes were red, and her face pale. She was looking at them both in extreme confusion.

"My dear child," Brunel said, stepping forward and taking both her hands in his. "I'm not sure that you should be out of your room."

"Mr. Brunel, thank you for... I can't stay there anymore," she murmured.

Henry gazed at her, a painful lump knotting in his throat. She was so far from herself, so dazed and lost, that she was barely recognizable to him.

"And Mr. Babbage," she said, her eyes settling on him. "How did you come to..." She frowned, as if the memories of the night before were slipping in and out. "Were you... did you...?"

"Mr. Babbage stayed with you last night, Miss King," Brunel supplied, as Henry felt his voice go dry and disappear. "I gather you were quite distressed."

She looked at him, and her eyes shimmered. "Yes... I remember." She held out one hand to him, and Henry took it in his.

"Is there anything we can do, Miss... Annabella?" Henry said, his voice sore and hoarse. He felt Brunel's gaze on him, but he ignored it.

"I...I don't know..." Annabella murmured. Her hand had slipped from Brunel's, and her fingers rested limply in Henry's grasp.

"You should eat something, my dear," Brunel said, looking at Henry for support.

Annabella shook her head quietly. She looked around her, unable to settle her gaze.

"Is there anything that would give you comfort?" Henry said softly, holding tighter to her fingers. "Playing your violin, perhaps?"

Annabella frowned. "Playing... no. Yes, playing." She brushed past him suddenly, and seized her violin from its stand. Instead of playing it, she whisked out of the room, and down the hall.

Henry followed, Brunel behind him. He knew where she was going before he reached the room. He could already smell it, the smell of metal and grease, smells that were wrong for this gentle and quiet house. He stopped in the doorway.

Annabella stood in the room, facing the hulking form of the Analytical Engine, that was still attached to the little bells. She was standing with her violin and bow in one hand, staring up at the bulk of the Engine as if entranced by it. She suddenly stepped around to the back, and with her free hand, began pulling out punch cards, stacking new ones in, rearranging them swiftly.

"My dear, I really don't think-" Brunel began, but Henry held up a hand and stopped him. He recognized the danger, watched with trepidation at the flowing folds of her nightgown, and waited for the moment when the Engine would trap them. It didn't. Instead, her work done, she stepped back, and pulled the crank of the Engine.

The Engine groaned into life, and clicked its familiar rhythms for a moment with no other sound. A moment later, the bells began, sweet and sad and solitary, ringing one at a time, as had once been all they knew how to do. Annabella put her violin to her shoulder, curled her three good fingers around the neck, and began to play.

Henry didn't know the song. He wasn't sure that Annabella did either. It wasn't so much that she was playing a song as that she and the Engine were singing to each other. It was a lullaby, to comfort and soothe them. It was a dirge, the groaning of the Engine and the cry of the violin singing out in grief. It was as if both she and the Engine were wailing the loss of their mother. He watched her with an aching heart, as he thought of when she had first demonstrated the bells, in this room, with this Engine. She had been so full of joy, and so free of sorrow.

The bells slowed, and the violin slowed to long mournful tones, and then brightened, and finally ceased, both ringing their tones through the room. Annabella turned to face the two men who stood in the doorway, her face wet with tears.

Brunel was gazing at her sadly. Henry's face was set in hard lines, his own tears refusing to fall.

XXIX

Alas! Is even love too weak
To unlock the heart, and let it speak?

~Matthew Arnold~

Annabella sat back in the chair in the drawing room, and rubbed her eyes. She looked down at the notebook in her lap with grim satisfaction. After weeks of feeling like a stranger in her own mind, she had managed to write out some of the code patterns that she could test on her return to the works.

Ada's funeral had been only two days before. Annabella had largely stayed in her room for the days preceding it, not so much because the doctor had advised it – though he had – but rather out of a desire to avoid her father. Sarah had come to tell her that Lord King has returned, and was preparing to move her mother's body to Hacknall. She was to be buried next to her father, Lord Byron, Annabella's grandfather.

Annabella had quietly absorbed the information, and had asked Sarah to prepare her a traveling dress, and her mourning dress. Sarah had looked uncomfortable, and had replied that she had heard Lord King say to Bancroft that Annabella needn't come to the funeral "in her present state."

Annabella had stood mechanically, and walked downstairs, Sarah following her in concern. She had found her father in the study, writing at the desk.

"I will be going to Mother's funeral," was all she had said. By the time Lord King had looked up to reply, she was walking out of the room.

She had travelled up to Hacknall on the train with Sarah, separately from her father. So far from London, the group that was gathered was sparse; her father, herself, and Charles and Henry Babbage. Her brother Byron had still not returned, and no word had been heard from him or his naval vessel. Annabella might have been concerned, had she not been too full of grief.

It had been on a warm, grey Sunday. Every yard of her black mourning dress clung to her body, the flat black satin absorbing the thin light. Annabella had looked over the top of the grave, at the churchyard shrouded in warm rain. Charles' eyes were focused on the casket, already lowered into the ground. Henry's flickered up to look at her, and then looked back down at the grave. His black clothes made his features seem sharper. Her father had avoided looking at her at all.

In her drawing room, Annabella closed her eyes as she recalled the scene, like a painting of a funeral, rather than a real one.

"Annabella?"

For a moment Annabella considered not looking up. She wondered if he would leave. She finally looked into the doorway.

Lord King was standing there, as though he were awaiting permission to enter. He was dressed in a black suit.

"Father," she said, looking back at her notebook.

"Will you not speak to me, Annabella?" her father said, stepping into the room, but not sitting down.

Annabella closed the notebook slowly. "What would you like me to say?" she said, raising her eyes to look at him.

Lord King lowered his gaze to the floor, and stood silent for a moment. "I thought... we might speak of what happened."

"Of what?" Annabella replied. She couldn't bring herself to say anything more.

Lord King looked up, his expression between weary and exasperated. "Of your mother, or of-"

"The fact that you were not here when she died?" Annabella offered, her voice flat. "That you left when she needed you most?"

Lord King winced. "Annabella, you don't understand-"

"What exactly do I not understand, Father?' Annabella said, unable to keep the bite out of her voice.

"What your mother told me... I had reasons for not being at her bedside when she...," Lord King trailed off, and looked down at his hands.

"Yes. I know your reasons," Annabella said. *I have even met your reason, and allowed him to set foot in your house*, she thought, but did not say. "I do not accept them as an excuse."

Lord King frowned at her. "Do you intend to remain angry at me forever?"

222

Annabella turned her head to one side. "Angry? No. That would be exhausting. But I will not forgive you for it."

"Annabella-"

"I don't care what reason made you go," she said firmly, setting her notebook down on the table beside her. "You sidestepped your duty, and left it on my shoulders."

"That wasn't what happened, Annabella," Lord King said, shifting his feet.

"It was what happened. You only don't think so because you did not see it. You left me to do your duty for you." She could see anger and embarrassment mounting in his face.

"I do not have to listen to this," Lord King said in a thick voice.

"True," Annabella said. "But it was you who came here to ask my forgiveness."

"I have never denied you anything, Annabella," Lord King said pleadingly. "When you wanted to work on the Engine-"

"How can you compare this to the Engine?" Annabella cried out, unable to restrain herself. "Mother is dead. That can never be undone. Your absence can never be made right."

"And you will hold that one action over everything else?" Lord King said, his voice rising. "I have given you everything, Annabella, every freedom, everything that I never gave your mother."

Annabella rose to her feet. "Do not make this into-"

"Even when I saw Henry Babbage's feelings for you, when I thought he would make you happy, I did not object - "

"What *possible* objection could you have had to Henry?" Annabella snapped, facing her father.

Her father threw up his hands. "I didn't object to his lack of title, to the fact that he-"

"Father!" Annabella cried out, aghast. The idea that her father could ever have had mixed feelings about her marrying Henry had never crossed her mind.

"Of course," her father said in disgust, as though he had read her thoughts. "Because you assumed that you could have exactly what you wanted. It never occurred to you that it was *privilege* to be allowed to even *consider* marrying an untitled engineer!"

"I can scarcely *believe* you," Annabella said, lifting her chin to glare at her father. "Mother's death has nothing to do with my feelings for Henry. And even if it did, at least *Henry Babbage* was here to comfort me! Where were *you*?"

Lord King turned away, and leaned his hands on the back of the chair in front of him. "You have to understand, Annabella, the principle for which I left your mother, I-"

"Principle?" Annabella said, with a dry laugh. "Is that your excuse for casting aside the person you love?"

"It was yours, wasn't it?" Lord King snapped in irritation. "When you refused Babbage?"

Anger crackled inside her. "That is not the same."

"How is it not the same?" Lord King said, his voice rising again. "There was no lack of love, only principle. For that damned Engine."

"It is not the same," Annabella said, "because I didn't harm anyone except myself, and-" she felt her voice strangle around his name – "Henry. You wanted to punish Mama, but you abandoned *me* when you abandoned her." She could hear her own voice, rising to a wail. "As if I could endure alone what you could not."

"Couldn't you?" Lord King, his voice softening.

Annabella glared at him. "Yes. Which is why you will ask nothing of me. Not forgiveness. Not obedience. Nothing."

Lord King frowned. "I am the father of this house-"

"Oh yes," Annabella said with a hard laugh, "you could compel me to do whatever you like. I am heartily aware of that. But you can't compel my thoughts, and I will never see you as I did before. You have been a coward, and I will never forgive you for it."

Lord King took a step back, and stared at her. His face saddened, softened, and he turned and left the room.

Annabella sank to her chair, in a rustling of black crepe, and angrily brushed her tears off her face. She wanted to pretend that nothing had changed, that she could share her grief with her father. And she couldn't,

224

because it was not the same grief, not the way that it would have been if he had stayed. She didn't regret her words; they were true.

She knew, even as she calmed down, that some of her tears were angry ones. Her father's words about Henry had rung painfully true. She was, wishing that her father had given her mother a second chance. A chance she had never given Henry.

Not yet.

"She's back, Master."

Henry looked up from the plans that he was poring over, and saw Bentham framed in the doorway of the overseer's office.

"Back, Bentham?"

"Miss Annabella, Master Henry," Bentham said, in a voice that bordered on exasperation. "She's here. In the training room."

Henry's heart jumped. Which was stupid, he reminded himself. It wasn't as if he hadn't seen her recently.

He had thought that he had endured all the heartache that he would have to, until he had seen her at her mother's funeral. The face that looked out from under the black bonnet was pale and tired. She had lifted her eyes to meet his, and had nodded, as though he understood everything that she could possibly say. There had been no other greeting. He had watched her as she stood staring into her mother's grave, the soft rain leaving a silver fuzz on her black dress, like the blurring at the edge of a telescope lens. She had seemed so infinitely far away.

And yet she was here. Now. Working in the training room. Where he could see her.

"Master?"

Henry coughed. "Yes, Bentham, I'll be there, I, … once I've finished these orders."

"Master Henry," Bentham began, insistence behind his voice.

"Bentham," Henry said sharply, looking up to meet Bentham's eyes. "In my own time, thank you."

Bentham met his gaze, and gave a small shrug. "As you say. They don't wait forever." He closed the door behind him as he left.

Henry set his hands down on the surface of the desk, and stared blankly at the papers in front of him.

"Damn," he said after a moment. He picked up his hat, and strode out into the works.

Henry rested his hand on the outer door of the training room, and hesitated. He could hear the murmur of voices, and the shunting, clicking sound of the Engine. It had seemed so obvious that he should come barreling down to meet her, but it occurred to him now that that was insufficient. What could he say to her?

He pushed the door gently, but not fully open. The sounds became louder, the Engine's hissing and shuffling becoming the full thunder of an Engine in motion. He looked through the gap in the door, at the analysts walking quickly and quietly, holding stacks of cards and sheets of paper. As a group of young men in dark brown clothing passed him, Henry caught sight of her, her dress black in a sea of brown and grey, as though all light disappeared when it met her.

She was bent over a table, her hair pulled tightly back into a knot of braids. She wore a dress of deep black wool, with a band of flat crepe fabric around her waist. Her goggles hung around her neck, and her leather gloves were pulled up to her elbows. Her dress and hair made her look older, sadder, but her cheeks had colour in them, and she was gesturing towards the table in an animated way. She looked, all in all, more alive than Henry had seen her in weeks. Evy and Rosie stood at her elbow, looking over notes on the table. He stepped quietly into the room.

"... but then why haven't they shut the Engine down if it's catching?" he heard Annabella say.

"Because it isn't catching all the time, Miss," Evy replied, pointing at the table. "The instructions for the track change between Folkstone and Staplehurst are all working."

"And beyond Staplehurst?" Annabella asked.

"They're fine too, Miss," Rosie said. "They say it's only the timetables that are wrong."

226

"So the problems is in the codes, not the Engine," Annabella said, drumming her fingers on the table.

"I checked them before they went in," Evy protested softly.

"Just you?" Annabella said, looking up. "You could have-"

"No Ma'am," Evy struck in. "Mr. Bentham went over them as well. We ran them twice to be sure."

Annabella sighed, and began to play with a necklace of jet beads around her neck.

"I can't tell from here," Annabella said with a sigh. "We'll have to go look for ourselves."

"I'll go, Ma'am," Rosie said.

"No," Annabella said. "It would be easiest if it were the people who worked on it to begin with. Evy, I'll take you, and Bentham. And Sarah."

"Tomorrow, Miss?" Evy said with a nod.

Annabella looked up, and her eyes met Henry's. Henry saw her look change to what seemed to be genuine pleasure.

"Yes. We'll leave by the 10:15 train," Annabella finished, her gaze continually flickering back to Henry. "Go let Sarah and Bentham know."

Evy and Rosie scooped up the papers on the table, and rounded the other side of the Engine, leaving Henry and Annabella looking at each other across the room.

"Mr. Babbage," Annabella said, closing the space between them.

"Miss King," Henry said, unable to stop the smile that broke over his face. "Forgive me, I didn't mean to intrude on your work. I just wanted to welcome your return."

"Thank you, Mr. Babbage," Annabella said, playing the formal name across her lips with a small smile. "Bentham told you, I assume."

"Of course," Henry said. "He's nearly as delighted as I am to have you working here again."

Henry swallowed, feeling stupid, but warmed as Annabella returned his smile.

"Will you walk with me, Mr. Babbage?" she said. "I could use some fresh air."

Henry nodded without speaking. Annabella collected a black bonnet and shawl from a peg by the door, and walked out the door that he held open.

The fall day was brisk and clear, though in the grey of the yard, it was hard to tell the exact season. Henry watched Annabella walk down the stairs before him.

"You have to travel, I understand?" he said when he reached her.

Annabella tightened her shawl around her. "Yes," she replied. "Some code is catching up in Folkstone and Staplehurst, and no one's sure why without seeing it."

"Could it be the users rather than the code?" Henry said, as their walk began to take them towards the gate of the yard, and out into the street beyond it.

"It could be," Annabella replied. "The cards may have been inserted incorrectly. That's why I'd like to see it myself, instead of going to all the work of correcting it here, only to find out that they fed the machine incorrectly."

They both fell quiet as they rounded the corner of a long brick warehouse, and the road wound along the river. The wind came up, and lifted the tangy sour-salt smell of the water, and blew it down the street. From somewhere upriver came the pungent smell of fish and tar, mixed with the soot and smoke that Henry barely smelled any more.

"When will you be back?" he asked softly, as he and Annabella turned back towards the works.

"I can't be sure," Annabella replied. "I'll send Brunel a telegram as to when to expect our return."

Henry held the edge of his hat to keep it from flying off in the wind, and thought of all the things that he'd like to say. That he didn't want her to go, not when she had only just returned. That he could go with her, and help, in spite of all the work that he had to complete here. That he would be awaiting her return, because the time that he spent with her was precious to him even if it wasn't to her.

He took her left hand, and placed in the crook of his arm. She squeezed his upper arm with her three good fingers and her thumb. Henry didn't speak. The lump in his throat made it impossible, and he couldn't tell whether it came from their shared joy, or their shared sorrow.

XXX

Wandering between two worlds, one dead,
The other powerless to be born,
With nowhere yet to rest my head,
Like these, on earth I wait forlorn.

~Matthew Arnold~

The Analytical Engine at Staplehurst Station was new even by the standards of the Engines themselves. A glass wall partitioned it from the rest of the station, but the towers of cards and cogs were visible to the passersby, the cards still white and their edges still clean, the cog towers shiny with new metal. Daniel Withers had operated an Engine for as long as Staplehurst station had had one; he had been the only station hand willing to take on the task. He couldn't see why – the Engine did most of the work. It sent light signals to the nearest signalman, it printed out the timetables when needed, and even when the timetables had glitches in them, as they had had recently, it wasn't his job to fix it. Daniel had a chair in the small room that enclosed the Engine, and even in the chill of fall, his work was warm and easy.

Daniel yawned, and picked up his book of codes. He input the time of day, and pulled the crank to set the machine in motion. The Analytical Engine whirled through its options and sent its signals, and Daniel sat back in his chair.

He was about to fall asleep in the warmth of the room when a screech tore across his ears, so shrill that he felt as if it were inside his head. He sat up in his chair, and at first, couldn't see what the problem was. The Engine was still churning through its calculations, but it gave a groan of protest that told Daniel that something was wrong. Then Daniel smelt it. Slowly at first, then picking up intensity, he smelled the choking smell of smoke.

Daniel glanced nervously around him, and crept around the back side of the Engine. He put his forearm up over his face as he did so – flames and smoke were pouring out of the back of the Engine, its stack of cards curling

230

back in the fire. He needed to stop it, to stop the steam power – but if there was a way, he had never been told how.

Daniel staggered back to the other side of the Engine and to the door of the small room. His eyes burned, and his head was cloudy. He didn't know what to do, only that he had to get outside.

He threw himself against the door, and staggered out onto the station platform, gulping down the fresh air outside. He looked back to look at the smoke pouring out of the room, and turned back to the platform.

"Help!" He yelled. "The Engine! The Analytical Engine! It's on fire!"

Two miles outside of Staplehurst, the 2:20 train to London pulled through the countryside, rattling swiftly across the tracks. There had been no switches to the line, no changes to the track, and as he closed on a mile and a half from the town, the conductor of the train began to feel nervous. There was something off. But it wasn't until he saw a red flag on the line that true fear gripped him.

Panic rippled through the train. The brakes were thrown on, and the train howled in protest, sparks flying from the wheels as they attempted to slow down several tons of locomotive. The engine reversed, hissing and spewing steam. The passenger cars shook and shuddered, as they fought against the sudden attempt to stop the thrust of so much weight.

The train thundered across the trestles of the bridge, as the steep banks of River Beult opened up beneath it. The brakes squealed, straining every inch of steel to stop the weight of the train. The locomotive and the first brake van shot across the bridge, and leapt over the small, almost insignificant piece of track that had been removed for repairs. They pulled safely to the other side of the bridge.

The carriage behind them hit the gap, and slid off to one side. The coupling tore loose from the car, and the carriage careened down into the ravine, pulling the remaining carriages after it. They hit the muddy banks with the shrieking of metal and the snapping of wood siding, crunching one carriage into the back of the other, before coming to rest in the water and mud.

The last brake van came to an uneasy stop, uncoupled from the rest of the train, and stopped just short of the edge of the missing track. There was a ringing, hushed silence.

The brakeman pulled in a ragged breath, and leaned heavily on the handle of the brake, as the screams of the passengers began to rise from below.

Henry ran one hand over his face, staring at the codes on the table in front of him, and stretched his neck to one side. The Lloyd's order for a program to create insurance tables was not all that complicated, so the catch couldn't possibly be either.

"What have we missed?" he muttered to himself. He flipped his watch over the knuckles of his right hand, and cast a glance at its face. It was pushing towards five o'clock, and he still didn't have an answer. He felt sure that if Annabella and her students had been here, they would have found one by now.

"We've run it three times, sir," the young man next to him said. "It isn't the machine. There's something in the code that's making it catch."

Henry rubbed his forehead. He wanted this fixed today, but there was nothing new that he could see. The pounding sounds of the works around him, the shouting and screams of the machines, filled his head and made it hard to think.

"From the start, run each sequence," Henry said finally. "Adding them one at a time, and -"

"Babbage!"

The call rang across the works in a hard bark that made even Henry jump. He turned, and saw Brunel coming across the works at something approaching a run, holding a slip of paper in his hand.

"It's the catch again," Henry said, looking down at the codes again as Brunel approached. "We'll run them from the beginning, and try-"

"Henry."

Henry looked up at Brunel's face, and stopped. Brunel was pale and visibly shaken, and was holding the slip of paper out to Henry.

232

Henry turned slowly and took the telegram from his hand. *"Derailment at Staplehurst of 2:20 from Folkestone,"* he read under his breath. *"Unconfirmed cause, possibly fire in A. Engine at Station. Deaths and injuries unknown.* Dear God," he breathed, handing the slip back to Brunel. "Who sent the telegram?"

"It came in from Tonbridge," Brunel said quickly. "Nothing is getting through from Staplehurst, but Henry-"

"But they're saying the Analytical Engine was-"

"Henry!" Brunel shouted, as he stepped forward and grabbed the lapel of Henry's jacket. "Annabella King was on that train."

Brunel's words hit Henry like a fist to the center of his chest. The air left his lungs, and there was nothing to replace it. This couldn't be. It couldn't. He could not place Annabella amongst the damage that he imagined, amongst the fire and the smoke and the cracking and shattering train cars. It wasn't possible.

"I... no," Henry said, the fear bubbling inside of him reflected in Brunel's face. "How do you know?"

Brunel gently let go of Henry's jacket. "You knew that she and some of her analysts were in Folkestone. To fix the catch in the Engine-"

"Yes, but if they fixed it, how did the train derail?" Henry said, barely hearing his own voice.

"It was the Engine in the Staplehurst station that caught fire, not Folkestone. I don't know why," Brunel said, bleakly. "Miss King sent me a telegram this morning, to tell me that they would be on the afternoon train from Folkestone through Staplehurst-"

"But there's another, surely?" Henry demanded.

Brunel gazed up at Henry, his face tired and pained. "The afternoon train from Folkestone, Henry. You know there's only one."

Around him, the men had gone still and silent, and were staring at him. Henry felt his hands grow cold, as fear made his heart pound.

"No," he whispered.

"Henry," Brunel said with surprising gentleness. "They haven't-"

"No, no, no," Henry said, shaking his head, as if the force of it could push away the images that fought their way into his mind. His mind was good at recalling images of violence. It was not good at getting rid of them.

"Where are they taking survivors?" he said abruptly.

Brunel looked at him and shook his head. "I don't know. I don't know if there were any-"

"*No,*" Henry said in a hoarse whisper, gripping Brunel's arm. He met the older man's gaze. He saw fear and anguish written there, and abruptly let go of Brunel's arm.

He walked quickly away, and took the stairs up to the overseer's office two at a time. He threw the door open as he reached the top and snatched his overcoat off a peg inside the office, just as Brunel tentatively entered, and carefully closed the door behind him.

"Henry, they will send word once they know what happened, and where they are sending the injured."

Henry pulled on his coat, carefully buttoning it down the front. It was water tight enough for a ride, though not a long one – but it would have to be enough. It would take too long to go home for heavier clothes.

"There are no trains out to Staplehurst. All traffic will have been stopped," Brunel said.

Henry opened the desk drawer. There was a small flask in it and a leather folder with a five-pound note and some coins in it, as well as a worn pair of gloves. It would be enough. He put the flask and the folder into the pockets of his coat, and began to pull on the gloves.

"For God's sake, Henry, talk to me!" Brunel burst out.

Henry looked up. His movements had been smooth and methodical, but in looking into the anguish on Brunel's face, he felt his throat squeeze. Brunel was staring at him, his face betraying all the things that Henry could not bring himself to consider, even in his own mind. Not yet.

"I'll ride out of the city on the high streets and change horses at Croydon," Henry said. He flexed his hands in his gloves, and picked up his hat. "From there I can ride across country to Staplehurst."

Brunel moved in front of him as Henry made for the door. "Henry, you're riding tomorrow, surely?" he said, with a frown at Henry's coat and gloves.

"No, now, of course. As soon as I have a horse. Please stand aside," Henry said. He felt tense inside, like a coil that had been wound too tight. He moved towards the door.

"Henry, wait, dammit!" Brunel said, as Henry brushed past him and down the stairs.

Henry strode swiftly out of the works into the yard. A thin, persistent rain was falling; there was no wind yet, just the beginnings of an aching October cold. Henry called over one of the hands, and spoke to him quickly. By the time he had sent the young man to hire him a horse at the closest stable, Brunel had caught up with him.

"Henry!" Brunel said, catching the sleeve of his coat. "What are you doing?"

"Riding to Staplehurst," Henry said, feeling the chill already beginning to seep into him.

"In the morning," Brunel all but pleaded.

"I am going now, Isambard," Henry replied, his voice thick and weary.

"They will send a telegram, surely," Brunel protested. "As soon as the lines are cleared."

"You said yourself that nothing is getting through," Henry replied, clearing his throat. "And they will send… numbers only. They won't know … who to look for."

"Henry, for God's sake," Brunel said, pulling Henry to face him. "It's near dark, you'll never find her at this-"

"It will be nearly light when I get there," Henry replied, scanning the entrance of the yard for a sign of his horse.

"You cannot seriously be suggesting that you'll ride through the whole night!" Brunel shouted.

"I am not suggesting it. I am doing it," Henry replied, his voice wavering slightly.

235

Brunel opened his mouth to yell at him again, and closed it slowly. Henry wondered what Brunel had heard in his voice that made him stop. Henry didn't know himself; he felt a tension that he couldn't identify, far more terrifying than fear or grief.

"Staplehurst is forty miles at least," Brunel said softly.

"Yes," Henry said. "A long night's ride, but only one night. And then I will know."

"Henry, you would have to ride as though Death himself were behind you to-"

"I have to find her," Henry said, clearing his throat, facing Brunel. It was not a choice. He had to go. Somehow, it had to be him.

"It's not that that I fear," Brunel whispered. "It's that when you find her, you won't be able to bear it."

They both fell silent, the hiss of the rain muffling the clatter of the city.

"If I stay here," Henry began, his voice thick and slow, his breathing painful, "it will be worse. I will imagine everything that could have – that might have – " He lowered his head, and droplets of water rolled down the brim of his hat. "I have to, Isambard. You know that I do."

"You will be beyond exhaustion when you get there," Brunel said feebly, in a voice that said he knew he had lost.

Henry nodded. "Yes. But I –" Henry looked up at the sound of hooves coming into the yard, and walked towards the man who was leading a chestnut horse. He turned back to face Brunel. "You need to get a telegram to Lord King."

Brunel nodded, as Henry gripped the horse's bridle. "Of course. You will get word to me when you know?"

Henry nodded, and swung himself into the horse's saddle. He looked down at the worn and pained face of his employer. Brunel held up his hand, and Henry gripped it in his own.

"God speed, Henry," Brunel choked out. "I hope to God she's alive."

Henry's fingers clenched around Brunel's hand one last time. He snatched up his reins, squeezed the heels of his boots into the horse's sides, and dashed out of the yard.

236

XXXI

Thou wast the mountain-top – the sage's pen –
The poet's harp – the voice of friends – the sun;
Thou wast the river – thou wast glory won;
Thou wast my clarion's blast – thou wast my steed –

~John Keats~

Henry tried to remember a time when he had felt even close to as exhausted as he felt now. His hands had been cramped around the reins of his horse for so long that he could barely uncurl his fingers. He was onto his second horse of the night, rented from a livery stable outside of London. The rain had stopped, and had been replaced by a numbing wind. The countryside flickered in and out of the light of a half moon, causing his horse to stumble on the small country road. Every missed step sent a jolt of pain through his back.

He wavered between total conviction that his actions were right, and an equally total conviction that he was being an idiot. Surely it would have been faster, more expedient, to simply send a telegram to the nearest town, to wait for news – even, to wait for Annabella herself to return? But then each time he thought that, he dragged himself through all the possible reasons why the authorities at the next train station wouldn't be able to tell him what he so desperately needed to know.

Annabella could not yet be conscious, and could be unable to tell them who she was. She might be perfectly well, but be helping those around her, too busy in the chaos to get word to them that she was all right. There were any number of reasons why Annabella couldn't tell them herself that she was alive and unhurt.

Deaths and injuries unknown.

Or she could be dead.

Henry hunched himself over in his saddle and squeezed his hands to try and coax some warmth into them.

It was only when the River Beult came into view that Henry realized he had been riding slower for the past hour. His mind had wavered as he rode, between his gnawing exhaustion and the mounting fear of what he would find when he reached his destination.

It was still early morning, the sky a pale thin grey. The River Beult itself disappeared from view as Henry rode closer. There was no sign yet that anything was wrong, only the tracks stretching directly onward, towards the wide riverbank. He couldn't yet see the damaged bridge.

The road meandered away from the tracks, and Henry was beginning to regret that he hadn't followed the railroad instead, when the road mounted a small rise near the riverbank. Henry looked down at the bank below him.

He no longer felt numb, and he wished that he did. Instead his stomach roiled inside him, and he clenched the reins of the horse as his heart began to pound.

Spread out on the riverbed was the wreckage of the crash. Smoke rose from small fires that still burned in the stagecoaches that had caught fire; the blackened remains looked like the second class carriages. More than one carriage was fully overturned, their wooden frames bent and crushed under the weight of the exposed wheels. Wooden planks had been pushed under the carriages, to keep them from shifting in the mud. Figures moved amongst the wreckage, dressed in dark clothes, strangely silent as they lifted pieces of wood and steel away from the cars.

Henry nudged his horse forward across the field, and coaxed it down into the ravine. As soon as they reached the bottom, he reigned in the horse and slid off. Pain shot up his legs and into his back, and Henry staggered and gripped the horse's saddle to avoid collapsing into the mud.

He turned slowly, the horse's reins in his hand, and stared at the carriages. After a moment's uncertainty, he tied the reins to the remains of a tree that had been snapped off, and began to walk towards the site of crash. Against the protests of his aching body, he began to run.

"Annabella," he whispered under his breath, looking over the carriages.

He purposely didn't look at those that were blackened, or crushed.

"Annabella," he said out loud.

Panic was mounting in him, and he stared in confusion at the men around him. What were they looking for? There didn't seem to be any passengers left.

His eyes settled on a cluster of men who surrounded one carriage, and he walked slowly towards them, dread swarming inside him. They were lifting one of the carriages a little at a time, sliding more planks under it as they strained to raise it out of the mud. Henry took a step closer, and saw why.

Stretched out in the mud was a woman's hand and forearm, and the edge of a plain brown dress. The fingers were splayed wide in the soft ground, stretching straight out from the carriage, as though the hand were trying to pull itself out from under the train.

Henry took a slow step forward, until he could see the shattered form under the carriage. He could see a mass of blond hair, and the edge of a stained and ragged blue cloak. He stumbled away from the men and up the bank onto the wet grass. He fell to his knees, and retched onto the ground.

He stared at the ground, his head swimming. He felt ready to collapse. The images of bloodshed crowded back into his mind. He would have thought that years in the army would have made him impervious to violent death, to the wave of pounding nauseous that overwhelmed him now. Apparently it didn't. Yet under his shaking came the quiet, calm, and selfish reminder: *it wasn't her*.

"Babbage?"

Henry lifted his head slowly, as he heard his name and felt a hand touch his shoulder. He turned wearily, and frowned at the man who stood over him.

"Mr. Dickens?"

The man in front of him wavered into a steady image of the writer who he had met more than once at his father's home. Yet his doubt didn't disappear – how could this possibly be Charles Dickens, here, in this place? How?

"Mr. Dickens," Henry said, as his nauseous quieted enough for him to speak. "How are you-" He coughed, his chest giving a painful spasm.

239

"Here, let me help you," Dickens said, and took hold of his arm. He eased Henry to his feet, and turned to look at him with a concerned frown.

"Mr. Dickens," Henry said with a cough, as he struggled to stay on his feet. "Why are you here?"

"Just helping, if I can," Dickens said wearily. "To see if there are any souls left alive. You weren't on the train, were you, Babbage?" Dickens added, as if seeming in doubt of his own recollection for a moment.

"No," Henry replied. He blinked. "Wait, do you mean to say you were?"

Dickens nodded, and Henry finally noticed that the author seemed badly shaken. "Yes, in one of the first cars. Terrible business," he murmured, and seemed to stare past Henry, at something he was remembering.

Henry ran a hand through his hair. "Then you would know-" He stopped as realization dawned. If Dickens knew his father, he likely knew Annabella as well.

He grabbed the writer by both arms. "Mr. Dickens! Was Annabella King on the train? Did you see her?"

Dickens blinked and started to speak, and then frowned. "No, I can't recall that she was. But if she were, she would be at Staplehurst station by now. There's a makeshift infirmary there, and they-"

"Where is *there*?" Henry asked, violently gripping Dickens' hand.

Dickens stepped away from him at his visible agitation. "Why, in the train station, of course."

The Staplehurst train station smelled like war. Henry could smell it from the outside, the caustic smell of ash and smoke mixed with the metallic smell of blood. The voices that seeped out of the train station as he approached it were low, with an occasional cry that rose above them, only to be swiftly cut off.

Henry stepped into the main train shed, and had to grip the edge of the red brick wall to steady himself. The smell had intensified, and seemed to blur the scene that lay before him.

In the center of the platform was the charred hulk of what had been the Analytical Engine shed. Henry could see the stacks of flaking ash that had

240

once been the punch cards; they sat whispering in the moving air, held precariously in place by the blackened metal of the cog towers. Shattered glass surrounded the Engine, where the windows to the shed had been broken. Henry stepped none too carefully through the shards, glass crunching under his boots, and looked down the platform.

Unlike the grand swooping glass ceilings of the London train stations, this station only had slopping metal roofs – enough to keep off the rain, but not enough to keep out the wind. Scattered down the platform were people clustered in small groups. Some were huddled around small fires built right on the platform. There were maybe fifty such people, all dressed in damp travelling clothes.

Henry began to walk slowly down the platform, moving past people who looked up at him in weary numbness. No curiosity showed in their faces – one more exhausted man in a riding coat was not a surprise to them. Henry checked each of their faces slowly, then looked up, and stopped.

He had reached the infirmary. Or at least, what passed for one. A number of injured passengers were spread down the platform. Most were laid directly on the stone and cement of the platform itself, though some were covered in blankets.

Some of the forms were still, with blankets pulled fully over their faces.

He stopped next to one of the bodies, covered with a coarse piece of blue cloth. He had ridden this far. He should check this one. He stood frozen, staring at it, then turned abruptly and walked on. He would check the dead last. It would, after all, make no difference if he did.

Henry walked slowly forward. Nightmares crowded into his mind, of infirmaries like this one, makeshift and exposed to the elements, sweltering in the heat. The smell of blood and wet fabric made his stomach twist, but he walked on. There was nothing left in his stomach anyway. He lifted his head.

And froze. Only thirty feet or so down the platform, her head bent forward over a person that Henry couldn't see, was Sarah. She wore a brown wool travelling cloak, her light brown hair tossed hastily up on her head. She was reaching out with tenderness towards someone, and speaking to them.

241

The first step forward was the hardest. Henry walked past two bodies, without even looking at them. Then suddenly he was running, devouring the ground between them, until he reached Sarah just as she stood up, and turned to face him.

"Mr. Babbage-" Sarah said, her eyes wide with surprise. Henry stopped. He barely registered her weary, tear-stained face, as he looked over her shoulder at the person lying on the platform.

It wasn't Annabella. It was Bentham. His head was resting on what looked like a woman's black shawl. It was tossed back at an awkward angle, his face pale and sweaty. He still had on a white shirt and a coarse woven jacket, but his lower body was covered with a cotton sheet.

Henry's eyes came to rest on the sheet, and his mind churned. There was something wrong.

"Oh, Mr. Babbage," Sarah said in a sob. "I don't know where you've come from, but I'm glad to see you."

Henry continued to stare at Bentham. There was something wrong.

"Sarah," Henry said in a strangled voice.

Henry's chest tightened. It was his leg. His left leg ended where his knee should have been.

Sarah looked up at him, and then down at Bentham. "He was… his leg was… crushed in the accident," she choked out. She covered her mouth with a gloved hand as tears formed in her eyes.

"Sarah," Henry breathed. "Is he... Is he alive?"

"John? Yes, he's alive." She swallowed, and more tears ran down her face. She turned to look at Bentham.

Henry looked sideways at her. *John*. He wasn't even sure if he had known Bentham's first name before she had said it, but he heard in her voice the same emotions that he felt. He could see it, written in every tear-stained line of her face. The same aching, weary waiting. The same mix of fear and love.

"Henry?"

XXXII

I have found Demetrius like a jewel,
Mine own, and not mine own.

~William Shakespeare~

Even before he turned around, Henry felt the warmth of relief begin to spread through his chest. He turned slowly, and met Annabella's gaze.

She was unharmed. Entirely, beautifully, unharmed. She was wearing a navy blue cloak, its wide hood resting on her shoulders, cradling her face. Her hair had been pulled hastily back, with damp wisps of it coming free at her temples. Her dark eyes looked worried. She was tired, but she was there, alive and uninjured.

Henry took one step forward, and felt his legs giving out underneath him. He reached out to her, and she was there, supporting his arm on her shoulder. He fell to his knees, and she was there, holding him as his body wavered with fatigue.

"Anna," he breathed. He wanted to kiss her, but couldn't lose sight of her. He clumsily tore off his gloves and rested his hands on her head. He could feel the soft waves of her hair under his aching fingers. He could barely understand that she was real.

"Henry," she said. She cupped her hands around his jaw and looked into his drained face, her eyes clouded with concern. "Why are you here?"

"Why…" Henry gasped, worried he would begin to sob himself. "I… the train,… the accident. You're not hurt," he whispered.

Annabella touched his cheek, and Henry closed his eyes. "Henry," she said softly. "I was not on the train."

Annabella looked over Henry's shoulder at Sarah, and back at Henry. His coat was soaked through, and there was mud well up his boots and trousers, and even on his face. He was exhausted. She knew that they needed to find shelter for Bentham, but she felt sure that if she moved Henry would collapse.

Henry was staring at her in incomprehension. "Not... you were..."

"Sarah and I stayed in Folkestone to fix some problems. Neither of us was on the train. Bentham went on with Evy," Annabella said, swallowing the lump forming in her throat.

Evy.

Not now. There would be time later.

"Henry..." she murmured, "Dear God, did you ride from *London*?"

Henry's face was close to hers, his green eyes clouded and desperate for rest. "I thought..."

He tried to pull her towards him, but fell forward instead, and Annabella wrapped her arms around his back as he sagged against her shoulder. His left hand gripped the shoulder of her cloak, and Annabella felt him draw a shaking, ragged breath.

"I was afraid I had lost you," he murmured, his mouth close to her ear.

Annabella felt her heart beat hard and warm in her chest, and closed her eyes. She wanted to hold him there and let him rest, but she looked up again at Sarah, and her worried expression.

"We need to go to the inn," she said, gently pushing Henry away from her. "I have two rooms for us." She stood up, and extended her hand to him. He looked up, and took it, and pulled himself to his feet.

"How can we get John– Bentham there, Miss?" Sarah asked, her voice shaking.

"They have lent us a cart," Annabella replied. She turned to look at Henry, who was wavering on his feet. She took one of his arms, and lifted it over her shoulder. He didn't resist, and instead leaned against her.

"We just need some help to get him outside."

Henry opened his eyes and sat up with a jerk, and groaned out loud. He had been dreaming of crashing train cars and the screaming of metal and humans. Every inch of his body ached. The room was dim, and through window, Henry could see the clouds lit red by the setting sun. He considered for a moment dropping back against the pillows, but instead grimaced and swung his legs over the side of the bed.

244

He was sitting on top of a lumpy double bed, wearing only his trousers and his shirt. He looked around the small room, and saw his jacket and waistcoat, as well as his greatcoat, carefully hung to dry on pegs by the door. His boots were underneath them. Henry blinked. He couldn't remember having undressed himself. His last recollection had been leaning heavily on Annabella's shoulder as she opened a door.

He moved his shoulders experimentally, and instantly wished that he hadn't. His muscles were tight and throbbing, and his lower back was a constant, burning ache. He got gingerly to his feet, and hobbled across the floor.

As he sat on the end of the bed and pulled on his boots, the thought flitted across his mind: *what now?* Annabella was safe. That was all he had focused on during his ride. Now that he was here, and she was unharmed, he didn't know what to do. He didn't know if he was welcome here, or if he should simply find his way back to London. As soon as he thought it, he realized he didn't know how he would even do that; there were no trains, and even the thought of getting on a horse again made his muscles burn.

He stood up, winced, and reached for his waistcoat.

The small inn in Staplehurst had a parlor that faced out towards the street. The windows were small but clean, and low tables were surrounded by worn but comfortable chairs. Annabella sat in one, the saucer of a cup of tea resting in her lap, the cup itself forgotten in her hand. She was staring out one of the windows, watching the sky turn the colour of blood with the setting sun.

Her body was frozen and sore, not from too much activity but from too little sleep. She and Sarah had caught the evening mail coach out of Folkestone as soon as they had heard about the accident, and they had travelled through the night. It was only just getting light when they had arrived in Staplehurst. She had caught snatches of sleep when the rocking coach allowed her to, but she knew that Sarah had not, in her anxiety for John Bentham.

Annabella took a sip of her tea, and tried to organize the events of the previous day in her mind. Bentham had been barely conscious when they had arrived, and it had taken them a few frantic, agonizing minutes of searching before they found him. He had awoken for a moment, long enough for him to recognize Sarah, and smile through his agony, before crying out in pain. Through gritted teeth he had told Sarah what had happened to Evy, before another wave of pain made him pass out. Sarah had moved her shawl under his head, and had scarcely left his side since.

Annabella had left them, and gone to search for what shelter there was in the small town. She had had to be rather liberal with her money, but had at last convinced the landlady at the inn to take a wounded man and two women, and had acquired two rooms for them.

It was on returning to the station that she had met the one surgeon of the town. He was walking out of the station, and she had run up to him to catch his arm.

"Sir!" she had gasped out, turning him towards her. He looked tired and frightened. Thirty injured people at once was more than the country surgeon had ever had to deal with.

"There is a man in the station," she had pressed on, ignoring his look of confusion. "His leg... have you seen to it?"

The surgeon had frowned. "I'm not sure who-"

"His name is Bentham," Annabella had said, grasping his sleeve. "Brown hair, tall, he would be about-"

"The one with the crushed leg?" the surgeon had replied abruptly. "Yes, I've seen to him. His leg was amputated during the night."

Hearing it said aloud had made Annabella more sick than she had known it would, and she had forcibly pushed aside her memories of her own injury. The surgeon had told her that he would return to bind the leg again the following day, and Annabella had instructed him to come to the inn.

And then she had entered the station, and Henry had been there. She had seen him from down the platform, gripping Sarah's arms, looking over her shoulder at where Bentham was lying. She had walked down the platform as if in a dream, unable to comprehend how, with everything else going on, he could possibly be there.

She had never seen him like that, never seen him so helpless and exhausted. She had never imagined a moment when he would all but collapse

246

into her arms. She thought back to him carrying her into Ockham Park after she had fallen off her horse, and smiled.

"Anna- Miss King?"

Annabella turned, and set her tea down on the table in front of her. The same gentle voice said, "No, please. Don't get up."

She turned to look at the door of the parlour, and her heartbeat quickened. Henry stood in the doorway, his head slightly hunched as he ducked through the low frame. He closed the door behind him. Dried mud flaked off of his riding boots as he walked, and his waistcoat was open over his shirt. The collar of his shirt was open, and Annabella felt her gaze being drawn to his neck, to the hollow of his throat. He still looked half asleep, his hair ruffled and his eyes red. He moved into the room stiffly, the pain of each step evident, and sank into an armchair across from her. He leaned forward, and took her hand in his.

For a moment neither of them spoke. They both looked at their clasped hands, Henry's red and chapped from his hours of riding, and Annabella's with a smear of Engine grease across her thumb.

Annabella cleared her throat. "Are you hungry? I can call for something to eat."

Henry continued to look at their hands. "In a moment," he said softly.

Silence descended between them, until Annabella spoke. "I hope… you slept well," she murmured, feeling how stupid the words were.

Henry looked up at her, his eyes the colour of the sea on a fitful day. The light of the fire and the lamps danced across them. "I'm not sure. I don't remember a great deal after leaving the station. Did I… that is… who undressed me?"

Annabella couldn't help herself; she giggled. "I did," she said, and grinned when Henry's eyes widened. "Well, once I got you upstairs you collapsed on the bed wearing your soaking wet coat and boots. I couldn't wake you, so… yes, I undressed you."

It hadn't been easy, either. She had been tired herself, and hauling off his tight riding boots had been sufficiently difficult that she had had to brace her foot against the bed to manage it.

More difficult still had been pulling off his jacket and waistcoat, and breathing in the smell of him, damp and masculine. He hadn't opened his eyes as she had untied his necktie. His head had lolled sleepily towards her hand, his lips parted in a soft, breathy moan that made her heart skip. She had let her fingers linger on his neck for a moment, feeling his pulse beating in his throat, and had let her fingers find the puckered scar that ran below his collarbone. She had lowered him clumsily to his bed, and had felt a deep longing to collapse down next to him.

She thought of it now, and felt her cheeks reddening.

Henry's own cheeks were flushed, and he coughed, looking down at their clasped hands. "How is Bentham?"

Annabella swallowed. "He is asleep. Sarah is with him, though the last I checked, she was asleep as well."

"Will he... will he live?" Henry said in a small voice.

Annabella nodded. "The doctor came and changed the bandages. As long as he can keep off infection, he will live." She paused, feeling the pain welling inside her as she thought of what Bentham had told them in his brief moment of consciousness. "We... we lost Evy." Her throat tightened, and tears threatened her eyes.

Henry looked at her, frowning for a moment, and then his face went white. "Evy," he breathed. "She was blond, wasn't she?"

Annabella looked at his face, suddenly so shaken, and felt him squeeze her hand painfully tightly. "Henry, what do you-"

"I saw her," he breathed, lowering his head. "At the crash."

Annabella put one hand over her mouth, blinking tears down her face. In the hours that Henry had been asleep, she had confirmed what Bentham had told them with the men searching the crash. The description that they had given her alone had made her feel ill.

"Oh God, Henry," she said, still holding his hand, and sinking to the floor in front of him.

Henry was hunched over, still clutching her hand, running his other hand through his hair. He was breathing hard. "It must have been her. She was, I saw her, and she-"

"Henry, stop!" Annabella cried, letting go of his hand, and gripping his head in her hands. He looked up at her, his own eyes red. Annabella swallowed, and felt tears stinging her eyes.

"Oh dear God, Annabella," Henry breathed, as he slipped off his chair and fell to his knees in front of her.

He seized her against his chest as Annabella began to weep. Her cries were painful, wrenched from somewhere deep inside, burning as they slowly bubbled through her throat. The memory of her mother's death swept through her, entwined with Evy's.
Henry held her now as he had then, as she smoothed her hand against his chest. Henry stroked her hair, as fear and grief rocked through her, his chest shaking with ragged breaths beneath her hand.

Annabella's sobs slowed, and she looked up at him.

"I trained her," she said in a voice that was little more than a whimper.

"I know," Henry said with a small smile.

It's only a stepping stone, Evy had said. Just one more stone along a path with so much sorrow.

"How did you... *Why* did you ride out here?" she said, gulping down her tears.

Henry reached one hand behind her head, and cradled it in his hand. "I had to know you were alive," he whispered. "I thought you were on the train."

Annabella nodded. "The telegram to Brunel."

Henry nodded in return, and brushed a wisp of her hair from her forehead. "Yes. I couldn't... I couldn't just wait to know what had become of you."

Annabella reached up a hand and brushed it against Henry's cheek. "I am glad you are here," she said softly.

"I love you, Annabella," Henry said.

Annabella froze, her hand on his cheek. It was too much, all at once. Too many emotions fought in her mind, and made her heart beat painfully.

She pulled away from him, drawing herself back towards her chair. "Henry, please, not now, I-"

Henry caught her wrist, and pulled her back towards him. He knelt facing her, holding her elbows in his hands. "Annabella, please, I have wasted enough time that I could have-"

"Henry, we have already-" Annabella began.

"I was wrong, Annabella," Henry said quickly, still holding one elbow, and touching her face with his other hand. "I was a coward. I thought I had to protect you from the world, and I couldn't see that… that you don't need me to protect you. That you are not a coward, and that you can face the scorn of this world with or without me."

"It was not…" Annabella looked up into Henry's frantic face, riveted by his eyes. "You are not alone to blame. I did not give you the chance you deserved, because I… I was too afraid of losing what I had fought so hard for."

"The chance I…" Henry breathed.

"Yes," Annabella said, feeling her chest tighten. "To prove that you… that you loved me enough to change … everything around us, and let me be who I am."

Henry's eyes brightened, and he touched her cheek with one trembling hand. "I will not ask you for your hand. Not now. I know this is the wrong time. I know you have sorrow to bear. But… let me help you to bear it. Even if you don't need me to. Let me share your sorrow, and your joy." He drew a shaking breath. "Or else tell me that you truly don't love me, and I will not ask again."

They gazed at one another for one fragile moment, knelt close together.

"I do love you, Henry," she said finally. "I never stopped loving you."

"Annabella," he said. His voice was breathless, as though breathing were painful. "I am going to kiss you."

Annabella slid her hand beneath Henry's waistcoat, and rested her palm against his chest, feeling his warm skin and the beat of his heart through his shirt. His breath caught.

"I am going to let you," she whispered.

Henry pulled her towards him, and tilted back her head to press his lips against hers. She slipped her hand inside the open collar of his shirt. He

250

sucked in a breath and stiffened, and groaned against her mouth as she traced his collarbone with her thumb, and wove her fingers around the back of his neck. His hands grasped her neck and waist with a longing that was finally free of despair, and he sank against the chair, pulling her with him. She could feel the warm length of his body beneath her, and ached to be cocooned in this moment forever.

She lifted her face from his and drew a deep breath. He didn't let go of her, but grinned up at her. He was slumped against the chair, warmth flooding his tired face. Annabella reached her hands under his waistcoat, and against his back. He jumped away from her, and laughed.

"And what is funny, Mr. Babbage?" she said, with a slow smile.

Henry shook his head. "Every inch of my body hurts," he said with a laugh and a wince.

Annabella pushed herself reluctantly away from him. "Perhaps you could use a drink. And something to eat," she added.

"Hmm," Henry said with a slow nod.

They both rose slowly to their feet, Henry holding out his hand to help her. They found themselves face to face, and stood awkwardly for one moment, before Henry seized her around the waist and kissed her again, nearly lifting her off the ground.

He looked at her and touched her cheek, his gaze sober. "Please tell me that I'm not dreaming," he murmured.

"You are very much awake, Mr. Babbage," she said. "Surely your aching body tells you that."

XXXIII

The heart will break, but broken live on.

~Lord Byron~

"You look like hell, Master."

Henry lifted his head off the back of his chair, and blinked. His neck hurt, and it took a moment for the room before him to come into focus. Bentham was awake, pushing himself up against his pillows.

Henry stretched his neck, and stood up. He pulled the chair closer to Bentham's bedside, and sat down. It was dark outside, probably the middle of the night, and a single low oil lamp burned next to Bentham's bed.

"You look a little beaten up yourself," Henry said softly.

"You're not going a-pitying me, are you, Master?" Bentham said. His tone was light, but perspiration beaded on his face. He frowned. "Where is Sarah?" he said, with an urgency that Henry all too clearly understood.

"She's with Annabella," Henry replied, his throat tight. "They're both asleep."

It had been hard to part from her. They had lingered together in the hall, holding onto each other, neither of them quite convinced that the other was real. Her touch felt like fire on his skin, and he could still feel every place where she had touched him, her fingers lingering on his neck and tracing down his aching back. He felt guilty for even having such thoughts in his mind, as he sat next to the injured man's bed.

"You came for her," Bentham said, with a faint smile.

Henry looked up at him, and back down at his hands, and smiled. "Yes."

"And she finally took you," Bentham said. It wasn't a question.

It was four days later that two carriages drove into the yard of the small inn in Staplehurst. One bore Lord King's family crest on the side. The other was Brunel's.

With Bentham and Sarah in one carriage and Annabella and Henry in the other, they made their slow way back to London. Annabella was faintly aware that propriety dictated that it should be she and Sarah in one carriage together and the men in the other. She refused to care. It was cold and rainy, and she nestled against Henry, watching his sleeping face as they made their way home.

The carriages clattered across the cobbles into the yard of Lord King's London home, and as Annabella emerged from the carriage, she met her father's worried eyes. He strode across the yard towards her, and stopped short as Henry got out of the carriage behind her.

"Annabella!" he frowned.

"Please, father," she said wearily, "anything you have to say can wait until our patient is inside."

"Our patient?" Her father said with a frown. He looked pointedly at Henry.

"Mr. Bentham was badly injured in the crash. He will be staying here until he is well," Annabella said briskly. She walked quickly across the yard towards the door of the house, leaving Henry and her father no choice but to follow.

"And perhaps you would like to tell me who Mr. Bentham is?" Lord King returned irritably. "And while we're about it, perhaps you'd like to explain why you're travelling alone in a carriage with Mr. Babbage?"

Annabella laughed, and enjoyed the shocked look on Lord King's face as she pushed open the door. "No, Father. I have other priorities. Bancroft!" she called into the house. The butler shortly stepped into the hall, and looked between Annabella and Lord King.

"Please see that a room is prepared for Mr. Bentham. He will be staying here until he has recovered," Annabella said briskly.

Bancroft shot a glance at Lord King, but when he received no contradiction, he gave a slight bow, and a murmured "Yes, Miss," before walking up the stairs.

Annabella turned back to face her father's questioning gaze. "Mr. Bentham is one of my students. I work with him," Annabella said.

"A *factory* hand?" Lord King gasped. Behind Lord King, Henry drew his lips in, his irritation evident.

"Yes, Father," Annabella said calmly, pulling off her gloves and setting them on the hall table. She began to remove her cloak.

"Annabella!" snapped Lord King as he recovered from his shock. "You are not turning my house into an infirmary for *factory* workers!"

Annabella threw her cloak over the banister of the stairs, and leveled a glare at her father. "*A* factory worker, actually," she returned. "Only one."

"You are not-" Lord King said.

"I am, actually," Annabella said, taking a step towards her father.

"Annabella," Henry said in a warning voice.

"Know your place, Mr. Babbage," Lord King snapped, as frustration played across his face. "You will refer to my daughter as Miss King."

Annabella looked past her father and met Henry's gaze. He had recovered from his initial surprise, but his eyes snapped with anger.

"He has always known his place, Father," Annabella said softly. "It is you who have forgotten yours."

Lord King blanched. "This is not about-"

"No, this is exactly about that," Annabella replied, trying to keep her voice level, and failing. "Because Mother's death was what made me see clearly. That some things are worth crying over. And rank and position are not one of them."

Lord King stared at her, and Annabella could see his resolve leaving him. "Annabella-"

"Mr. Bentham will be staying with us until he has recovered from his injury. And Mr. Babbage will refer to me as Annabella if he so chooses." She lifted her jaw to glare at her father. "They have both earned it."

She brushed past her father, to see that Bentham was safely conveyed from the carriage.

The small churchyard, not far from Brunel's works, was covered with a fine layer of black soot. Annabella looked at the small circle that was clustered around a freshly dug grave, swallowing a lump in her throat.

Rosie stood staring at the freshly turned ground, her eyes studiously avoiding the cream-coloured gravestone. Her eyes were vacant and seemed to gaze past the earth, as if she could see right through it. She looked as she had ever since Annabella had told her of Evy's death – hollow, as if she had been emptied from the inside and could never again be whole.

Sarah and Bentham stood beside her, Sarah in her blue wool dress, Bentham in a rough brown jacket and trousers, both with black silk bands around their upper arms. The leg of Bentham's trousers were folded back and pinned under his missing limb. He held a long crutch under one arm, his other arm around Sarah's shoulder. She leaned into him, as though he were supporting her, and not the other way around.

There could be no doubt of Sarah and Bentham's feelings for each other after the crash, and yet Annabella had still found herself faintly surprised when Sarah told her that they were to be married. Annabella had gently pointed out the challenge that Bentham's injuries would pose, and Sarah had only stared at her in incomprehension, before asserting that it changed nothing. It had only made her more certain.

Brunel stood next to Bentham, holding his hat in his hand. The loss of Evy to an accident caused by the Engine had cut him deeply; it was a failure of his progress, in the most destructive of ways.

Henry took her hand, and she looked at him, standing next to her, looking pale in his black coat. She herself had not had the chance to stop wearing black since her mother had died; the black wool was soaking in water at the hem, making her feel heavy once more.

It was Sarah that moved first. She nudged Bentham gently, and the two of them moved wordlessly off, making their way down the path away from the grave. Rosie left next, giving a choking sob and turning abruptly away. Brunel put on his hat, and stopped next to Henry to shake his hand, before walking away.

Annabella stared at the limestone gravestone. *Evelina Hayward, born 1833, died 1851. "Our dead are never dead to us, until we have forgotten them."* She wondered where Evy's sister was; she had realized only after Evy had died that she didn't even know her name.

"This is my doing," she said softly.

"Annabella," Henry said in protest, turning towards her.

"It is," said Annabella. "I am responsible for them all. Evy, Rosie, Bentham, Sarah. I brought them so much destruction."

"Annabella," Henry said gently, turning her to face him. "I know what it is to be responsible for the people that I have led to death. That is not what this is."

"They would not have been with me if-"

"They all made a choice to follow you. Because they believed, because they still believe, that the Engines can let us do more, can make our lives better."

Annabella sniffed. "But their work, ... it has taken so much from them."

"Annabella," Henry said, taking her arm and wiping away a tear from her face, "the Engine is made by human hands. It is not perfect. But it is potential, it is progress. That has not changed." Annabella opened her mouth to speak, and he held up his hand to stop her. "When you were injured, when the Engine took something from you, I blamed myself. I thought there was some way that I might have protected you, and kept you safe. But that you should never have worked on the Engine at all... is that what you would have wanted?"

Annabella shook her head. "You know it isn't."

"You told me once that sometimes our choices would ask sacrifices of us." Henry pressed on. "That you could make that choice, and were willing to pay the price of progress."

"Not with someone else's life," Annabella said with a sob.

"Evy made the same choice."

Annabella looked up into his face, at the slight frown over his grey-green eyes. "What of Bentham? His life is – " she said.

"Changed, yes. But if Bentham had lost his limb working as a factory hand, he would have no livelihood now," Henry said soothingly. "He does, because he works with his mind as well as his hands."

Annabella remained silent, and looked back at the grave. It didn't seem right, that Evy was quiet and cold in her grave next to them, while they were still so alive, still so dear to each other.

Henry pressed a kiss against her forehead, and pulled gently at her arm to lead her away from the grave. They followed the same path that Sarah and Bentham had taken away from the cemetery. They could see the works from the small hill they were on, looming above the river, full of threat and of promise.

XXXIV

Ye stars! which are the poetry of heaven!
If in your bright leaves we would read the fate
Of men and empires,—'tis to be forgiven…

~Lord Byron~

On top of Brunel's works, two voices resounded through the night air.

"Henry, it's freezing up here."

"Well, of course. Winter is the best time to see it."

"Is that a fact, or something you are saying just to stop my complaints?"

"It can't be both?"

Henry swung himself over the ladder onto the top of the building, to the sound of Annabella's laughter. He turned and looked over the ledge to watch her climbing up the side of the building.

"Are you all right?" he asked, worried for about the tenth time that this had been a bad decision.

"Yes, yes," Annabella returned impatiently. "I'm taking my time. Remember, I have one less finger and significantly more skirts than you do."

Henry winced at the mention of her finger, but waited until she climbed closer. He held out a hand to her and pulled her onto the top of the building. She landed with one hand on his chest. He caught her, and didn't let her go.

"Oh my," Annabella said, turning her face to the sky.

London was no less brightly lit than ever, but it seemed as if the stars were closer tonight, vibrant and scintillating in the winter sky. The brassy ribbon of the Thames, lit by the gas lamps, wound its way through the buildings, and a light wind lifted the smells of tar and murk from off the water. Henry saw none of it. His eyes were on her, her unturned face alight with joy.

Annabella turned her face towards his. "I'm still freezing, but… yes, it might just be worth it."

"Just wait here," Henry said, grinning in the darkness, even though she couldn't see him. He moved across the roof towards the boxes that were scattered on it.

"Can I help?" Annabella asked, resting a hand on his shoulder.

He smiled to himself. "Look at the sky. Let your eyes adjust to the dark."

He lifted the tripod into place, and glanced over his shoulder at her before getting to work. He could see her silhouette in the dark, her eyes upturned to the heavens.

They had not spoken of what they felt for each other in the two months that had followed the accident at Staplehurst; there had been too many heartaches to heal first. But nor had they let each other out of their sight. In the days following the accident, whether Annabella was helping Sarah to nurse Bentham to health, or at Evy's funeral, or at the works, Henry had never been far off. He had seen her every day, to talk about the Engine, to get her out of her house, and to help her bear the burden of her mother's death that still weighed on her.

"You will need to forgive him one day," Henry had said to her one day when they had been out for a ride.

Annabella hadn't asked who he meant – she knew that it was Lord King. "Perhaps," she had said softly.

"He can't lose you as well as his wife, Annabella," Henry had said, trying to make his voice as gentle as he could.

Annabella had turned her eyes full of tears towards him. "We all make our choices, Henry," she had said in a hoarse voice.

"Yes," Henry had said. He had taken her hand. "But some of us have a second chance."

He had been relieved when she had squeezed his hand in return.

"What are we going to look at?" Annabella asked, still looking up at the sky.

"Just wait," Henry said.

He shouldn't have been surprised when Annabella returned to work as soon as Bentham and Sarah did. It was just as well that she had. Strangely, the Staplehurst accident hadn't made much of a dent in the demand for Analytical Engines.

"I would have thought that no one would want to buy one now," Henry had said to Brunel when they had met to look over the recent orders.

"I would have as well," Brunel had admitted. "It was in the papers that it was part of the accident, but everyone seems to be caught up in the train itself."

Henry had frowned. "The newspapers didn't print that it was caused by the Engine?"

Brunel had shrugged. "They did. But very few understand how the Engine really works, so why would they understand when it doesn't work? Did you and Miss King ever find out why?"

Henry shook his head. "No," he said, frustration edging his voice. "It might have been a combination of a mechanical flaw and a catch in the codes, but with the cards burnt, we can't tell." He didn't like not knowing, and he knew Annabella liked it even less.

Brunel nodded slowly. "It doesn't seem to have slowed things down. Progress rolls on."

Henry pushed the conversation with Brunel from his mind, and set the telescope into the mount. He spun it to face the direction he wanted. The eyepiece of the telescope came level with his chest, and he carefully searched the sky until he found what he was looking for.

"All right, ready?" he said.

Annabella walked quickly towards him. "Yes. And still freezing."

Henry grinned in the dark, and pointed at the telescope. "I'll hold it steady. Just look."

Annabella bent her head, and rested one eye on the eyepiece. She gasped, and gripped the eyepiece in one gloved hand. "Henry," she breathed. "What is that?"

Henry smiled at her. She looked not unlike what she was looking at; lit by the starlight, she was all blacks and blues and silvers, the swirls of her hair like the black stardust she could see through the lens.

"It's the Nebula of Orion," he said.

"It's..." Annabella looked back through the lens. "It's breathtaking. And the stars in it..." she whispered. "They're ... so bright. What is it?"

"We don't know yet," Henry said softly. Of all the wonders he had

260

seen in the sky, the black dust cradling the fire white stars drew him most.

She lifted her head from the telescope, and turned to face him. He could just see the lines of a smile on her face, and he took a step towards her.

"Annabella," was all he said, before he found himself pulling her to him, and kissing her upturned mouth. He held her tight as she slipped her hands around his neck.

He pulled his mouth away from hers. "Will you marry me?" he said in one breath, before he could hesitate.

Annabella slid one gloved hand against his cheek. "Has anything changed?" she said softly.

"Everything has changed," he said, as he held her close to him. He knew his voice sounded desperate, and he didn't care. "I wish I had more words. And a better promise. I can only tell you that I love you, and I would give anything to make you happy."

Henry's heart fluttered as Annabella gave a breathless laugh, and tilted her head back to gaze at the sky. "Even the stars?" she said.

"Even the stars," he whispered. Henry's eyes traced the line of her neck and her upturned jaw, and resisted the urge to pull her to him and kiss her bare throat. The sounds of the city dropped away, as he heard only the wind and his pounding heart.

Annabella's gaze came to rest on him, glittering in the darkness. "I will marry you, Henry."

As though they had both been teetering on the edge of a cliff, they fell into each other. Henry pulled her close, as Annabella's body curved to fit against his. The wind off the water whipped her hair around his face, as they clung to each other in the cold and the dark.

Annabella swung herself up the stairs to the training room door, and tried to regain her composure. It wasn't easy. Her heart felt lighter than it had in… good God, had it been a year? Even her dress made her happier. For the first time since her mother had died, she wasn't wearing black, but instead a pearl grey wool dress. After months of death and mourning, it seemed like the brightest of colours.

She pulled open the door of the training room, and stood gazing at it for a moment. It felt… like it was hers. Every movement in it was familiar, including the determined faces of the women working alongside the men. There had been four new ones, since Evy had died.

"He took his time about it, didn't he, Miss?"

Annabella turned to see Bentham's grinning face, as he came out from behind the Engine, and smiled back. "Sarah told you?"

Bentham leaned easily on his crutch. "Of course she did," he said. "No less than you both deserve."

Annabella smiled, feeling warm inside. She turned as she heard footsteps pounding quickly up the stairs, and nearly collided with Henry as he reached the door.

"Annabella, you'd better come see Brunel, he's asking to see the – good morning, Bentham," Henry stopped, and held out his hand to Bentham.

Bentham gripped it, and with one quick pull drew Henry towards him and clapped him on the back. "You took long enough to ask the poor woman!" he exclaimed.

Henry's confusion lasted only a moment before he glanced at Annabella with a warm smile. "Sarah?"

Annabella nodded.

"Thank you, Bentham," Henry said, firmly gripping the other man's hand.

"You'd both best be off to see Master Brunel." Bentham gave a quick nod towards the door, and then moved away, darting around the Analytical Engine on his crutch.

Annabella took Henry's arm as he led her down the stairs. The ground of the yard crunched cold under their feet.

"Did you tell Brunel that we were engaged?" she asked, squeezing his arm.

"I did," Henry said with a wry smile.

"And?" Annabella asked. "What did he say?"

"He said, 'it's about damn time.'"

31112707R00160

Made in the USA
Lexington, KY
15 February 2019